THE FIVE WORLDS

Book Six of The Arizona Series

JAN KELLY

THE FIVE WORLDS

Book Six of The Arizona Series

Western / Adventure / Romance

set in the Modern American West

Author: Jan Kelly

Copyrighted ©2023 by Jan Kelly

Published 2023 by Jan Kelly

Cover Design: SelfPubBookCovers.com/Island

For my mother

Book Six of The Arizona Series
Western/ Adventure/ Romance Novels
set in the Modern American West

CONTENTS

PROLOGUE

The Yaqui

Yomumuli understands. She does not like the strange tree's message, but she—and she alone—can comprehend it. Since she made them all—the desert people, the river tribes, the mountain clans, those dwelling on the plateaus—it's her job to explain the tree's buzzing to them. But she does not really want to; it's a disturbing message, to be sure.

Can you even call the thing a tree? It has no branches, there isn't a leaf on it. It's a barked pole, a giant stick rooted in the earth. And the hum-hum-humming sound it makes is like a swarm of aggravated insects. Trees sigh, rustle, or stand mute in still air. Trees might house bees, but they don't sound like them. Normal trees, at least. This tree is very odd.

Of course the people have noticed it and marveled. They circle it, arm in arm, and stare up at its wooden spire. The elders confer, their heads together, rubbing their chins, but since none of them have seen anything like it before, they can reach no conclusions. Only Yomumuli understands, and she does not like its meaning.

How to tell them?

She becomes twin boys and speaks: "The tree is humming to explain to the animals how to live." The boys are mirrors of one another, and their words come out in unison. "It's telling the mice and rabbits and deer, the crickets and badgers and turtles and frogs to eat grass," they chant. "But the coyote and fox, the bobcats and cougars, the snakes and even birds are to hunt."

This is by far the easiest part of the tree's message, but even so, the elders scrunch up their noses and crease their brows into frowns. "What is this echoing coming from your mouths, boys?" they ask. "Such nonsense!" One old woman even cackles out a laugh.

Yomumuli is not pleased. But these people are her creations; she feels she must pass on to them the huge stick's meaning.

So she comes to them as a very young girl, her black hair in braids, and in her tiny voice she spells out the worst of it: "Jesucristo is coming. The Conquest is coming. You will be given laws to live by that are not of your own choosing."

This is the part that Yomumuli dislikes very much. It is not good news. It is not.

Sure enough the elders scowl and the people look at one another in dismay. Some become so furious at this news that their faces turn bright red and spittle forms in the corners of their mouths as they shout: "No! This will not come to pass. It cannot be true!"

But Yomumuli knows what the stick says *is* true.

She grows angry in turn as many move away from her,

refusing to believe. She does not like to know this future that is to befall them. She does not want to even witness it. So she rolls up her river into a tight ball and shoves it under one arm. "I am leaving. I will go north," she announces as she floats up and up and into the clouds.

"Well, we are leaving, too," some of the people shout after her. They gather their belongings and enter the earth; they live to this day under the mountains.

"And we will go, as well." This group leaps into the ocean and remains there, under the waves.

Those who made one of these two choices are the Surem, very little, very strong people who will sometimes offer help to those who become lost in the wilderness or find themselves floundering in the sea.

But some of the people do not want to leave. They will wait, they decide. They stand up tall and grow taller still.

These are the Yaqui.

I. ATONEMENT

"Push, damn it!" you will tell the girl. You won't even be able to see her—it'll be too dark—but you'll be able to hear her. "Stop your blubbering and push!"

Only she'll be sobbing too hard to really help you; she's steering through the opened window, but she isn't providing much leverage against the VW's sill, having to keep wiping at her face because of the blood in her eye and all of her snuffling, and wailing: "I can't believe I did that! Oh, God, I can't believe it! Can you believe it, JC? My God, oh my God."

"Yes. I believe it," you will yell at her, full throated. "Now stop being a wimp and push the damn car, push hard!" Then you will shove, head down, shoulder against the fender, and together you will force the tires off the asphalt, through the gravel, over the scrubby grass, and just barely squeak the vehicle past the guard rail.

You'll catch her shoulder and hold her back as it teeters, holding your breath; finally it will slide-fall into the ravine, snag a bumper on an outcrop on the way down, and flip onto its roof. A puff of dust and exhaust will rush over you, then you'll lean forward with her, arms still threaded, and peer down at the hissing and ticking, tire-spinning, upside-down turtle barely visible through the dark brush below.

CHAPTER ONE

ASH WEDNESDAY

February 10, 2016:
Almsgiving, Prayer, and Fasting

"Take care not to perform righteous deeds
in order that people may see them."
Mt 6:1-6, 16-18

Guy's old pickup rattled bad enough on the blacktop, but when he turned down the Far View Ranch road, then under the arch of the sign bearing their logo and passed over the cattle guard, the steering wheel nearly jumped out of his hands. He grit his teeth, which caused that molar that had been bothering him to send a jolt of pain through his jaw, and clenched the wheel so hard the arthritic knuckles in his right hand started their familiar aching. His old truck had been falling apart for decades now—the rebuilt engine and tranny Trick had helped him install couldn't keep the dashboard from jiggling free of its mounts or do a damn thing to help its shocks—so the vehicle's clatter and jarring wasn't what bothered him. It was the fact that *he* was falling apart, getting leather-skinned, stooped and grouchy, and hell, turning 50 not so many months away that forced an involuntary growl out of him.

His son, Trick—soon to be 21, a near-grown man, tall and stocky and out-weighing him now by a good forty pounds—turned in the seat beside him, pushed at his sunglasses, and said, "You can buy a new truck anytime you want, Dad. We can afford it—pretty much any kind you want."

"The damn truck's fine," he grumbled. Trick was just off the shuttle from the university in Tucson; Guy knew he shouldn't be making the young man wish he'd stayed at his graduate studies there instead of taking the time off for a visit, so he straightened in his seat, rocked the kinks out of his neck, and tried a smile.

It didn't work. Trick shook his head at him and asked: "What are you snarling about now?"

So Guy shrugged and set his eyes on the distance. There were fine views all over this southern Arizona rangeland, but his favorite was this one, the one heading home, either from Tucson, a 45-minute drive north, or the short haul from Sonoita where he'd gone to pick up Trick and a couple of bags of groceries. Apache Peak crowned the Whetstones and loomed over the Imperial Cienega Resource Conservation Area that set their small ranch's eastern and northern boundaries. The weather had been warmer and dryer than normal for this time of year, and the wildfires scorching the grasslands had already started. But the windmill they passed was still churning up sweet water and their small herd of white-faced Herefords gathered around it seemed happy enough. The driver's side window was at half-mast ever since it'd gotten knocked off its shelf—which was downright chilly on these early spring mornings but fine much of the year—and the wind of their passing lifted Guy's long, grey-brown hair and resettled it around his shoulders. It was a good day. A fine sunny 60-some-degree day, and Trick was home for a time.

"You growing your beard out again?" his son asked him with a sidewise glance.

"I don't know. Maybe." Guy risked taking a hand off the steering wheel to scratch at what was now quite a bit more than stubble. It was growing in mostly brown but flecked with white, and Guy wasn't sure he would keep it; he already knew Star didn't like it. *That's* pretty much why he was growing it—in protest.

"Well, you're looking kind of scruffy," Trick said, turning away.

When the out buildings and then the casitas and finally the historic ranch house came into view, Guy's smile turned genuine and a familiar burn warmed his chest. And sure enough, just as they pulled into the yard, Sally, his and Star's five-year-old, was slapping out the screen door and running full tilt for the truck. Only this time it wasn't "Daddy!" that came squealing out of her but Trick's name in Spanish: *"Truco, Truco, Truco!"*

"Guess she missed you," Guy mused as he shifted into park. The driver's side door was the only one that still opened —JC had done a post-pivot that had jammed the mechanism on the passenger's side—so Guy shouldered it open and stood aside while Trick maneuvered out of the vehicle and swooped up his half-sister. He looked enormous compared to the little girl in his arms, then he swung her up on his shoulders and they really were a giant, a two-headed one, and much too tall to fit under the roof of the porch.

"Watch her head," Guy cautioned, then "Jesus!" popped out of him as Trick squat-walked up the steps and the curly-haired girl ducked down; they cleared the wooden support beam by inches.

"Come on, monkey, get down now," Trick instructed her, and Sally knocked his sunglasses off unhooking a leg from his shoulder, then she half climbed, half slid her way to the weathered wooden boards of the porch. The screen door opened again, and Mariana was there, smiling her greeting at his son. "*Buenas tardes, señora*," Trick said as he bent to plant a kiss on the middle-aged woman's smooth, brown cheek. "Happy Ash Wednesday." Trick bent to retrieve his sunglasses but then paused as she backed up into the deeper dark of the entryway and asked her: "It's okay to be happy, right? I mean, on Ash Wednesday?" Her musical laugh was the only response Guy could hear. Unless there was something wrong with his hearing now, too, because he saw they were head-together whispering when he followed them inside. His son looked normal-sized again; he was just a little taller than the willowy Yaqui woman.

Mariana turned to him. "Groceries," she said to remind him, and Guy spun around with a muttered, "Oh, shit" to retrieve them from the bed of the truck. Damn if his memory wasn't going, too.

But Trick caught his arm. "I'll get 'em," he said. "I gotta grab my backpack anyway." Then he nodded at Mariana: "*Solo un minuto.*"

"Daddy," his daughter said. Her voice was suddenly pensive, and when he bent over, she took his hand. Her face had gone from beaming happiness to too serious: "Momma called."

They were seated around the dining room table, its dark wood crowded with serving dishes filled with enchiladas, refried beans, rice, and a salad. The candles were lit, for a change, and Mariana had set out their best plates on colorful placemats. They'd started eating before Guy noticed what Trick must have when they'd first come in: a black smudge across Mariana's forehead. So it *was* Ash Wednesday again, and time for the weekend ceremonies at Old Pascua in Tucson to begin. Every Friday Mariana would be taking the afternoon off to watch the Lenten processions into the plaza, and she'd stay over at her son's house for the dances that began early the next seven Saturdays and lasted until Sunday afternoon. The ashes must have come from the Our Lady of the Angels Mission church on the southern outskirts of Sonoita, but all the weekends of Lent Mariana would be celebrating with her people in Tucson, and things around the ranch would seem to slow to a stop.

Guy knew he was out of line to resent her absence during those weeks, and it wasn't negotiable—it had been a condition for her employment that he'd agreed to readily enough when she'd started working for them—what was it?—over three years ago now. But it meant their weekend meals would go back to the chilies and soups that he could manage once the leftovers ran out, and if they had guests in the casitas—which they didn't, but a couple of times they'd had a few unlucky tourists during this time—they would be fed the same fried eggs, dry toast and usually-burnt bacon that he and his daughter ate on his most ambitious mornings. JC would disappear for days at a time as if Mariana's absence detached him from the ranch somehow, and Sally would stop minding him and start terrorizing the place. Hell, even the horses, even the god-damned cattle, would all start acting up—he'd been through this three times before and knew it with a certainty.

"What are you getting all morose about now, Dad?" Trick asked him.

It made Guy raise his head and stop shoveling food into his mouth, but he just kept chewing instead of answering his son. Trick would be back at school while it happened, Star would most likely still be staying at her father's in Tucson; he and Sally and the absent JC would have to bear it all alone this time. But Mariana was making a motion with her napkin, so Guy stopped his interior rant and imitated her; food in his beard again, apparently.

Then Mariana got Trick talking about his research results and how the chair of his committee was going to co-publish an article on some kind of equine virus with him; simultaneously she stilled Sally's attempt to squirm from her chair with a look that somehow got the girl to resettle with her hands in her lap; then she rose, asking, "Who wants desert?" as Trick finished up. The flan she brought back to the table was creamy and sweet and had Guy licking his plate, but he knew better than to ask for more—*she* was watching his weight, even if he wasn't. Guy had always been skinny, and having a little spare tire to tote around with him was a sign of his contentment, in his mind —except now there'd be weeks of it wasting away. He thought about maybe sneaking into the kitchen later and finding it in the refrigerator.

"I made you a dentist appointment," Mariana told him as

she plucked his fork from his hand. The tug of war over the empty plate was brief. "It's all paid for—I gave him your credit card number. You just gotta show up on Monday morning, 9 a.m. Of course if you miss it, that's money down the drain." The last came from over her shoulder as she carted a pile of dishes into the kitchen.

"What's wrong with your teeth?" Trick wanted to know. The young man was dark-skinned like his Yavapai mother had been, and wore his long, black hair in a braid that fell to the middle of his broad back, but now that he wore contacts instead of glasses, the light blue eyes he'd inherited from Guy and a white grandmother were even more noticeable.

Guy was about to tell him: "Not a damn thing," when Mariana called from the kitchen: "Not a damn thing a dentist can't fix."

Sally was off her chair and climbing onto his lap, her sticky hands on his cheeks, then trying to pry open his mouth: "Lemme see," she insisted, but Guy pushed back his chair and rose with her in his arms instead.

"*Gracias*, Mariana," he said over his daughter's, "I wanna see. Please?" as she squirmed in his grip. "That was a fine meal, as usual." But he knew there'd be no amount of praises or raises that would keep her from taking all the coming weekends off. "Let's get you ready for bed, girl," he said to his daughter, leaning an ear away from her, "Noooooo!" No wonder he was going deaf.

But he clearly heard his son, still at the table, as he started up the stairs: "When you get done there, Dad, we need to talk."

Trick and Mariana had moved from the dining room out onto the porch. They'd left the front door ajar, and Guy could see the empty chair with a glass beside it, waiting for him. If it was a pitcher of water or lemonade they had on the rickety little table between them, there was nothing really wrong—just a normal, family conference. Minus Star, of course. But as he took his jacket off its hook and put it on, then eased out of the screen door and settled in his seat, Trick reached down and grabbed the bottle of Jack Daniels by its neck.

"What?" he demanded, immediately regretting how surly he sounded. But, god-damned it, the two of them—Mariana holding her glass like it was forgotten in her hand, staring off into the dark yard, Trick poised to pour with that serious set to his jaw—they had him on the defensive. He fumbled for his glass, held it out.

If it was about JC, he could handle that. The fifteen-year-old—Jack Crawford—had been trouble from the start, but that's why Guy had agreed to take him from his folks, Kate and Richard. The boy had briefly been helping Rose with the horse training and riding lessons she gave at Kate's old ranch outside of Winslow, but even Rose hadn't been able to handle him.

That was saying a lot—Rose had been about as crazy as kids come, back in her day. But apparently JC's "destructive habits' and an obsession with knives had created a situation where the kid's family's choices had come down to a stint in juvie or a move. Guy's new home in Sonoita was "the move."

That's why he and Star had hired Mariana. Back then they had been holding their own, raising their just-a-baby, Sally, and starting their new B and B business, but they could tell right away JC was a complication that couldn't just be folded into the mix. They needed help, and Mariana had stepped up to the challenge admirably.

But as soon as Trick asked him, "Where is JC off to, anyway?" Guy knew that wasn't what this "big talk" was about. He sipped his whiskey thoughtfully and let Mariana answer for him.

"He makes himself scarce whenever you're around," she told Trick, her eyes still unfocused on the distance. "You know that. You can use his bed—I put clean sheets on it."

"No, I don't mind bunking in Sally's room," Trick hurriedly assured her. Then "So where is he off to?"

This time Mariana turned to Guy, her chin cupped in her hand. "You want to explain what's going on?"

Frankly, no, Guy didn't. The two boys—or rather, the young man and the wayward youngster—had started off wrong and gone worse from there. Guy had always felt a bit responsible for JC's troubles, having gone through his kidnapping and rescue—and being the one who'd shot the perpetrator right in front of the then five-year-old. But Trick didn't have that history and wasn't inclined to cut the foul-mouthed in-your-face smart ass any slack. The first time JC ran away—not long after his arrival at their Sonoita ranch when Guy had confiscated the stash of knives JC had secreted under a loose floor board in his room—Trick, home on holiday, had been the one to find him, and Guy was certain some of the pre-teen's bruises —like the spot purpling on his chin—had been sustained *after* his discovery along the side of the 83 with his thumb out.

"Guy," Mariana said.

Guy roused himself. "He's staying with his girlfriend's family." But they both just kept looking at him. He took a swig of whiskey and held it in his mouth to ease the pain of his sore tooth. After he finally swallowed he said: "She's a few months older and has her license already. She takes him to school."

Mariana made a little growling sound. "When they go."

Guy sent a scowl her way. "He *mostly* goes." But she was right—they'd get a call from the school at least a couple times a month about JC being absent.

"That pimple-faced girl? What's her name—Heather?" Trick wanted to know. Guy nodded so Trick went on. "Jeez, Dad, you know that girl's family is trailer trash—I mean, literally. The dad's a junkie. And don't they have four kids or something all squashed in there? Where the hell does he even sleep?"

When Guy just shrugged Trick took a slug of his whiskey, coughed, and looked away; Mariana didn't seem to have touched hers. Guy followed her gaze to the stars powdering the sky over Mexico, ruminating.

So maybe they were ganging up on him again about Sally. "What's the big deal about kindergarten, anyway?" Guy demanded suddenly. "It's called 'first grade' for a reason, and it's comin' soon enough." Of course the truth was he just liked having his daughter around, and between Star and Mariana, she'd been getting a fine—and bilingual—education right here at home.

But "Why are you harping on that again?" Mariana wanted to know. Trick gave a heavy sigh, then stuck his long legs out and leaned back in his chair, making the wood squeak. Guy wasn't used to his son looking so blue.

That left Star. Guy took a gulp from his glass and realized it was nearly empty. They kind of had him there; he was worried about her—about *them*—too. He'd understood her desire to spend more time with her father when he'd first had the stroke; Guy had even encouraged her. But it seemed every time she left for the old man's house up in Tucson she stayed longer. There were never enough caregivers to satisfy her, or they'd quit all of a sudden, or there were doctor appointments she'd want to stick around for. This time she'd been gone a good ten days. Guy had wanted her to pick Trick up at the university and bring him home with her, but she'd said no, to have him take the shuttle, that she'd try to make it home by the weekend and give him a ride back up to Tucson, instead.

But Guy had no intention of letting on to Mariana and his son that he was feeling a bit deserted. "If it's about Star then you're just wasting whiskey," he told them, then he drained his glass to emphasize his point. "Her taking care of her dad is just the right thing to do." But he couldn't help muttering under his breath: "The old fart can't last forever."

Mariana heard him, shook her head and tsked at him. She gathered her shawl around her and set her full glass down on the little metal TV tray between her and Trick. "You better put your father out of his misery soon," she told Trick. "He's running out of suppositions."

Trick leaned over, picked up her glass, and handed it to Guy. "I got a call last night. From Jasmine."

"Whoa." Guy sat up, looked at the glass in his hand, and knocked back a big swallow. News of Jasmine, who Guy always thought of as Trick's girlfriend, no matter how many times he was corrected, was never good. She'd disappeared just days before her father—and Trick's foster father—had moved down to Tucson with Trick, and Guy was sure his sense of abandonment didn't even register on the same scale as the young girl's. She'd run away on Guy's horse those many years ago, good old Sweet Pea, one of the most reliable mounts Guy had ever had or known about. But Sweet Pea had found her way back home, while Jasmine, the runaway, she'd stayed missing for years. By the time Star had finally located her socked away in the juvenile justice system, she'd made one hell of a mess out of her life and had caused the family even more heartbreak.

"Daddy, I have to talk to you," came through the crack of the doorway.

"I thought you said you were putting her to bed," Mariana said, rising.

"I said I was getting her *ready* for bed," Guy corrected her as he waved at her to sit back down. "What, honey?" he asked the one eye he could see peeking out at him.

"Momma called." It was barely a whisper.

"Okay, honey—I know. We talked about that before dinner."

A little hand appeared, waving him inside.

Guy set his glass on the porch and made an effort to suppress the groan as he pulled himself to his feet. He pushed through the door and lowered himself carefully to one knee. His back was bothering him again; if Star had been home, he would've had her work her magic on him. But Star wasn't home and hadn't been for quite a while, maybe even longer than 10 days.

"Grandpa's real sick," his daughter informed him solemnly.

"Yeah, I know, baby. We talked about it—remember?"

"She said he's gonna die."

"She did? Well, I guess you didn't tell me that before." And Guy earnestly wished Star hadn't done any such thing.

The little girl's eyes welled with tears. "I don't want *you* to die, Daddy. Ever."

"Oh, sweetie. Don't . . . don't worry about that." Guy pulled her into his arms.

"Momma says everybody dies, that I'm not to be sad."

"Well, of course you can be sad," Guy murmured into her mousey-brown curls. "I don't know why your momma was even talking to you about that."

"But not you, Daddy—right?" Sally persisted. "Not you ever."

"No. I mean . . . ."

"Don't lie to her, Guy," Mariana admonished him as she stepped around him in the entryway. She swooped up the sobbing child. "There's got to be death, babe. There's no way around that. Even your father. Even Jesucristo."

"Wait now," Guy broke in, but Mariana was making her way up the stairs. His daughter was still crying but quietly now, her full attention on Mariana.

"I'll tell you the story again." The Yaqui woman's voice receded with each step. "It starts out sad—*muy triste*. But it has a very happy ending—*ya verás*."

"Dad?" Trick towered over him, his whiskey glass still in hand. "Jasmine's been cleared for release next week, if she can find a sponsor." He lowered his head and said: "She doesn't have anybody else."

Guy had to grab on to the door jamb to creak and crack his way back onto his feet. He knew that was true; the young woman's father had died several years before in a car accident; her mother was in some kind of home with mental problems. Guy sighed, took his jacket off, hung it on its hook beside the door, and squared his shoulders.

"Dad?" Trick said again. "I said she could come here. That's the right thing to do, isn't it?"

"Aw, jeez, son," Guy sighed, fingers rasping through his scruffy beard. He didn't remember having to look up to meet Trick's eyes—black wells ringed with blue; was it possible the kid was still growing? "Look, I know Star's a healer, but I'm sure as hell not. So I don't understand how we suddenly get to be the home for all the messed-up youth in the world."

"Jasmine's my age," Trick countered. "She's not a kid anymore."

Guy took a step back. "And that helps how?" He sighed and shook his head, no, then nodded. Then he took his son's glass out of his hand and chugged it empty, handed it back again. He let that be his answer and trudged up the steps after Mariana and his daughter, thinking he probably needed to hear that story again, too.

CHAPTER TWO

ROSE

Winslow, northern Arizona

There's only so much you can do for another person. It really doesn't matter how much you want to help them, if they won't even try, it just won't work. I guess that doesn't stop you from feeling bad about it, though.

Jack had been a normal enough little kid when it'd happened, but I guess you don't survive a kidnapping and come out the same. And he wasn't alone; we were all changed by what happened that day, that night, Guy maybe even more than Jack. Guy took off on Sweet Pea while Bane was still a body under a tarp, but then there wasn't a body, only scuff marks where someone had fallen and scrambled up. It was a mystery that went on for weeks, and Guy's absence only made it worse. The whole time we—the family Guy had left behind: Richard and Kate, Grace and Jack, me and Cody—had huddled on the ranch and kept in each other's eye sight. I swear, Cody would stand right outside the bathroom door and pester me with questions to make sure I was still in there. I finally let him take his showers with me.

It was just we so desperately didn't want anybody to get taken again. Too late for Guy, though—he was already gone, and he stayed that way, although he finally wrote to Kate and let us know where he was gone to. Turns out he had an eleven-year-old son from some old girlfriend he had never even told us about. Of course Guy was never much of a talker, 'cept to Grace; I bet she knew. And Kate didn't seem all that surprised, come to think of it.

Eventually Bane—the guy who'd grabbed Jack—turned up shit-faced on a neighbor's ranch and they hauled his alcohol-damaged ass back to prison for being drunk and disorderly on top of the class 2 abduction charge, which would have put him away for what was left of his miserable life. But for some reason that I will never understand, Kate and Richard argued for the class 4 and a judge agreed. Personally, I don't think Bane is any better off out of prison, and Cody doesn't think so, either. He's got fetal alcohol syndrome pretty bad; he's not really able to take care of himself. But I don't guess he's our problem anymore.

Me and Cody getting together, that was the one good change that happened afterwards. Like I said, he appointed himself the family watch dog—not that Shane hadn't been doing his job; he'd actually been the one to find Jack. But Cody parked himself right next to me, anyway, starting that next day, and I don't think we've been apart for more than a matter of hours since. He gets my bipolar thing and just rolls with it, and it has gotten better now that I'm finally on the right meds and all.

He was good with Jack, too. Grace seemed really resilient; she was only eleven at the time, still she seemed to be the least affected. But it was clear from day one that her little brother had been traumatized back into a kind of infant that we all had to accommodate, but mostly Cody, I guess because he was so good at it. Kate would just melt when Jack started crying, and Richard would get mad, for some reason. Well, maybe I'd get mad at Jack's weirdness, too—it just made everything so much harder. A trip to the grocery store turned into a shriek-fest if Jack was in the cart and any strangers got within shouting distance. I'd feel like grabbing Jack and running for the truck, but Cody wouldn't even flinch; he'd speak softly into Jack's red-faced, open-mouthed, slobbery howls, pat his back, gone all rigid, and move on down the aisle, looking for his favorite breakfast cereal. At home Jack followed Cody around, doing the stuff Guy used to do. We did end up auctioning off the buffalo, though; neither of us wanted to mess with them anymore.

If things had stayed like that, we could have managed. As it was, Richard took early retirement and he and Kate left the ranch for Cody and me to oversee; they moved with the kids to Flagstaff where the schools were better able to handle Jack's freak-outs. They doped him up with a bunch of tranquilizers, eventually, and speaking for all the kids who've suffered such "medical interventions," it only makes life easier for the people doling out the pills. The developing brain rewires itself, all right, and Jack shut up. But totally. He was a fidgety mute when they'd come out to the ranch for a visit. He did do okay around the horses, though—they calmed him down, just like they had me when I was such a fucked-up teenager. That's why

I thought we could take him when he started looking like he was a danger to himself—and others.

I remember Kate calling me the first time it happened. Like all good moms, she thought the school was just blowing things out of proportion. Coming at a teacher with a pointy pair of scissors? Not her baby, no way. But changing teachers didn't stop the attacks. Richard tried home-schooling him, but surly and disrespectful doesn't even come close to describing that kid's behavior around his dad; there certainly wasn't any learning going on, just a lot of frustration. So we took him over the winter break; he was only 11. We got a tutor to come out to the ranch, and he stayed with us several months before Cody— and the juvenile justice system—caught on to what he was up to.

It wasn't theft—he didn't *take* things, he just destroyed them. He'd evaporate soundlessly from the house, push Kate's old car down the lane and jump it—this kid was 11, remember, and we don't think he had any help. He'd drive into town and find a former schoolmate's house, cut the screens to get in, then he snipped, slashed, stabbed and ripped upholstery, couch pillows, draperies. He pissed on boots and boxes on the floor of closets—even took a shit once. He poked car and truck tires, lifted hoods and pierced hoses, sawed through wires. It was an orgy of mindless destruction, and then he'd reappear at the breakfast table, tousle-headed, surly—from exhaustion, no doubt—wanting to be waited on like his mom used to do instead of getting his own damn cereal like Cody and I.

Even today, I'm pretty sure, when Jack's around you better lock your cars, bolt your doors, and latch and bar the windows, even if you live out in the country like we do. Hell, *especially* if you live out in the country. And for God's sake, don't try saying "no" to Jack, or try to discipline him in any way; he'll go for your eyeballs—and your nut sack, if you got 'em—and watch your throat because he'll be aiming for the jugular. It's out of proportion, all right; he just goes berserk.

We wanted to help him; we really did. And I truly regret we weren't able to. But now it's Guy's turn to try.

And I wish him all the luck in the world.

CHAPTER THREE

JASMINE

Along the Verde River, north central Arizona
Late Summer 2010

Sweet Pea knew the way. Trick had told me how he'd practiced his escape on her, like he even needed to escape, that asshole. Everybody loved Trick, even my mom, the one ally I had left after I'd pushed all Trick's "mad at my dead mom" buttons and got him to explode.

I was—and am—really good at pushing people's buttons; I've had lots of practice.

The night I took Sweet Pea and ran away was about a week after my 15th birthday—I was finally the same age as that stupid shit Trick again. We were *not* boyfriend and girlfriend; I had already figured out that type of deal wasn't for me, and, Jesus, he was my foster brother, for Christ's sake. My folks had been fighting again—oh, yeah, I'd started it, and slammed and locked the door to my room, but I could still hear Mom tell my asshole father that she wouldn't miss him at all once the divorce was over and he'd moved with Trick to the school in Tucson, but she sure would miss Trick. I was used to hating my dad—he was such a know-it-all, dictator-type—but the news, only days before, that he was divorcing my mom had sent me reeling. And now Mom saying how Trick was such a nice boy —and so smart. Well it pushed me right over some edge. I'd known Dad liked Trick better than me from the start. Now Mom—she was already showing signs of the dementia, forgetting stuff I'd told her right after I'd said it. If she was going to be a traitor, too—well, I wasn't getting stuck with that.

Yeah, Trick was so smart, all right. Smart enough to steal all the school's horses. Jesus, what an idiot. Like he could get away with that!

Trick was taking them to his uncle's ranch on the Yavapai rez over on the Verde; at least, that's what he'd told me he was going to do. I'd pushed his buttons, pushed my folks' buttons, slammed my door, crawled out the window once I heard Mom's pronouncement of undying love for asshole Trick, and had gone by his house to stop him. Well, maybe that's why I was there.

It didn't matter; he was already gone. I must have missed him by minutes because I'd just grabbed the backpack someone had left lying on their living room floor—the magic backpack all us kids had heard stories about, part kitchen, part closet, part survival kit—when a car's lights coming down the driveway sent me scooting out their bathroom window and up the hill towards the stables. I was just about there when I heard the horses running; it kind of shook the ground, and they were neighing back and forth, like asking each other what the hell was going on. It was a really good question—since when do goody-goody kids like Trick turn rustler? Ha ha. I'd had to work hard to goad him into it: "You're no Indian, you don't give a damn about your uncle, you're such a chicken shit, you lied to your mom, your poor dead mom, so just do it, already. You've been bullshitting about this since you first came here." Yeah, I went on and on. But it finally worked.

It was dark as hell, but even I could pick out their trail. I walked all the way to the back pasture where the fence was still strewn along the ground, stumbling around in the turned-up earth where about fifty horses had passed through it and then down along Ash Creek. I had no intention of following Trick to his uncle's; I'd heard he was one mean bastard. But I didn't want to go home, either—like *ever*, and I haven't—so I turned for the stables, hunkered down in a pile of saddle blankets, and went to sleep smelling horse. Then in the early, early morning Guy brought me one, the best one: good ol' Sweet Pea.

He was doing all that lovey-dovey talk like he does with her and a lot of the other horses, telling her he'd be back soon, not to worry, but he had to see to his son, his stupid son that everybody thinks is so nice and sweet and smart—and who'd run off with all of the school's horses. That's when I decided to go, too, only I knew Trick would be found and forgiven—that Guy certainly *would* see to that—and my plan was to just *stay* gone.

Maybe I haven't managed to do that, exactly. But I *have* stayed unforgiven.

As soon as Guy was out of earshot, I was saddling Sweet. I could hardly get on her wearing that stupid backpack—it was so damn heavy—but I managed, then I found Trick's trail again just as it was starting to think about getting light. The magic reflectors he'd nailed along the trail were not working so well for me as the dawn came up—the asshole had been so proud of that part of his plan—but I only needed to follow them for a while; Trick had told me how hard it had been to find a culvert under the interstate big enough to accommodate a horse. Once on the other side, Trick's plan was to turn the herd north along the river so he could give all those horses to his mean-as-shit uncle.

A couple of hours later, me and Sweet Pea were on the banks of the Verde.

I made her go south.

CHAPTER FOUR

WILDERNESS WORLD

The moon has set and the sun is just a smudge of lighter grey at the eastern horizon when Mariana pulls her shawl tight around her shoulders, drops her head, and closes her eyes; her fingers come together in the familiar, intimate, intertwining of prayer. *Rattlesnake, scorpion, Gila Monster, stay asleep. Puma find your way back to your children now.* Mariana knows that in the wilderness world all creatures—plants, animals, even rocks—are one, but these wild beings are still dangerous if not properly placated. She turns to look back at the old ranch house with its circle of casitas, their occupants still in the Dream World. Beyond them a few of the horses stir in their pens, and farther off, the windmill turns its blades in the winter breeze. Mariana makes the sign of the cross: finger-tips to her forehead, to the center of her being, to her left then right shoulder. *Huya Ania bless my way.*

Normally she would have been starting a load of laundry on her way into the still-dark kitchen at this time. But her son has called to tell her he finally has enough javelina skins to make his poncho and ferocious mask; the animals' hooves he would now be able to fashion into rattles to wear around his waist. Using these he will transform himself into a *Chapeyka*, one of the evil ones who follow the *Pharisios*, Pontius Pilate's soldiers, into Old Pascua's plaza during the Lenten processions. Only one thing is missing, but the one is many: the cocoon rattles that will drape his ankles like rows of bracelets. He is dancing for the fourth time this year, which tells Marianna that her husband has been gone five years now, and she very much wants her son to continue in his father's footsteps—oh, so literally. So instead of making tortillas she is on a search for the pupal stage of the *mariposa de noche*—the giant silk moth.

If this was the Sonora Desert south of Tucson, she would know exactly where to go to find cocoons. But Mariana is still relatively new to this high desert rangeland around Sonoita, so the path of her gathering seems aimless. She lets herself through the first pasture gate and in the dim light she can just make out the small herd of white-tail deer gathered around the salt block; they are familiars and do not startle, only lifting their heads to watch her cut through that pasture and then another one. Now the ground slopes into a ravine and she passes under a small oak before her feet find the wash at the base of the hill, which she follows like a road until it peters out. By then the birds are awake and traveling with her, wrens darting from bush to bush, a thrasher calling, doves cooing, quail in a ragged string. When she climbs the next small knoll, gamma and lovegrasses, a faded brown now in the winter chill, rustle underfoot, with clumps of agave and mesquite, the occasional prickly pear, to avoid. There are beetles and buzzing flies, but no sign of moths. There are scurries of lizards, ground squirrels, and mice, but no twigs laden with spindle-shaped cocoons. There is a rabbit that sits up on its hind legs to watch her pass.

Seeing the *taabu* makes Mariana recall one of her father's favorite stories about Rabbit. He told her *Taabu* had a comfy house dug deep in the side of an arroyo and shaded by a desert marigold. But one day when Rabbit was not at home, a hungry snake came slithering along, tongue flicking, and he slid inside Rabbit's house to wait for his next meal to return. But when Rabbit came near, he saw the sinuous track of his enemy, knew he lay in wait, so he called out to his house: "Good morning, House!" Snake lowered his head to the ground and stayed very still. When there was no response to his greeting, Rabbit called out again: "House, are you angry with me? I said, 'Good morning!'" Snake stopped even his flicking tongue, even his breathing. A third time Rabbit addressed his house: "If you won't say 'hello,' house, I shall just move somewhere else!" At that the snake lifted its anvil head and hissed: "Good morningsssss." "What?" Rabbit exclaimed in mock alarm. "How could this be? Everyone knows that houses don't talk! That is the voice of my enemy." And Rabbit hopped off to find a new place to live.

Sally, Guy and Star's little girl, would like that story, Mariana decides; she will have to remember to tell it to her. The child is almost always the first one to join Mariana in the early-morning kitchen. She smells the bacon sizzling in the pan or the chilies broiling and hauls her blanket and an armload of stuffed animals downstairs with her. If there are guests staying in the casitas, Mariana sends her back upstairs with the various creatures—bears and dogs and kitties clutched to her chest, a giraffe tucked under one arm by its long neck and a monkey that clasps around her neck. Notably there are no horses—the little girl is afraid of them, despite all of Guy's patient instructions.

But on days like this one when it's just the family, she lets the little girl play underfoot with the menagerie while she makes the chorizo hash or *chilaquiles* and cuts tomatoes for a salsa. Once their voices grow loud enough Guy will appear, wanting his coffee; when Star is home, he'll take his own cup and a milky one for her back to their bed for a time. And finally, when everyone else is just about done eating, JC will tromp into the dining room, grab whatever is left on the platters, stuff his mouth and pockets, and clomp out the door to do his chores.

Only this morning Mariana has left the table empty except for a note: Gone Hunting.

She stops as the sun clears the horizon and takes her bearings: she's been keeping the Santa Rita Mountains behind her on her left; the Rincons near Tucson rise in the northern distance; the low humps of the Whetstone Mountains are ahead and to her right. She's in the Imperial Cienega Resource Conservation Area now; she knows "cienega" means "marsh," and that Imperial Gulch and Cienega Creek lie ahead. But she hopes she will not have to travel that far. Any water—a spring, a pond, even a stock tank—would cultivate the plants the caterpillars needed to attach their chrysalis to. Or perhaps there is a cave nearby, where Surem would be—they would surely help her. She knows of these places around Tucson, but to travel there would require her son to come and get her or for Guy to take her there—she knows how to drive but does not like to. So she keeps walking, tugging the shawl from her shoulders and draping it over her head as a *rebozo* to shield her eyes as the sun climbs the sky. She pauses at the lip of another wash, sniffs the air, then finds her way down a slope to its sandy bottom.

The warm earth slows her feet, and with each step she says five syllables in her heart: *Ave Maria*; then eight: *llena eres de gracia*; then seven: *el Señor es contigo*; she goes on until eventually she has recited a rosary. But even though she pauses in her prayers at the end of each decade to contemplate a sacred mystery for a time, the mountains look no closer when she stops walking, tilts her head back, and uses her shawl to wipe her glistening face. So she shifts tactics and calls out loud for the Surem to assist her: "*Muéstrame el camino por favor!*"

Almost immediately a breeze moves through the lowest branches of a nearby mesquite and sets a silken bulb swaying. "*Gracias!*" she calls out, and it does seem the Surem have done her a great service, for after collecting a few of the moths' cocoons from that plant, Mariana spies another batch in a neighboring red-barked manzanita crowding the edge of the wash. She inhales again, deeply, then moves toward the scent of wet earth and finds a hidden, shaded place where the ground dips into a catchment basin someone dug a long, long time ago around a seep. There stood an ancient Emory Oak loaded with the hardened, water-tight skins of the moth's pupa.

The small pool of *ba'am* is lined with brush except for the trails worn by hooves and paws down to its murky water, and seemingly every lower branch of the surrounding plants is weighted with the dark lumps of the silk moth's oversized cocoons. Mariana begins carefully stripping their leathery husks from the branches and has been busy at the undertaking for several minutes before she sees the mouth of the *teeso*—the Surem's cave—nearly covered by the jumble of boulders resting against the steep side of the wash; the sight of it makes her dip her head and hurry to complete her task.

On this day, instead of cleaning up the kitchen, moving one batch of laundry into the dryer and starting another, and then roaming from room to room through the house with a rag and a dust mop, Mariana is on her knees in the moist earth steadily picking cocoons from their anchor-twigs. She finally knots her collection into her shawl, stands, and swings it over one shoulder.

"*Gracias. Muchas gracias,*" she says first to the cave, then to the earth, the water, the plants, and the blue, blue sky. When she turns and starts for home, her shadow is a hunch-backed Kokopelli traveling beside her.

February 14, 2016:
Temptation

"... Jesus returned from the Jordan and was
led by the Spirit into the desert ...."
Luke 4: 1-13

Guy's first temptation upon awaking was to skip breakfast entirely, just let Sally and Trick go hungry —JC hadn't been around since the day Trick had arrived—and make the horses and all the rest of the critters wait while he rolled over and went back to sleep. He'd been lonely the night before and had drunk a six pack of a strong craft IPA by himself, then when he'd realized the next day would be Valentine's Day and that Star would not be home, he'd made a drunken phone call that he now regretted. So he closed his eyes again and tried to let sleep retake him; maybe another forty winks would ease his headache, if not the pain in his molar. But of course the cats had other ideas.

There were two of them, an almost pure white Burmese mix named Caicos and his orange tabby brother, Turks—apparently some islands Star wanted to visit—and they knew how to launch a coordinated attack. They were Star's cats, and normally she fed them and cleaned their litter box, but she was missing in action. She hadn't made it down for Trick's weekend visit, after all—her dad had fallen again. Nothing broke this time, but he had a sore hip and was having trouble sleeping because of it. So during his maudlin phone call, she'd agreed that Guy and little Sally should drive Trick back up to Tucson later in the day, and then stay the night up there with her at her dad's; they'd bring Mariana home with them on Monday.

The "cat attack" would be funny if it wasn't so damn annoying. It was usually the tabby that started it, jumping up on Star's side of the bed and making its way over to Guy when she was absent, which was currently the case. He'd sit inches away from Guy's face and switch his tail just enough to tickle his nose. Then Caicos would scramble up—he had super short stubby legs and was a tad overweight, so leaping wasn't exactly in his repertoire anymore—and lie on Guy's legs. If Guy made any movement at all under the covers, there'd be a claws-out pounce. If he tried to stay perfectly still, eyes closed —as he was doing now—Turks would lean in and gently nibble on his nose—like that.

"Stop it," Guy told him with a wave that shot the cat from the bed. But the tabby only raced to the room across the hallway to sit in front of his empty bowl and meow. Guy sighed and rubbed the thick stubble on his sore jaw, leaned forward and met Caicos' cool blue eyes. "Do I have to?" he asked the cat, but he knew the answer to that.

Sally must have heard him rustling around in the cats' room because before he could finish dishing out their breakfast and cleaning their litter, he had a tousle-headed five-year-old pressed against his knee, along with her tattered baby blanket and an armful of stuffed animals. "Daddy?" she said like a question, but then she didn't ask him anything.

"Morning, honey. Okay, let go. Let me finish this," he told her, but she hung on tight, and he had to sling her along with him as he worked, then he picked her up and carried her into the bathroom so he could wash his hands. He splashed some water on his face, then got the washcloth wet and tried rubbing some of the grime off the girl's cheeks—she hadn't wanted a bath the night before, had wailed in protest as he ran the water and then had taken off running. By the time Guy had hunted her down and brought her back to the tub, the water was cold, and the girl had refused to sit, just stood there naked in the knee-deep water, hugging herself and shivering. "I think maybe this is child abuse," Trick had said with a flip of his long braid before leaving the bathroom doorway he'd been filling. So Guy had just wrapped the girl in a towel and pulled the drain.

But Star wouldn't like her daughter coming to visit with ratty hair and a smudged face, so Guy gritted his teeth against the pain in his jaw and his head and kept struggling with cloth and comb until the girl's squeals brought Trick back to the doorway. "Don't even say it," he told his son without looking up from his wrestling match.

"Well, could you take it out of here so I can pee?" Trick asked.

When they passed him in the hallway, Guy's arms full of

child, blanket, and menagerie, he noticed Trick had his glasses on, and it made him smile; the man was still the boy he remembered when he wore his glasses, and looking at him made his heart burn.

So maybe he would rustle up some bread and cheese for these scoundrels, after all.

"BECAUSE I SAID SO," Guy told his children in the breezeway of the mare motel. "I'm in charge here, and what I say goes." The two of them had saddles and bridles at their feet; Trick had even loaded the old, black backpack onto the pile. "You two put all that gear back now—don't make José do it."

Sally's "Noooo, Daddy! I want to" was overlaid by Trick's "Come on, Dad. Marianna says you're too much of a homebody these days. A little exercise will do us *all* good . . . ."

"You don't even like horses," he challenged his daughter, and he turned back for the house. Then Trick's "I promised her I'd show her that secret cave Mariana told us about" made him stop and snarl over one shoulder: "Well, why the hell did you do that?" A Sunday trail ride when they had paying guests in the casitas to escort around was one thing; traipsing through the wilderness on a quest for a hidden cavern and a mysterious seep hole that probably didn't even exist on a day when he was finally going to get to see Star was another thing entirely. "We're going to Tucson. Pack up, and let's go."

Just a few minutes later Guy parted the living room curtains and saw that the two of them were in the yard, Trick mounted on Amigo, the largest of their trail horses, with Sally behind his saddle, invisible except for the hands she had wrapped around his waist; he led Guy's horse, Dice, by its reins. Guy moved over to the porch's screen door, sighed, and pushed it open. So much for exerting his authority.

But he hadn't done as Trick had asked and packed them a lunch, a decision he greatly regretted a short hour into the ride. Sally's enthusiasm about all things horses had waned, as Guy had known it would—she'd just been showing off to her big brother—and a snack might have provided at least a moment's distraction from her nervous chatter: "Why is he so sweaty? I don't like flies. It's not much farther, right? Right, *Truco*? Don't make him skip, *Truco*—that's scary! Stop, okay? When can we get down? My hiney hurts. He's too bouncy."

Guy was riding point, as usual, and he let Trick answer or not answer his sister as he saw fit. This was another reason he had resisted the morning's excursion—he just could not understand how a child of his, who he'd done everything in his power to raise right, could be so adverse to horses. So he tried to concentrate on finding a way through the rolling grasslands and the cuts of oak-cluttered arroyos; Trick had said to keep the Santa Ritas to their left and thread the gap between them and the Whetstones to the northeast. He'd been over this section of BLM land several times and had never seen a single cave, let alone any magical seep or catchment basin, so he expected to be turning things around here pretty soon.

But he also realized he owed Trick a little down time to do what he really loved out here. He'd kept him busy almost every minute of the day since he'd gotten there, filling in for JC in the horse barn, helping him with what little ranch work their small herd of Herefords required, and even doing some "honey-do" chores around the house and the casitas—Guy wanted things to look nice when Star finally *did* come home—

so this was the first occasion Trick had had to enjoy himself. He'd let the kid decide when he'd had enough of his sister's squirming.

"When are we going to get there? *Truco*—how much farther? This is no fun. I'm hungry. I don't see any caves at all. Amigo is pooping again—gross!"

Yep, any time now Trick would be pulling up; Guy kept one eye on their aimless path, weaving through hock-high grasses and around the occasional fairy duster shrub or agave, and the other cocked over his shoulder so he'd see the moment when this would all get turned around and he could pack them up and start them on the road to Star. Eventually Guy had been doing so much cockeyed, backward-looking that he realized his horse had strayed from his intended course over to within eyesight of the highway up to Tucson.

Trick's the one who noticed it: "Hey, I can hear the 83— we're supposed to be heading more to the . . . ."

When the young man didn't finish his sentence, Guy swung around again. There was Amigo, swishing his tail, and his daughter behind the saddle, eyes wide in alarm. The empty saddle.

Guy spun Dice and spurred him over the rough ground to the other horse. When Amigo jerked back at his panicked approach, making Sally squeal, Guy worked to soothe him, not his daughter: "Hey, hey, hey, now, boy—it's okay. It's okay." He leaned over to grab his reins before looking for Trick, already berating the young man: "God-damn it, Trick. What the hell are you . . . ."

"There's a car down here," Trick called from the edge of a ravine. "It looks like . . . . It could be . . . . You better get over here."

Something in his son's tone of voice silenced the rest of Guy's tirade. He swung down, led both horses over to a large mesquite, and secured their reins to it with a Highwayman's Hitch. He considered helping Sally down but decided against it. "You," he said, pointing at her, instead. "Sit there and be quiet. Don't move, and for God's sake, don't kick that horse."

"Noooo, Daddy," Sally said, her eyes still wide. She held out her arms to him.

But he wasn't sure what had bothered Trick about the car, so he said, "No, you just sit there and be good," to her imploring reach. It was another thing he didn't do that morning that he'd soon regret.

If she'd been there it might have stopped him.

He was tempted to just jump. The car was upside down, so he couldn't really tell from the undercarriage if it was JC's girl-friend's beat up yellow bug or not, but it was most definitely at least partly yellow, and it certainly looked like a VW. The sight of it made his stomach clench; he had to check it out. Even if it wasn't the girl's car, he felt guilty as hell that he hadn't made JC at least call him now and again over the past few days. The boy had resisted all of Guy's efforts to parent him, but that didn't mean he wasn't Guy's responsibility. If it *was* Heather's car—God, he couldn't even think about that. He tugged his hat down, made sure it was snug on his head, and rubbed the bristle on his sore jaw. The first ledge was quite a way below the canyon's rim, but he was still thinking about making the leap when Trick—who'd been scouting the ravine's edge toward the highway—rejoined him.

"I can't see any damage to the guardrail," he said as he came up. "It'd be tight fit past it, but I guess it's a small car." He tilted his hat back on his head and added: "Not much traffic on a Sunday to send for help." Guy noticed he had his cell phone in his hand and pointed at it with his chin. "Naw, no service. We'll have to go back. Or maybe the land line over on the Imperial Ranch is closer."

"Did you check the mile post?" Guy asked him, then he had to look over at his son to see him nod. "Any way down from the bridge?" If Guy could at least get closer, make sure of the make of the car, and—oh, man, his stomach hurt—check for occupants . . . . But Trick was shaking his head, no, this time.

"We gotta call the cops," Trick said softly. Then he raised his eyes from the wreck to his father's. "Right?"

"Who knows how long it's been there," Guy mused instead of answering him. "I mean, I don't hear anything." But just as he said that, "Daddy?" came floating over the waving grasses from where he'd left Sally with the horses, then a moment later: "*Truco?*" But he ignored it. "If it was recent you'd hear the motor ticking, something . . . ."

"Yeah—right?" Trick agreed. "Somebody must have seen it already and reported it."

"I don't know. There's a lot of brush down there." It wasn't that far of a jump, Guy was thinking. They both stood, hands on their hips, looking down on it a good while longer.

A car rushed by on the highway, then he heard: "*Truco, Truco, Truco. Where are you?*"

"The ravine's not that deep." In his head Guy added: *They could be okay.* He rubbed the ache in his belly through his shirt, tried to unclench his sore jaw.

"Dad? Daddy?"

"I'm pretty sure there's a couple of bungee cords in the backpack," Guy said finally. Trick had loaded the old pack behind the cantle of Dice's saddle.

Guy didn't turn, but he felt his son's eyes shift to him. "You're going to bungee jump off the highway bridge," the young man stated flatly.

"No," Guy scoffed. He was actually thinking about making an anchor out of one of the bushes beside them on the edge of the ravine. A belch escaped him. "Okay, you take your sister over to the ranch, make the call, get some help out here, maybe something with a winch . . . ."

"We don't do that anymore, Dad, remember?" Trick countered. "Star taught us different. We stick together."

Guy looked up and squinted his son into clearer focus.

"Let's all go," Trick added.

Guy considered, and yep, Trick was right—that's exactly what Star would have said. It was also the lesson the old O'odham woman had tried to teach him a long, long time ago: tribe spirit. Besides, JC wasn't down there, not anymore, anyway. Maybe. Probably. It wouldn't be neglect to leave him now; the neglect had come before this.

But he was going down there.

"Okay," he told Trick. "Get a move on. I'll be right behind you two." He jammed his hat down as tight as it would fit.

"Dad?" Trick said, eyeing him. Then they heard Sally again, a piercing, impatient scream: "Dad!"

"Go on, now," he told his son. Then as soon as he heard his daughter exclaim: "Finally. I thought you guys were never coming back," he made the jump.

CHAPTER SIX

KATE

Flagstaff, northern Arizona

I miss him.

When Richard first retired, we spent all our time together. Even before that, figuring out how to manage Jack's anger and depression had us putting our heads together in thought, our hands together in prayer; we had to figure a way out of the mess that our lives had become once . . . , after . . . when . . . .

Then deciding to hand over the ranch—that one was hard. The place had been in my family for four generations. But we didn't outright sell it to Rose and Cody—they couldn't have afforded it, anyway—we just leased the house and yards to them. We put the canyons with the rock art into a trust, slaved side-by-side packing up a lifetime of stuff, hell, four times four lifetimes.

And then planning the move to Flagstaff, only an hour and

a world away from the high-country rangeland around Winslow. Finding our new home, the right schools. Grace was easy; she was always easy. But Jack . . . .

Once we were settled we fell into a routine: I rousted the kids out of bed while Richard made breakfast, we drove them to school together, first dropping Grace off at her middle school and then driving over to Jack's charter because it took so long to pry him, screaming in protest, out of the car. Then we'd run errands together: grocery shopping, taking library books back, stopping at the hardware store. I even took up swimming—Richard would joke that I "paddled" rather than swam, but I got wet, anyway, and enough exercise to lose some weight; besides, I did it just so I could be with him instead of home by myself. Tuesday afternoons—discount day at the theater—we tried to fit in a movie before picking up Jack. Grace found her own way home, usually catching a ride with friends. Jack didn't have friends. The new doctor had upped his meds and he kind of turned into a zombie, but at least he wasn't acting out in class anymore. Or acting, at all, actually. I feel bad about that period of time now, but several months later when Jack stopped taking the pills we'd been giving him, things got even worse, so I don't know . . . .

When we had to take Jack out of school and Richard started teaching him at home—well, trying to teach him—all of that "together" time disappeared. I'm embarrassed to admit that I could no longer—can no longer—stand to be in the same room as my son. Or my husband when he's around my son. The dining room table became a battlefield, the kitchen a wrestling ring; even the garden I'd started at the back of our little lot was close enough to hear their shouting matches. I'd melt out the back gate, wander out into the pines, haunt the public library and bookstores, disappear into the open doors of churches or a coffee shop, then slink home in the almost dark to make a dinner that only Grace and I would eat. I really don't know how the boys survived those years; I'm not sure how I did, either. I wish I had been able to take better care of Richard, at least, because now that he's moved out, I really miss him.

Mea culpa.

I MISS HIM.

Not the him now—that would be crazy—but the old him, the sturdy little boy whose smile showed off the new front teeth too large for the rest of him, with my hazel-brown eyes and long, dark lashes, too pretty, maybe, for his own good. I could never punish that boy; he was just too adorable. He loved animals, could become them. We knew early on that he was on the autism spectrum—he had a tell-tale arm-flappy thing—but high-functioning, and real smart. And a touch of ADHD, but whose kid doesn't have attention problems these days?

The "maladaptive behaviors" didn't start until after . . . when . . . later. Personally, I think it was Jack's way out of the years of panic that had swallowed him. His way of fighting back against the fear was to become too brave, too unmindful of the consequences of his actions. At first I thought it was like kids in the old days going out on "cow tipping" escapades, but cars are the horses now—he started rolling mine down the driveway and joyriding around town when he was only eight or nine and just barely able to see over the dash—which is a lot more dangerous. And guns are the wooden swords we used to bash things with. But Jack didn't like guns. In fact, he hated them; he told one of his shrinks it was because the Indian man who'd abducted him had had *my* little pearl-handled pistol, the one his grandpa had given to me. Bane, the bane of our existence, had threatened him with it.

But Jack did like knives. Anything sharp, really, but especially knives, of all shapes and sizes: boning and paring knives, jackknives, utility knives, hunting knives. And other pointy things like ice picks and screwdrivers and tiny little files. It was quite a shock when I snuck into his pigsty of a room and dug deep enough into his closet to find his collection. Some were old and rusty, undoubtedly gleaned from the ranch's tool shed; others were newer, pilfered from God knows where. I made Richard go in there and look at the cache with me later, but I didn't do anything else about it. I just wasn't ready to believe it —he was only ten. I still needed to hold on to my notion of him as my tousle-headed, long-lashed, mooing or peeping or meowing, always smiling little boy. The boy I miss so terribly now.

Mea culpa.

I MISS HIM.

I honestly don't think Jack would be as bad, that our family would be as broken, if Guy hadn't left us so abruptly when . . . after . . . because he'd . . . . I know I felt physically ill for days after he took off on Sweet Pea, running from the law again, from what he thought he'd done, and I'm pretty sure my roiling nausea wasn't from the shock and exhaustion of Jack's abduction and return but from the loss of *him*, the man I'd come to rely on—whose physical presence had come to sustain me— even more than Richard. God, *so* much more than Richard.

Maybe a month after he left, Grace brought in the mail and I saw Guy's boxy scrawl on one of the envelopes—he'd never learned cursive, apparently—and I'd felt my heart take a huge leap in my chest. For some reason—some *crazy* reason—I thought he was writing to claim me, to tell me that he could no longer live without me, me and . . . . Well, me, at least. I know I had felt that way—hollow inside—since he'd ridden off and out of our lives. But it was just a short note—Grace read it after I'd dropped it on the kitchen table—telling us he'd found his son and work at that school near Prescott, and that he hoped all was well with us. That was pretty much it.

All was definitely not well with us.

I wrote him back, several times, careful to lie convincingly about our new and evolving circumstances. It comforted me to know that he really wasn't all that far away, especially once we'd relocated to Flagstaff, though I was fairly certain we would never cross paths again. But then Jack got so bad that even Rose couldn't handle him, and she was the one who reached out to Guy.

Now he knows what our lives have truly been like. I don't think he'll ever know how much I miss him though.

Mea maxima culpa.

CHAPTER SEVEN

JASMINE

Along the Verde River, north central Arizona
Late Summer 2010

Some asshole juvie judge once asked me if I was sorry about all the shit I've done. I lied and said yes, of course, because that's what he wanted to hear. Then I fed him a bunch of other crap about wanting to turn my life around, and how glad I was that I had such a caring man overseeing my case, and how I'd been thinking about going into social work or even law so I could be just like him—you get the drift. I mean, sometimes during my wild years there were periods of suffering—starting right away, in fact—when I wished for a soft bed, a hot meal, a nicer me, but sorry? Shit no. That just ain't who I am.

Sweet Pea knew the way to the water, but she didn't want to go south along the Verde, that was clear. She kept stopping, swishing her tail, swinging her head around and looking at me with one or the other big, brown eye. She was balky, and slow, and stopped a lot to snuffle grass, but she didn't outright refuse to go on when I gave her my heels and a bunch of, "Gee up, now, Sweet. Go, go, go!" She was too well trained for that. She stalled—all morning long, in fact—but she never stopped.

It was hot and muggy by the water once the sun cleared the trees, and I was already starving—I'd been too busy antagonizing my parents the night before to get any supper and occupied since by running away—but I knew I wasn't going back, would never go back, so there was nothing to it but to keep kicking that stupid horse down the trail. It got pretty brushy once we were downstream from Camp Verde, and I was wearing my regular "uniform" of cut-off shorts and a sleeveless T-shirt, so I was getting scratched up bad, and sunburned, practically nodding off from exhaustion, thirsty as hell because I didn't dare get off that horse to drink from the river—which the horse, by the way, did frequently—for fear that she'd run off or not let me back on again, and did I mention I was stomach-achy hungry?

So I was miserable, yeah, even before the mosquitoes or some little, gnatty things started welting up my arms and legs, and soon I was bleeding where I scratched them, bleeding from the scrapes of branches along my arms, bleeding from the slap of mesquite on my legs, and bleeding from one big gouge on my cheek from a broken tree limb that damn near took my eye out.

But it wasn't any of those discomforts or disfigurements that got me to stop harassing old Sweet Pea down the river. I get really determined once I set my mind to something, even when it's a stupid thing to do, and no amount of sleep deprivation, thirst, pain or even hunger—and *man* was I hungry—could have dissuaded me from my course.

It was a tiny little hummingbird. Damn that ziggy-zaggy, screech-screech-screech-screech-screechy thing; it was weirdly insistent. And I didn't even seem to be the object of its intentions—Sweet Pea huffed at it like it was an old friend, and she started ignoring me and following it.

Stupid horse.

Stupider bird.

CHAPTER EIGHT

ENCHANTED WORLD

Hummingbird floats from the fog of *Yo Ania* just as Mariana comes quietly out of the house. *In the same way, Deer emerges into view of the hunter, prepared for its sacrifice.* She pauses to admire the tiny bird's iridescent throat, its thrumming wings, then takes the steps down to the dirt of the yard. *Deer will lay its life down in a spray of blood.* The hummingbird zips toward her, the whir of its wings the only sound in the peace of the early evening, then turns its attention to the bright floral print of Mariana's scarf. *Each drop will transform into a beautiful, fragrant flower the very moment it hits the earth.*

In the dying light, Mariana glimpses behind the shimmer of the hummingbird's movements a world that is full of song and mystical events and inexplicable alterations. Once, before the Talking Tree, all Yaqui inhabited this enchanted realm, but when the Jesuits brought them *Jesucristo* and the

Conquistadors threatened domination, the ancient ways transmuted. Now *Yo Ania* with its formidable dark powers overlaps just the edges of things.

Mariana's son, who is to dance again as an evil *Chapeyka*, will channel the old, old spirits who opposed the crucified one, and they will be redeemed, just as her son has been. Her son, who as a younger man had scoffed at his father's devotion to his faith, now respects the ancient, mystical ways of their people. Like the awkward dancer who passes through *Yo Ania* on his way to the village where he is to perform and arrives filled with grace, her son is changed. So once again this year, Mariana is preparing the cocoons for his ankle rattles.

Mariana re-enters the house after the hummingbird has finished its inspection of her scarf. Later, alone at the table after the others have all gone to bed, in the kitchen still fragrant with the *arroz con pollo* she prepared for their dinner, she will shake each little chrysalis to hear the pupa bounce inside, then cut one end open and insert the tiny pebbles she has gathered from the yard. She will roll the sinew taut and use her sturdiest *bachia* to stitch the cocoons closed, then attach them, one after another, to the long, leather string. The thong will encircle her son's ankle many times, each tiny cocoon adding its small rattle to the cacophony.

For some *Yo Ania* is a physical place, but for Mariana it is the memories and voices that occupy her mind while her hands are busy at their task: her father's creased face comes to mind, earnest with his telling of the spirit realm, her mother's sly smiles while she chopped or stirred and spoke of it: "It is part of our lives but not *of* it, made of something different. *Yo Ania* is the world of the Surem and their power and seeps from their caves." These caves, their *teesos*, Mariana knew, could be caverns, rock shelters, lava tubes, anyplace cool and dark and safe.

Mariana snips and punches through the tough leather until her fingers cramp. In her mind's eye she watches Guy in a recent morning's dusky light, his long hair pulled back in a pony tail, as he approaches the herd of deer at the salt lick, hand out but fingers curled under, walking slowly, using his string of calming words, his settling voice, until the nearest one, ears flicking, takes the salt from the man's skin instead of crowding the white block with his brothers. She hears an old Navajo man, a hand trembler, tell a woman—her name is Sweet something, Sweet Kate, but Mariana doesn't know her—to look for her father in the mesas, "but down, below the ground," and then listens to a young man, an Apache, chant his death song, knowing, somehow, he is still alive. She sees her sister animate again, a young girl again, sticking out the tongue turned blue from her melting slushy as they stand on the side-lines of the dust and commotion of the *La Gloria* ceremony. She hears her own voice using words she has not spoken yet: "Yes, *hijo*, it is good to be happy today because we know of our resurrection."

Mariana stops, stretches her hands wide, and rolls her head one way and then the other. Then she takes a sip of her tea and reaches into her *waari* for another cocoon, relaxing her mind to visit these other times, other places: She sees the old O'odham woman spit the egg into her hand and rub it into the center of Guy's chest, hears his involuntary gasp as the burn of overpowering love—until then absent from his life—overtakes him. She hears her husband's jokes over the music of the drum and flute, the violin and harp at the saint's day festival when he first got up the nerve to approach her, feels her body relax into an exhausted sleep as her newborn son's squall erases all the pains of a torturous labor. She suffers again her sister's long exhale into death as she passes through to the other side. Each memory, each voice fills a cocoon and rattles around inside it; sewn together, they form a tribe.

The needle slips, and Mariana jerks the pricked finger back. There is a spot of blood on its tip, and the boy Guy has taken in, JC, fills Mariana's mind. He's standing in front of his cowering girlfriend; she holds a hand against a bloodied lip. JC is yelling at someone to back off, that they'll do it. Mariana looks up reflexively; she knows JC is in his room, can just barely hear his television turned down low, even though it's forbidden this late on a school night. She puts the finger with its pearl of blood into her mouth and hears the racing engine, a sickening thud, a man's scream, and Heather's shout: "Grab the drugs."

Marianna shakes the vision from her head and decides she's worked long enough for one night. She folds her basket and other supplies into the special blanket she keeps for this purpose only, packs it under one arm, stretches her long frame out of the kitchen chair, and travels down the hallway. On the way, as she approaches the room Star uses for her therapy sessions, she is surprised to hear the other woman's words echoing soundlessly in her head: she is intent on conjuring another child, a son, this time. Candlelight flickers and a cloud of skunky marijuana smoke dissipates just as Marina passes the suddenly-dark doorway. Of course the room is empty; Star's father has fallen and broken his pelvis, so she has had to go to him in Tucson. So Mariana does not pause but continues on to her rooms at the back of the house through a haze of cedar, sage and sweet grass incense, humming along with the soft melody of a flute.

CHAPTER NINE

SECOND SUNDAY OF LENT

February 21, 2016:
Transfiguration

"While he was praying his face changed
in appearance and his clothing
became dazzling white."
Luke 9:28b-36

"Ow! Ow! Ow! Shit! Fuck! Oh, my God!" Guy worked to stifle his noise, not wanting to draw the kids back, but his ankle hurt so badly after the jump that the yelps just kept coming out of him: "Oh, God. Oh, my God."

Sure enough, there was Trick's head poking over the edge of the ravine a good eight feet above him, his long braid dangling. "What the hell, Dad—what'd you . . . .?"

"Daddy!" came from Sally's littler head below her brother's; her curls sprouted around her pink baseball cap in corkscrews.

"Jesus, you're a crazy bastard," his son was muttering as he turned and extended a leg over the lip of the rock.

"No. Ow. Ow. Trick—no," Guy told him. "Don't come down here—just give me a minute. I'll be—ow—I'll be all right." But his ankle was *not* going to be all right; that much was clear. He raised his pant leg and carefully eased off his boot to examine the right ankle as gravel spattered down around him from Trick's attempt to find a foothold in the rock. "Get the fuck back," he paused to shout at his son. It wasn't a compound break, at least—no bone showed through or whitened against the skin; it just hurt like hell. A fracture, then, or—hopefully—just a bad sprain. "I'll be all right," he said again, quieter this time, probably more to reassure himself than his kids. He felt like a fool. He'd done this to himself and put his children in a fix in a questionable effort to save JC—holy crap, what had he been thinking? JC wasn't his child. Now what?

"Now what do we do, Dad?" Trick echoed him. "Jesus, I told you not to do that."

"You sound like me," Guy mused up at him.

"Yeah, well, I hope I'm a lot smarter than you," Trick said. He was back to kneeling on the rock above him. "I sure as hell would never have tried that."

"No, I wouldn't have wanted you to," Guy agreed. Now they were going to have to rescue *him*. "Aw, shit," he sighed. He wondered if he could still drive up to Tucson to Star's dad's in this shape. Nope, definitely not. "Damn it," he sighed again. He found his hat—it had been jarred off his head and lay, brim up, on the ground beside him—and leaned to look over the shelf of battered granite to find the bottom of the ravine where the overturned car was. It was just a short scree slope slide to get to it from here. "Find a mountain," he told his son as he settled his hat back on his head, "and pray for reception."

"There'll be something in the pack that we can use to haul you up," his son countered. "Those bungee cords, or maybe the clothesline is still in there. I'll be right back . . . ." Clearly, Trick still did not want to break up their little party.

And neither did his daughter, apparently, because moments after Trick's head disappeared, Sally was scrambling, feet first, over the ledge. She found a toehold, another, took a reach. "Sally, stop! No!" Guy shouted, but she kept coming; she looked like a spider scrambling over the rock. "Wait. Honey . . . ." Guy tried to stand—he had to get under her, catch her—but he just collapsed onto his side in a spasm of agony. Another "Shit," burst out of him. He heard the clatter of gravel onto the ledge, then she was there, squatting beside him.

"Don't cry, Daddy," she said soothingly. She scooted close on the rock and put a hand to his cheek.

"Sally! What the fuck," Trick sputtered above them.

Guy rolled over to look up at his son. "Use the bungee cords to lower the pack—I could use some water. Then get a move on. We'll wait for you here."

Trick towered above them, heightened into a giant again by the eight-foot wall of rock between them. He put his hands on his hips. "Well, no shit—you guys aren't going anywhere." Guy heard him cursing as he turned and disappeared. A moment later it was the old black backpack that was scraping gravel down onto them. Then Trick's face appeared again.

"Holy Moses, Sally—you really are a monkey," he told his sister as she grabbed the pack and stumbled over to Guy with it; it was heavy, but she managed. "I'll be right back—well, I'll be back as soon as I can, anyway."

"Don't worry, *Truco*," Sally said in her sweet, little girl voice. "I'll take care of him."

<hr>

"Ow! Stop moving around so much," Guy grumbled at his daughter; she was trying to find a comfortable spot on the rocky ledge beside him.

Sally had fallen asleep on his lap for a while, and he'd closed his eyes with his hat tipped over them, trying to nap just to pass the time. But he kept jolting awake anytime he or the girl stirred enough to jostle his ankle, and Sally had always been a restless sleeper; they had to unwind her from the bed sheets most mornings. He tilted his hat back when the ground around them went dark and, looking up, saw it was a cloud passing before the sun. A voice entered his head and Guy argued back wordlessly: *He's not* my *son.* But he sighed deeply and picked up the binoculars he'd been using to examine the overturned car again; that was definitely a wire wrapped around the exhaust pipe attaching it to the undercarriage. Then he shook his daughter's shoulder and said: "Come on, monkey. Wake up. We got work to do."

When Sally sat up, rubbing her eyes, she knocked over the propped-up umbrella Guy had positioned over her as a shade. "I didn't dream it," she said.

"Nope," Guy assured her. "Ow, so listen." He raised

himself up on both elbows, turned to look over the edge of rock toward the wreck. The backpack was within reach—they'd taken one of the space blankets out of it and spread it on the ground to rest on, had eaten an old candy bar, some trail mix, and a bag of crackers Star had stashed in one of its pockets, and finished one of the several bottles of water it contained—and sure enough, a little digging revealed the length of clothes line Trick had remembered. "Here," Guy told his daughter, "get this around you. I'll hold on to you while you go the rest of the way down there and take a look around, okay?"

It was a bad idea, he told himself while she got her arms and head and then shoulders through the loop he'd made in the rope. A terrible idea, in fact. But Guy tugged her close and made sure the knot at her waist was secure, then butt-slid over to the edge of the rock to watch her descend, one foot, the other, one hand hold then the next, no hesitation. She quickly made the bottom, then jerked them both—him forward with an "Ow" and her staggering back—when she tried to run the rest of the way to the overturned beetle; the clothesline was too short. There was a moment when Guy thought, no, he shouldn't let her go ahead without him hanging on to her some-how, but before he could say anything she'd shimmied out of the rope and was headed for the car again. "Be careful, honey. Don't touch anything—just look, okay? Just look inside and make sure it's empty."

Then there was a long, tortuous moment when her head disappeared inside the vehicle—the window had been left down. He couldn't help the sigh of relief when her pink hat reappeared again. "It's not empty," she called up to him. "There's books and two backpacks; I know one is JC's 'cause it's got that Iggy Pop sticker on it."

Guy groaned quietly—he didn't want to upset the girl. "At least there's no people—right?" Then he had a thought: "There's nothing, well, dark on the seats that you can see, is there?" He couldn't say the word "blood" to her.

Sally's head disappeared again, popped back out. "No. I mean, I don't think so. It's messy in there, though."

"Messy?"

"Yeah—school papers and Jack in the Box bags. Stuff like that."

Guy couldn't suppress his flush of irritation; the nearest Jack in the Box was in Sierra Vista, a good forty miles away. "Okay, sweetie. I guess you better get back up here now."

But Sally was moving around the wreck to its off side, steadying herself with a hand against its front bumper. "Eww," she said, wiping her fingers on her T-shirt, "Something wet. It's on the tire, too—gross."

Guy's stomach clenched, and he grabbed the binoculars and brought them to his eyes; the finger-smears across Sally's T-shirt were a dull red. "Shit," he wheezed. "You come on back here, now—that's enough."

"What's this?" she asked instead of obeying him; Guy had to use the binoculars again to see she was holding up a tiny, black stick. "There's a bunch of them all around here." Guy watched as she collected what he realized were burnt matches. "There's a lighter, too," she said, stooping over to retrieve it. "I think JC and Heather were playing with fire," she said, looking up.

No shit.

Just then Guy heard Dice give a whinny; someone was coming. "You listen, now, girl," he called down to her in his sternest voice. "You . . . ." He was about to tell her to put the lighter and matches back where she'd found them but changed his mind. "Stick that stuff in your pocket and come back here, and I mean *now*." He heard the siren now, too.

Sally, for a change, jumped to comply. She ignored the clothesline so Guy drew it in and stashed it and the binoculars in the backpack as she scrambled back up the slope to him. "Oh, no—I got Ariel dirty," she pouted, pulling her T-shirt front out toward him; sure enough, the Little Mermaid seemed to be wearing war paint.

"Come here. Quick. Come on." When she wandered over close enough—the siren had wailed up to the overpass and been silenced, but there were voices, now—he grabbed her shirt, yanked it over her head, reversed it, and was pulling it down again when he heard a man shout: "Hey, can anybody hear me?" Guy pulled Sally in close and stifled the "ow."

"Why did you do that?" the little girl wanted to know.

"It's the style now," he told her. "And remember, you don't talk to strangers, right?" Sally nodded, a serious look on her face, and Guy clutched her to his chest. Out loud he said: "Here! We're down here." Silently he kept repeating: *Oh, JC. Oh, my son. Oh, JC. Oh, my son.*

What have you done?

TRICK and three hands from the Imperial Ranch arrived right after the EMT's, and they'd helped haul Guy up off the ledge —Sally had scampered back up before anyone had even poked a head over. Once he was safely topside, they'd carried him over to the highway and stuck him in the ambulance for the ride of shame into Sonoita; Sally enjoyed it, though, and smiled the whole time the siren was running. Then it took Trick a while to get the horses back to the ranch and settled and then drive the truck to the urgent care center to collect them, so Sally was asleep again and Guy was sprawled across two waiting room chairs when he finally came in.

He told his son the x-ray had shown a bad fracture, and they'd wrapped his ankle up, strapped on a walker boot that went almost to his knee, and given him a pair of crutches before discharging him. Trick took one look at him and said, "I'll get the truck." Guy woke Sally and got her to help him stand, and they'd almost made it to the lobby doors when the cops arrived to tell him it was, indeed, Heather's little VW at the bottom of that wash. They'd spoken to Heather's dad, and now it was his turn.

But Sally was having none of it. "Nooo, Daddy, we gotta go home. We gotta go home *now*!" She nearly yanked his arm out of the socket, trying to pull him the rest of the way to the door.

Guy could have swooped her up and kissed her—if he hadn't been so woozy from the oxycodone they'd given him. He'd never liked dealing with the police, had a history of interactions with them that he was not proud of, and he wasn't ready to talk about his suspicions about what JC had done yet; he needed time to think. "Not right now, officer. I've gotta get this kid home and feed her," he said over Sally's: "Nooo, Dad—come on! We gotta go!" He told them to stop by the ranch and was spelling out directions when Trick pulled the truck up under the Health Center's overhang. "I'll be there. I ain't goin' far like this." Certainly not up to Tucson to see Star; he'd already called her to let her know what had happened.

But something must have delayed them because the cops

hadn't arrived at the house until after dark, and Guy had already been snoring on the couch in just a white undershirt and his boxer shorts when their headlights and then a spotlight had lit up the living room window. Even though he'd been upstairs in his room, Trick made the door before Guy could orient himself, find his crutches, and half-lunge, half-stumble to answer their rattle-pounding on the screen, but he'd shouldered his son aside and squared himself in the blindingly white space; his undershirt was all aglow in it. "I'll handle this, Trick," he told his son over his shoulder. "You go on back upstairs."

Because Guy had decided no way was he telling them the truth about what he and Sally had found at the wreck of Heather's car. He'd answered the officer's questions in slurs and mumbles, standing right there in the doorway, saying he didn't remember much after his fall because of the shock of it all, proclaiming intoxication, ignorance, and exhaustion, rubbing his eyes, his whiskered face, with both hands, the crutches clutched under his arms like broken wings. Still they seemed to suspect he knew more than he was letting on, and when he finally focused on their uniforms, Guy realized the lady deputy in front with the flashlight trained on his chest who was busy warning him about the consequences of tampering with evidence was backed up by an SUV-full of border patrol agents. That was interesting.

He did tell them he hadn't seen or spoken with JC since Ash Wednesday, four days before, when the boy had grabbed a burrito off the dining room table and headed outside to do his chores. As to why he hadn't filed a missing person report, well, JC was very independent. It sounded lame even to Guy, so he added: "You think I should have?" hoping they'd think him just callous and ignorant rather than willfully negligent. He tried to squirm out of it more by telling them JC was not *his* son, no; he was just staying with them for a while. He didn't elaborate on how the "while" was soon closing out the third year.

Heather's VW had a distinctive clatter to it—the tailpipe was just wired on—so he told them he was sure it was her who'd picked JC up before school that Wednesday because he'd heard it rattle in and out of the yard. When they asked if they could speak to Mrs. Thornton he'd told them with an umbrage he did not feel that there was no "Mrs." Thornton; he'd asked her once and she'd said "no." Besides, she was pretty much living up in Tucson with her father now. Guy did not tell them anything else, just sock-footed the tabby cat aside, making it look like it wasn't allowed outside—which it was— then took the business card the deputy proffered and backed up clumsily until he could swing shut the door. He was to meet with the chief marshal over in Patagonia in the morning.

At least that meant he wouldn't have to go to the dentist.

Guy turned and looked up the stairs in time to see Trick disappear back into the hallway; Sally still crouched on the landing, her face pressed between the railings. "Is JC bad?" she asked Guy.

He didn't know the answer to that yet, so he just told her: "Go on back to bed, monkey."

Trick drove him over to the marshal's office the next morning, but Guy made him wait in the corridor while he sat across the desk from the white-haired, hugely mustached man. Guy tried to find out about the Border Patrol's involvement and got a stern: "There are elements of this case that I'm not able to disclose." Then the marshal told Guy he knew that Sally had been down by the car—they'd caught her tracks. Their discussion, if you could call it that, both being men of few words, neither willing to disclose more than he had to, concluded with another warning about Guy taking any actions on his own to find JC and a promise to keep him informed of the progress of the "missing persons and possible homicide" investigation.

Guy sat up at that; he surmised it *was* blood on the front fender then, but he didn't say anything, just got to his feet and took up his crutches.

"Ow! Jesus, that hurts! Stop it," Guy told his daughter. He'd been sound asleep on the couch, dreaming about being back on that ledge again, when Sally had climbed first onto his sore leg then lay on his chest and peered close at his face, her way of trying to see if he was asleep and insuring that, no, he sure as hell was not—anymore, anyway.

"I made a tent, Daddy, so I can sleep down here, too," she informed him.

Guy groaned his head up off the cushion to look. Sure enough, she'd drug four of the chairs out of the dining room and hooped a sheet over their ladder backs.

"I'm gonna make one for *Truco*, too," she said as she slid off him and crawled under a corner of the sheet. Guy glimpsed one of the cats, the white one, curled up inside it.

"Well, I think you'd be better off sleeping in your own bed, girl," he told her, wincing from the pain in his ankle as he pulled himself up. "I sure as hell would be happier up there."

But Mariana had said he had to stay down here, that no way was she letting him and his teetering hobble anywhere near those stairs.

It had been a week, already, since his injury; the only good part of it had been Monday when Star had brought Mariana home from Tucson and stayed a couple of nights. But Guy had been so doped up on pain pills that he'd barely spoken with her; he'd felt overwhelmed by the need for sleep and had kept nodding off in the middle of their conversations. Besides, he hadn't liked what she was saying: Trick was going to take a couple of weeks off from his graduate studies to manage things around the ranch—meaning keeping *him* and Sally out of trouble whenever Mariana was too busy to—because Star's dad was failing, refusing to get out of bed, to bathe, even to eat; this notoriously ravenous man would now only rally if she was there, coaxing him, mouthful by mouthful.

And Star had been ragging on him: "Why haven't you called Heather's dad? Are you sure you didn't see anything that might help the marshal out? I think you should ask him again about the Border Patrol's involvement—that has to mean something. I know you can't walk much, but there must be *something* you can do to clear this up. I have a real bad feeling about JC, Guy. Aren't you worried about him, honey? And could you possibly start shaving again?"

No, Guy didn't want to share his suppositions with either Heather's dad or the Marshal—that the still sticky blood left on the VW's bumper and tire meant its driver must have struck someone or something hard enough to do grievous injury, and that the spent matches and lighter implied a failed attempt by JC and Heather to disguise their accident. They could have hit a deer—but then why try to hide it? And yes, he did think the connection to the Border Patrol meant trouble—drugs or immigrants or both; the border was so close. Of course Guy was worried and terribly afraid for the boy. And no, shaving was the last thing on his mind right then.

But he would keep this vigil on the couch.

CHAPTER TEN

GRACE

Flagstaff, northern Arizona

My brother wasn't always this way. He came back different after he got snatched for a night. That seems so terrible, I realize, but soon after his safe return I heard him telling the Winslow sheriff about what had happened and, you know, it didn't sound all that bad to me; it wasn't like Bane beat him or even really mistreated him. And it didn't last very long—we were all home before noon the next day. So it doesn't seem nearly as bad as what happened to me. But the trauma changed him. Just like it changed me.

It's just I'm much better at hiding things.

"I think I better get going now," I tell him. *I can't remember his name; maybe I never knew his name. "It's late. I should get home."*

JC was still plain ol' Jack back in those days on the ranch. I was trying to be "Ace"—that's what I wanted to be called. But, of course, nobody—nobody except Guy, that is—ever did. And, well, I guess I really wasn't much of an ace at anything, anyway. Except getting myself into the worst fucking possible situations.

And making sure nobody ever found out.

"Come on, don't be such a baby," he protests. "It's early—not even midnight. Here—take this; it'll perk you right up."

Everybody thought I was so mild and steady, such a good girl. And I was, I really was—that is, until Guy took off on all of us. He never even said goodbye to me. I mean, he'd told me he had found out he had a kid about my age, living somewhere over near Prescott, so I was actually the first one to know *why* he went, but I was an infatuated eleven-year-old and couldn't forgive him—wouldn't forgive him—still can't forgive him —anyway.

I don't think my mom ever will, either. And I for sure will never forgive myself.

I should have shook my head, no, with my jaws clamped shut. Instead—to please him, to be liked—I stuck out my tongue and tasted the cigarette smoke on his fingers, the chalky coating of the pill. I didn't even know what I was taking. Ecstasy? Speed? Or something else.

Eventually my little brother became such a pain in the ass with all his stupid knives and obsession with stabbing things that we all had to move to Flagstaff, and that's when I kind of reinvented myself—what was I? All of thirteen? Just old enough to know I had a choice: keep my old, country hick persona and hang with the boring, smart kids, or grow my curly red hair out into this huge mess, pile on the make-up, hike up the black skirt, pull on the black tights, the black everything, stop feeling sorry for myself and being all pissed at my parents for not liking each other anymore and even more pissed at my brother for being a crazy brat, and have some fun. What do you think I decided? But I couldn't let my parents know. I just couldn't do that to them, on top of all the Jack-shit they had to deal with, and with Mom gazing out windows all the time, wishing she was somewhere else with someone else.

While I was just wishing I *was* someone else.

"Here," he said, passing me the jug of Gallo wine that had been making the rounds of the house party. Whose house? Damned if I know. Where? Uhm . . . . "This will help it go down easy." To this day I cannot stand the taste of cheap wine; even the sickly-sweet smell of it gags me.

So all through high school I left home looking "normal" with a stuffed backpack that had hardly any school crap in it. The transformation occurred in the high school restroom. I kept it just a bit edgy-cool for school, then after the last bell: Watch out! Here comes Super Slut.

That padded bra was such a joke. What if a guy ever did want to feel me up? Didn't I think he'd notice the false advertising?

Nothing happened for a while. I went outside and bummed a cigarette from some girl. She warned me: "You're a little young to be out so late with this crew, aren't you? Some bad shit went down here last weekend." She took a deep drag of her own cigarette and squinted at me through the exhale of smoke. "Whatever you do, don't pass out."

Yeah, I thought I was so sneaky, but the real reason nobody ever found out about the new me was because once Jack became JC he provided so much cover for my illicit activities; they were all so worried about whether he was suicidal or homicidal or just plain old "disturbed" that I passed right under the radar. And if anything suspicious happened, man, he was so easy to blame. And he took it—at least for me he did. You could say he'd done just about anything, and he'd put a sneer on his face and just take it. That was part of the changed Jack.

No, that was part of JC.

It was almost as if the girl had conjured the effects of whatever that guy had given me with her words because right away I had to find a place to sit, I was about to pass out, and that guy was right there, believe me: "Hey, you better lay down."

Like taking the car out for a midnight spin. I'd gotten away with it a bunch of times, just practicing my fast starts and quick turns with whichever friend I'd been able to talk into sneaking out her window that night. I kept to the back roads around town, neighborhood streets, and we never got stopped. But then it got all wintery, and I wasn't that used to driving in the snow —hell, I wasn't used to driving on *anything*, really—and I hit an icy patch and sent us careening off into a ditch. We had to walk home, and even though it wasn't that far it started sleeting, so we were sopping wet and so fucking cold, and she'd smacked her head during the spin out and kept moaning about it. I was screaming at her to stop being such a wimp when I saw Jack walking toward us down the street that ran in front of our house, and he hardly even stopped, just asked me: "Where is it?" So I told him, and he went and sat in the car—in the driver's seat of the car—until the tow truck came.

I would never have done something like that for him.

I must have passed out because, when I came to, I was in one of the bedrooms. I could hear music coming from under the door—it was "I Kissed a Girl" by Katy Perry. What a stupid song. I hate that song. I hate it. I could barely lift my head up from the mattress because that guy was on top of me, pulling at my clothes. "No," I mumbled and pushed at his hands. Then louder, "No. Stop." "Shut up," he said, but I wouldn't. I said, "Stop. You're hurting me." And then he reared back and he smacked me—not on the face, on my boob, and it hurt like hell. "Shut up, bitch, or I'll really hit you." And when I still wouldn't, he did.

While Jack was waiting for the tow truck to finish winching up the car, I was sneaking back inside the house. I threw my sopping wet hoodie into the dryer, tip-toed up the stairs to my bedroom, used the wipes to slough off all the makeup, stuffed my clothes into their hiding spot, climbed into my sweet baby girl PJ's, and shivered under the covers. I was already asleep when the doorbell rang, but Dad's voice in the hallway woke me: "He's been up to it again, Kate—you'll have to come into the living room and talk to the police. No, you have to—I can't deal with him anymore. I swear to God I'm sending him away . . . ."

I don't have a brother anymore because I never told them it was me. I still have not told them.

And I'm sorry. I'm so sorry, but I never will. What I *will* do is get the hell away from here. I've already applied to the U of A down in Tucson, about as far from Flagstaff as you can be and still get in-state tuition.

It seemed to go on forever, and even after he slid off me and stood by the bed, adjusting his jeans, a smirk on his face, it didn't really end. It didn't end when he turned and sauntered out of the room, leaving the door wide open like an invitation: Who's next? It didn't end when I lifted my head and saw Jack in the doorway, crying; he'd found me somehow. He managed to help me back into my clothes, still all rubber-limbed and groggy but ambulatory enough with my arm slung over his shoulder. He's the one who propped me up against the wall while he dug my jacket out of the pile in the living room, and together we stumbled home.

And it didn't end after that either because when I saw that creep at school I'd feel a rush of shame. He would cover his mouth with one hand and snigger stuff to his friends, and I'd feel a nausea so intense I had to swallow, swallow, swallow—he was telling them!

But I never told anyone.

And I never will.

CHAPTER ELEVEN

JASMINE

**Along the Verde River, north central Arizona
Late Summer 2010**

Sweet Pea followed that damn, super-tiny bird all the way to within sight of this old house with a pasture full of horses. I recognized the horses—they were the very ones that asshole Trick had just run off with—and so did Ol' Sweet; she started whinnying at all her friends as we came up. So, what do ya know—the stupid jerk had actually managed to pull off his stunt. And that meant this was Trick's uncle's cabin tucked among the huge, old cottonwood trees, just into the Yavapai-Apache Rez along the Verde.

I sat the horse—she was being really grumbling, snuffing, she wanted to go forward; I swear she would have gone right up on the porch if I'd let her. But despite my stomach-rumbling, I wasn't going any closer until I was sure no one was home. There were no cars, but there was an open screen door with the grizzled face of an old dog in it, and other dogs yammered from some kind of kennel behind the house. So someone was home. Maybe several someones, including Trick.

But I was hungry, so I kicked and yanked and swore until I got Sweet Pea to turn back toward the water and finally swung a leg over the saddle and slid to the ground; I could hardly stand. Actually, I couldn't stand; I leaned, hunched over, one hand on the reins and the other clinging to a stirrup, for a good five minutes—man, my butt was sore! I finally sloughed off the heavy pack and let it fall to the ground; my shoulders ached like hell. But I was also thirsty, and so was the horse, apparently—she started shoving me toward the river, nearly stepping on me, throwing her head. So I hobbled down there with her and drank just like she did, face to muddy ripples. When I felt about ready to puke, I sloshed back up the bank with the horse in tow and stood at the edge of the row of cottonwoods and looked back at the house.

They say when you die that your life passes before your eyes. Well, standing there, considering my options, I was doing just that kind of inventory, only in reverse: okay, so if I go up there and knock, and Trick's there, and his uncle's not all that mean, I could get food. But maybe Trick's not there and his uncle *is* the drunk, White-hating bastard that everyone says he is, and I'd get a belly full of shotgun pellets, instead. Then what happens after they feed or don't feed me? Regular people would try to make me change my mind about running away. They'd make me call my dad. Or maybe they don't know I've run away. Maybe I tell them I'm just checking to make sure Trick made it okay, and I go back to the school with him, just like nothing's happened. Or they're not regular people and they don't give a shit and just let me go on my way. Or they kidnap me and hold me for ransom. Or they eat me instead of feeding me. Shit, how the hell was I supposed to know what they'd do?

The screen door opened and slapped shut behind the old dog, and it stood on the porch with its nose in the air. I decided it was a nice, old dog. I decided it wasn't going to bite me, that it wasn't going to betray me, that it was going to help me. Just then my empty stomach rumbled so loud it made the dog turn its head toward me, then it made its halting way down the steps and limped in my direction. It looked like it had sore hips; it didn't move very fast.

My animal brain was telling me: *Run. Go now. Get away. Grab the pack, jump on that horse, and make tracks.*

But I waited for the old dog to approach, holding out my hand; her whiskers tickled as she sniffed, and she wagged slowly. When she rested her frosted chin on my thigh and looked up at me, I saw how one of her eyes had a cloudy-blue color to it, but both were squinted up into a kind of doggy-smile. Sweet Pea watched intently, snuffling at my shoulder, while I gave the dog a good scratch behind her ears.

Then my stomach growled again, and the dog did a strange thing: she turned and took a few steps back toward the house, then stopped and looked over her shoulder at me, and I knew I was supposed to follow her. So I tied Sweet Pea's reins to a low branch—she kept nudging me, jerking back; she didn't want to be left—and fell in behind the dog. I was going to go wherever she led me, but I was relieved to find she wasn't headed back to the porch but was making her way, one back foot dragging a bit, behind the house toward all the noise of the other dogs in the shed. They got even louder as we approached, and I was sure we were going to be discovered, that I was going to be shot as an intruder, and I kept looking over my shoulder, waiting to be grabbed, to be wrestled to the ground, to be murdered right there in the stink and dusky light of an old shack filled with snapping and lunging dogs behind a flimsy-looking chicken wire fence.

But most of the other dogs quieted when the old dog padded in, and they all shut up when she sat down in front of a big, plastic garbage bin. I lifted the lid and used the coffee can inside to scoop up a bunch of kibble. "Is this what you want?" I asked her, and a couple of the other dogs answered for her with little yips. I was hungry enough to put one of the little pellets in my mouth, and you know what? It really wasn't that bad. And while I was crunching away I saw the cans of dog food on the shelf with an opener beside them, and I grabbed that thing and started cranking away, and was fingers knuckle-deep in the stuff before I even noticed the big kitchen spoon that was lying there, too. I swear to God, it was the best meal I'd ever had.

As I munched I went around and served up dinner for the dogs—a generous helping for everyone. What the hell, it wasn't my money, and it shut them up.

Unfortunately, the euphoria of food in my belly didn't last long because just as I'd finished up I heard voices—deep men's voices—distant enough to be coming from inside the house, but still *voices*, and the *Run. Go now. Get away* launched again. This time I dropped the spoon into an empty can and obeyed. I charged back across the dirt yard toward the cottonwoods and got to Sweet Pea just as she was about to wrangle the head piece of her bridle over her other ear—in two more seconds, she would have been free. "Oh, hell, no, you don't," I spat at her as I grabbed a handful of mane, jerked the bridle back into place, and reached to untie my knot in her reins. I left the back-pack propped against one of the trees—no time—launched myself onto the snorting horse, and started kicking her in the sides and sawing at her bit. "Gee haw!" I urged her, "Yaw!" but she kept turning in circles instead of charging off; it was like riding the rearing horse on a carousel, and I was getting nowhere fast. Sweet Pea did not want to leave whoever had spoken the words I'd heard—the person that stupid bird had led us to. That much was clear.

I hate to admit it, even now, but I forced her. I was ruthless, lashing her with the reins wherever they would reach, hammering her barrel with my heels, whipping, jerking, bouncing, until she finally faced the direction I wanted her to—south again—and took off with a last big buck that nearly unseated me.

One of those men's voices, I'm almost certain, was Trick's dad, Guy's, and Sweet Pea's devotion to him was legendary. So for ripping her away from him, for the abuse it took to make her do it—and that alone—I am sorry.

II. CRUCIFIXION

You'll tell her again: "Shut up, Heather—Jesus! I don't know why you're mad at me—this is all your fucking dad's fault, not mine!"

"But what'll we do now?" Heather will whine. She will have her hand pressed to her bloodied left temple where the sun visor had carved a cross in her forehead; neither she nor you will have been wearing your seat belts. "You said the gas tank would explode. You said they'd never be able to tell what happened . . . . Oh, Jesus, my dad's gonna beat the shit out of me. I told him I'd fuck up—I told him. You heard me tell him . . . ."

"Shut up, God-damn it. I'm thinking."

"They're going to find us. They're going to figure out what I did, and they're going to kill us. Oh, my God, why did I listen to you?"

"Me?" you'll ask. But when you shoot a look at her face, you'll realize it isn't just scared-white; it's being lit up by a pair of headlights coming from the north.

"Screw my dad—I gotta get the hell out of here . . . ."

Then she'll start running toward the lights, arms waving, and for a moment you will be sure that she, also, will be struck, will be killed. But the car will swerve and stop, and Heather will yank on the back door of the sedan, shouting, "Help! Help!" and sobbing, until somebody opens it from inside, and she will crawl in; the noise of her will be suddenly cut off with the door's slam. Then the tires will spray gravel, and she'll be gone.

CHAPTER TWELVE

NIGHT WORLD

Mariana drapes her shawl over the back of the chair and pulls her dress off over her head, then kicks out of her shoes and goes barefoot over the cool tiles to the dresser where she keeps her night gowns. She opens the drawer and fingers the material before donning it; a scratchy cotton. She steps into the slippers on the floor beside the wardrobe and opens it to find her burgundy robe, then standing before the mirror, Mariana brushes and braids her hair, finally wrapping it into a crown on the top of her head. She takes the vial of holy water from the dresser and places a drop on each wrist and on the top of each foot, replaces it. Then she kneels on the tiles before the crucifix she has nailed to the wall by her bed, makes the sign of the cross, folds her aching hands, and bows her head in prayer: *Padre nuestro que estás en los cielos . . . .*

So begins her nightly journey into the strange occurrence known as sleep.

Many creatures move easily through the darkness and are at

home in it. In the days before the talking tree, Mariana's people, the Yoeme, did, as well. There was the face of the moon and the patterns of the stars to guide them, their camp fires to warm them. It was a good time for storytelling, the dark adding its mystery to the lore. Mariana's father, sitting cross-legged in the dancing circle of light cast by flames, had heard the tales from his elders, and he had repeated them to her, sitting cross-legged on the splintered boards of the lamp-lit porch. By the time Mariana recounted them to her own child, he was sitting cross-legged on the braided rug before the couch, a television with its sound turned off flashing its electrodes. They had moved indoors because the stars had been absorbed in the surfeit of the city's lights and the flames extinguished by its ordinances. This is why Mariana feels her people's ceremonies are so important: it is the Yaquis' task, assigned by Yomumli just before she rose up to the clouds, to right the wrongs humans have done to this and all of the other worlds. There are no others to do this.

And it must be done.

"*. . . y no nos dejes caer en la tentación sino que líbranos del malo. Amen.*" Mariana repeats the sign of the cross and rises from her knees with a practiced ease, unafraid, now, of all the odd events of the *Tuka Ania*. She turns to open the French doors that lead into the back patio she shares with Star's treatment studio, hers alone now that Star's father has fallen ill, and steps outside into the chatter of the fountain, the cooling air. It is long past the time for the stealthy dip and rise of the night hawks, the flitter of bats, and she listens instead to the resident owl high in the oak beyond the courtyard and the chirping of frogs in the pond below the house. Mariana glimpses the stars through the branches—she is grateful she can see them again here, in this open ranch land—and there is the sliver of a moon. Then she reenters her room, latches shut the screen, drops her robe from her shoulders, and pulls the sheet back to climb into bed. To still the flutter of moth wings at the screen, she reaches over to the nightstand and switches off the lamp. Then she closes her eyes at the crickets' *chik, chik, chik, chik, chik, chik, chik*, remembering one of the stories she was told as a child and had, in turn, told her son:

The cricket loved a good party, so he said to his friend, the grasshopper, "There are people over there drinking wine. Let's drink with them and then ride our horses all over the mountains while we sing."

Usually the grasshopper was asleep by this time, but he told Cricket that sounded like fun, and they hopped their way over to the gathering where the cricket showed the grasshopper a tiny stick. "Sit here while I get you some wine," he told him, then he jumped over to the table and plopped right into a full cup. The chief saw this happen, and he immediately picked up the cup and emptied it onto the ground, giving the grasshopper a winey bath.

"Good stuff, am I right?" asked the cricket when he could stand again after the deluge.

"Yum," answered the grasshopper.

There is more to the story, a lot of singing and bothering mountain lions, but Mariana has already slipped from consciousness, the neurons in her brain slowing into steady ripples; she is cut off from the world, submerged, no longer capable of hearing anything. Minutes later, the electric bursts rise in quick succession, moving memories like weightless freight, connecting one to another, sorting, collecting, discarding: Sally's scraped knee, the tragedy mask she'd lifted to

Mariana while she howled over it, cemented to the day's vast and empty blue sky; catching JC sneaking whiskey from the cupboard over the oven linked to her son's nearly fatal opioid overdose on his twentieth birthday; Star's voice over the phone blended into her sister's wheezy laugh. Gradually even this activity slows along with Mariana's heart, and the last vestiges of awareness slip away.

She is breathing the air of *Tuka Ania* now. She is dead to the other worlds.

She is asleep.

CHAPTER THIRTEEN

THE THIRD SUNDAY OF LENT

February 28, 2016:
The Fig Tree

"For three years now I have come in search of
fruit on this fig tree but have found none."
Luke 13:1-9

Guy pulled the afghan tight around his shoulders and used his cane to move the heavy drape aside so he could peer out the window into the dead-of-night dark. He could barely make out the old fig tree one of the previous owners had planted in the side yard, its thick trunk and fat leaves a darker black against the adobe block wall. There was no fruit on it and never had been, as far as he knew, and its roots went deep and had started buckling the wall.

But when he'd directed José to cut it down, Mariana had contravened the order. José had just started up the chain saw, and the noise of it must have drawn Mariana to this very window. She'd come rushing out: "You've shown it your blade," she'd told the two of them. "Now give it another chance. It's just old and neglected, so fertilize it well, José. If it doesn't produce this year, then you can cut it down." Of course, Mariana's assessment prevailed.

That's the way things went these days, one woman or the other, making all the decisions. Well, he was just about fed up with that.

Guy dropped the drape and continued prowling the warren of the old homestead's downstairs rooms, each cane tap followed by a cast thump. The main parts of the house—the entryway and dining room, the long, back bedroom that they now called "the sun room," and the big-beamed, stone-fire-place-dominated living room—had been constructed in the late 1800's, according to the realtor lady, with additions tacked on as the original family grew. Most of these walls were fashioned of thick adobe bricks meant to keep the cool inside, the heat and Chiricahua Apaches' arrows out. The upstairs was the expansion of an old, open loft, and the kitchen and bathrooms all came much later.

But that was only about half of the sprawling ranch house. Star's treatment room and Mariana's rooms were down a long hallway and opened out into a shaded patio way at the back of the house, almost like the home's sprawl had encompassed another dwelling that had been just a little too close. Guy seldom ventured back there, but tonight not only Star but also Mariana were up in Tucson again, and he missed them, so he slowly made his way down the hallway, the rusty orange of the Saltillo tiles silvered by the moonlight cascading through the series of French doors that led out onto the patio. He paused at

Star's office and her treatment room, their doors closed to keep the cats out, and opened them.

Let the little critters have some fun.

Guy was wandering because he wasn't sleeping much these days, ever since Mariana had started hiding his pain pills, ever since that phone call from JC had launched Trick into his attempt at a rescue, ever since Star had decided her father was more important to her than him. It was a toss-up, which one was bugging him the most, but the physical aches would wake him—his tooth had started back in with a vengeance, not just his right hand but both sets of knuckles were swollen and achy with a flair up of his arthritis, the couch made a lousy bed and put a crick in his back, plus his throbbing ankle, of course— and then the worries kicked in, making him toss and turn until he finally put his feet on the floor, pulled the afghan onto his shoulders, and lumbered up.

The phone call from JC—that had to be the worst of it. Thank God Trick had been there because his son was right: Guy just was not up to the response it required.

Was there a way, he wondered, to water and fertilize a teenage boy?

Or more accurately, Guy wasn't sleeping much *at night* these days; he spent most of his daylight hours in a kind of comatose state in his spot on the couch, usually with one or the other cat curled up on his belly. The only thing that roused him, made him push the fur ball off and sit up and rub his eyes, was little Sally in her play; he could watch that—and did —for hours. She really liked her animals, had a backyard, barnyard, and zoo-full of tiny miniatures of them: dogs and cats and rabbits, bears and turtles and birds, a zebra and a lion, a pink pig and a whole herd of tiny, plastic cows. Just no horses; she didn't have any affection for them, for some perverse reason.

Guy pivoted at the last door—Mariana's private sanctuary; he didn't open that one—and tap-thumped his way back into the kitchen and stretched up to check the cupboard over the oven again to see if his Jack Daniels had magically reappeared, but of course it hadn't. Thinking about Sally and her distaste for horses had gotten him pining for old Sweet Pea, his rodeo horse and general side kick for those many years, but, hell no, there weren't any beers left in the refrigerator, either. There was pie, though, and Guy grabbed it, turned with it and set it on the table, then went back to the counter to wrestle the silverware drawer open and find a fork before sitting down in front of the half pan of it. He needed something to soothe the ache in his ankle, the many aches of his heart.

Pie would have to do.

THE HORSE'S death had haunted him for years, now. He carried the guilt of it around with him during the day, dreamed the pain of it almost every night. He kept seeing Sweet Pea, lathered and stumbling-tired, trying to do what he was asking her to, and he being so intent on his tracking of the young girl that he wouldn't let up on her, wouldn't stop to let her rest, wouldn't keep his heel from her ribs. She'd been such a sturdy quarter horse mare, and although nearly thirty years old, she was still tough as jerked meat, so when she dropped to her knees and keeled over, it was such a surprise he hadn't managed to clear his left leg, so he'd been pinned beneath her heaving side, forced to watch her take her last slobbering breaths, nostrils quivering, her eyes going wide with a fear that was taking hold of him just as white-knuckled hard. He had covered his face with his hat and wept, his heart burning so hot he was sure he'd be following right after her.

IT WAS APPLE, cinnamon-laced, with a lattice crust made crunchy with a crust of sugar and a bottom browned to perfection. Guy threw off his shawl and shoveled and chewed and sighed his way through most of it, then dropped his fork onto the tablecloth with a clatter.

Apparently pie wasn't strong enough.

BECAUSE HE WAS BACK at the start of it, before Sweet Pea's last labored breaths, in the yard at Stanton School, when Jasmine's mother had confronted him as he and Star were packing the rest of his household into his truck. He'd fixed up the bunk house at the neighboring Circle N Bar Ranch enough to make it habitable, and there was nothing holding him there at the boarding school anymore; Trick and his foster father had left for the high school in Tucson the previous morning. It had been depressingly easy to load up his life of the past five years, especially with Star's help. It all fit in his broken down truck.

Guy was carrying a box across the yard, distracted by thoughts of his son, when the woman—he couldn't remember her name—charged across the grass from her cottage and up his driveway; it was the ex-wife of the man who had taken Trick.

"What are you doing?" she wailed at him. "You can't leave. You have to find my daughter!"

Guy knew she meant Jasmine, who had taken off on Sweet

Pea four days before, chasing after Trick and the rest of the school's horses, he imagined. He and Star had found Trick and the herd he'd stolen at his uncle's. But, although the authorities had been notified and the Highway Patrol and everybody else was supposedly out looking, nobody had seen anything of the girl.

Guy shoved the box into the open bed of the truck and turned to face her. Four days was a long time to not know what had happened to your kid, Guy knew, and during that time the woman had changed: no more hand-wringing and little mousey voice. She'd turned into a lion. Her hair was a wild tangle, her eyes blazed, and she looked ready to strike him with that raised fist. Guy was happy when Star stepped up to intervene.

"Emily, my goodness. How are you holding up?" Star reached out for the fist and took it in both her hands.

"You *can't* go," Jasmine's mother continued, trying to move around Star. Thank God she held fast; Guy kept stepping back, his hands up. "It's your damn son who put this crazy idea in her head, now you find her." She was pointing at Guy's chest with her other hand now.

"Yes, of course they're going to find your daughter. Of course they are," Star said quietly, almost a whisper. Then louder: "Why don't you come inside for a moment? I'll make you some tea." Even though Guy knew every pot he owned was in the box he'd just carried out to his truck and the pantry was emptied; its contents were now in a couple of paper sacks on the floor of the cab.

GUY GRABBED his cane and used it to hoist himself from the table, then he tap-clomped the nearly empty pie dish over and set it in the sink. Mariana would give him the stink eye when she saw it there upon her return late the next morning, but he'd pretend to be asleep on the couch while she was doing it. Then she would set about making him another pie, when what he really needed was something to wash it all down with.

Then it struck him—there was plenty of wine. Star had stocked up just before her father had taken the turn for the worse, apparently thinking they'd be having full casitas with happy hours for their guests and lots of candlelight dinners to celebrate their new enterprise. But the casitas remained empty —they'd had to cancel all the reservations when Star had decided to leave for Tucson—and the subsequent celebratory dinners had, of course, never materialized. They'd made maybe $1200 before the pause in their operations, and Star had probably spent half of that on the wine.

That's what he got for letting women make the decisions for him.

Guy stalled out again in front of the French doors that opened into the patio off the dining room when Turks, the orange tabby, appeared, threading himself through the spaces between Guy's legs and his cane. The cat sat expectantly before the door, but Guy didn't open it for him, just stood there remembering how Jasmine's mother had exploded into tears that made Star wrap her up in an embrace and him keep backing away. The force of the woman's grief was overwhelming; all he could think to do was go back inside the house and look around stupidly at the stained carpet, the empty bookshelves, the cleared counters until Star called him back outside again.

"You said they're all out looking for her, right, Guy?" she called to him, still holding the sobbing woman. "It's too soon to take Sweet Pea out searching, though, right? She's got to rest. She does, Guy." The woman in her arms raised her head, but Star said the words to him, her blue eyes burning: "There's nothing you can do."

"I'm so sorry, Ma'am," Guy said, shaking his head. "The Sherriff, the Highway Patrol . . . ." He got no further than the porch, no further than the word before Jasmine's mother erupted again:

"They think she's a statistic!"

THE ONLY PROBLEM was the wine was stored down in the cellar, and Guy was not up to negotiating stairs yet. Still he tap-stepped back through the kitchen and down the short hallway that led to the wooden door marked "No Guest Access." The white cat, Caicos, had joined his brother, and after Guy rattled the knob and pushed the door open on its squeaky hinges, the three of them stood looking down the length of decrepit stairs.

Guy knew the railing and a few of the struts were rotted at the base, the boards of the steps warped and uneven. He'd hoped to demolish and repair it with Trick's help, but then he'd gone and broken his ankle, and Trick had taken off on the hunt after JC's phone call, *and* the "honey" who inspired his "honey-do lists" was nowhere to be found, as well. Guy felt around on the wall for the switch, flipped it, and a bare bulb at the bottom illuminated the shelves full of junk, the stacked boxes, old lamps, picture frames, assorted chairs, and glinted off the bottles of wine in their racks.

· · ·

GUY KNEW STAR WAS RIGHT: Sweet Pea had been worn to a frazzle by whatever had happened after Jasmine had run off on her. She was scratched and gouged and noticeably ribby when she'd shown up just two days before, saddled and bridled but with no sign of the girl or the backpack Jasmine had also taken. He knew a couple of night's rest was not enough, especially for a mare Sweet Pea's age, and he was putting his best horse ever, his best friend, at risk.

But the mother's grief unsettled him; he had to act. He'd tipped his hat back, sighed, and assured both Star and Jasmine's mom: "I'll find her. Sweet Pea and I will find her. We'll set out directly."

THE TALKATIVE CAT, Caicos, looked up at Guy and mewed a question; the curious one, Turks, lifted his tail high and scooted down the steps into the gloom.

If Guy hadn't been so heartsick about JC, he wouldn't even be considering this risky venture into the cellar. But the timbre of the boy's voice on the phone had really rattled Guy, even more than his words; it had been high, like he was a little kid again, gone breathless with fear. Then they'd been cut off so abruptly it suggested violence, but even as Guy had set down the phone and thrown on his clothes, in his heart he'd known he was in no way fit to go to his aid, to be the father the teen needed him to be right then. Still he'd rooted the old, black backpack out of the back of his closet and taken it up by the straps.

Fortunately, Guy hadn't been the only one that JC's phone call had upset. He hadn't realized Trick had picked up the upstairs' extension and was listening in on JC's call until he ran into him as he backed out of the closet.

Guy's words had been enough to get the girl's mother to stop her bawling and start wiping at her face. Star was scowling at him, but she put a hand under the other woman's arm, turned, and started walking her back to the teacher's cottage she'd shared with Trick's foster father and her daughter. Guy watched them go then squared his shoulders and, for the last time, reentered the house he'd lived in with his son. He strode across the living room into the kitchen, opened the refrigerator, picked up the only thing left in there—a half-full jug of water —and took it over to the sink.

But then Star returned. The screen door slapped shut behind her, and she took the jug out of his hands, set it on the counter, and said: "No, Guy. I know you're just trying to do what's right, but no. You sit this one out. Sweet Pea . . . ."

"Since when do you tell me what to do?" Guy snapped at her. He'd picked up the water jug and put it back under the running faucet, then he'd settled his hat and made for the door with not much more in the way of supplies. If he'd still had the backpack, he would have grabbed that, but he didn't; he wouldn't reclaim that until the next morning, after he'd run Sweet Pea into the ground and suffered the "lay it down" feeling of muscle and motion becoming dead meat. Guy had stumbled upon the black lump of the pack resting against a tree near Old Henry's place only after he'd gone to get his help with burying his all-time best horse ever.

Star had tried to stop him with a hand on his arm at the edge of the porch. "You need to listen to me, Guy," she'd said as he pulled away. "You go if you have to, but don't take Sweet Pea."

Guy had just frowned at her and said, "Sweet Pea's the only one who knows where to go." Then he turned to tromp down the steps. Star's, "No. Wait. You're not going to find Jasmine. And Guy—something bad's going to happen, instead" had followed him across the yard.

Well, he had *not* found her. And something bad *had* happened.

But he had gone looking.

And now Trick had, too.

GUY DUCKED his head to get a better view of the wine rack. He knew there were some really tasty vintages down there, some whites, but mostly the local, earthy reds that he preferred. The Sonoita area had a soil quality similar to Burgundy in France and people had been growing wine in the region since the 1500's, with a break for Prohibition, of course; the local vintners knew what they were doing. But Guy blocked the other cat, Caicos, at the door to the cellar with his cane. The white cat had stubby little legs and a hanging belly; maybe it wouldn't be safe to let him follow his brother down there.

There were plenty of women suddenly crowding Guy's head as he and the white cat stood in the opened doorway, looking down the length of steps. The two closest to him —Star, of course, and Mariana—certainly would not want him traipsing down there. But he doubted that Trick's mom, Sally, who'd passed away years ago when Trick was just a kid, would want him to, either, or his old boss back in Winslow, Sweet

Kate. Actually, he *knew* none of them would want him to do this. Even his sparring partner, Rose, would think it was crazy.

Even *Rose*.

He felt the weight of them on his shoulders as he hooked his cane over his right elbow, grabbed the rickety railing with his left hand, and took his first steps down the stairs.

FIRST SCRUTINY

I *didn't tell him, and I never would have.*

The only reason Guy found out he had a son was Trick figured out how to find him. He was only eleven, living at the boarding school, just a month or so after I'd died. He was always a bright child, our son.

It was warm enough in the barn, but when Trick led the horses outside, the motion-sensitive yard light illuminated the clouds of condensation their breath made around their faces in the crisp night air. Trick spoke to each horse in wispy puffs of it as he tightened their cinches and arranged his gear. Then he tamped his hat down, stepped into a stirrup, and swung his leg over Dice's saddle. With a creak of leather and a jingle of the bit they were trotting down the lane, Amigo in tow.

But I guess Guy does not realize how resourceful our son is; he doesn't trust him enough to find JC and has managed to worry himself into craziness. Why else would he trust those stairs to hold his weight, that cat to keep out from underfoot, the cellar door not to swing shut and lock behind him with a tiny "click"?

The directions JC had given during his panicked phone call were vague, at best, but Trick knew they had a hell of a long way to go, through rough country, and if they were going to get there and back within a reasonable amount of time, he'd have to take care of the horses and ride smart. So he decided that, now that the full moon was setting, it was too dark to trust cutting across the pastures and kept the horses to the center of the rutted drive back to the highway before turning them north along its shoulder. Amigo wasn't used to being a pack horse, and he kept sawing from one side to the other behind them, and Trick had to keep turning around to yell at him and lift the lead rope to keep it from slipping under Dice's tail; he wished the big chestnut Saddlebred would just pick a side.

He'd chosen to ride his father's horse instead of Amigo because, even though both were larger, experienced trail horses, Dice had benefited the most from Guy's attention, and if things went south—as Trick expected they would—he knew he'd need his father's presence in the form of the animal he had trained. Dice was a mostly-Morgan gelding with a distinctive snowflake coloring—white spots on his chest and haunches, otherwise black; hence the name. He was at the top of his breed standard for height at over 15 hands, with an almost-Arabian arch to his neck, but most of all he fit the breed's characteristics of being smart and powerful and of a generally good disposition. Trick had no doubt he would need all of those qualities over the coming hours and possibly days.

The white cat strikes first. He launches just as Guy posi-

tions his cane on the fourth step and manages to occupy the very spot Guy intended to place the walking boot. Caicos yowls, Guy swears, drops his cane, and makes a grab for the railing; the wood breaks in his hand, and he goes crashing through the banister, taking a section of the stairs down with him. He can't hear the whisper of the door shutting, the click of the lock engaging, with all the splintering, banging and clattering going on as the boards fall around him.

Trick shivered his chin down into the collar of his borrowed heavy Levi jacket. The coat was his father's too, the one concession Guy had made to equipping Trick on his search for JC. His father had run right into Trick just outside the downstairs closet door, the old, black backpack in his hand.

"What the fuck is going on with JC?" Trick had demanded of Guy, pushing his glasses back on his nose. Then, jerking his chin at the pack he was holding: "Where the hell do you think you're going?"

Guy had tried to get past him, but Trick was having none of that. "Dad? You can't go after him. You're in no shape . . . ."

"Since when do you eavesdrop on my private conversations?" his father had wanted to know.

"Ever since the phone started ringing in the middle of the night," Trick responded, the same heat in his own voice. He moved his glasses again and added: "I didn't want it to wake Sally." He reached over and took the backpack from his father's grip.

Guy started to answer, had his other hand raised, a finger all set to point, but lowered it and shushed himself at his son's words. "And what are *you* doing?" was reduced in volume to a harsh whisper.

Guy opens his eyes to a wooden cross hanging above him

—a section of the railing with a sideways board still attached —all that's left of the middle part of the stairs. He raises his head with a groan and sees that his body reflects the shape: he's landed flat on his back with his arms spread-eagle and legs outstretched over the rubble. The bare light bulb is still swinging on its chain, making the room pitch and sway, but the hands Guy brings up to his face look fine, if a little scratched and dusty, and although his right shoulder is sore, he's able to leverage himself up onto his elbows. Neither leg looks to be damaged; he lifts one, dislodging a board spiked with rusted nails, then the other. The black walking cast is now a powdered brown, but it's still strapped tightly around his broken ankle.

Trick pushed past Guy and crossed the living room to set the pack down by the front door. Then he made his way to the kitchen while his father followed, whispering: "What the hell, son. Wait . . . wait up. You can't . . . ."

"Somebody's got to," Trick told him over his shoulder, then he just let Guy bluster while he opened cupboards and set supplies out on the counter: "Hold on, now. Stop and listen to me. It's the middle of the night . . . ." Trick went to the refrigerator, grabbed the nearly empty gallon jug of milk and chugged it down, then rinsed it at the sink and started filling it with tap water. "It's friggin' freezing out, and you don't even really know where you're going . . . ."

There's his cane. Guy pulls it close, rolls with a wince to his side, and uses it to get on his knees. It's awkward, but he gets his good leg under him and struggles the rest of the way up, then starts brushing the dirt off the sweat pants he sleeps in— or more accurately, doesn't sleep in—and rifles dust from his hair and scruffy beard. When he looks up again, two sets of eyes—blue and copper—are peering out from under a metal shelving unit by the nearest wine rack. Aaah, the wine rack.

Guy sighed as he watched his son move to the pantry and grab a couple of Mariana's canvas grocery sacks off the hook on the back of the door and start filling them with canned goods, then Guy straightened from his hunch over his cane. "I'll go then. You stay here and take care of your sister."

Trick stopped his packing long enough to turn all the way around and look at his father. He didn't say anything, just adjusted his glasses and gave him a good up and down, shook his head, and went back to the refrigerator's vegetable bin to grab the bag of apples, paused in thought, then took the carrots, too, and started searching the shelves.

"What?" Guy asked his son sourly.

"You can't hardly walk yet. What are you gonna do—bring your crutches? Maybe you could hold them out like wings," came muffled from inside the refrigerator; Trick was pulling stuff out of the meat bin now.

Guy takes a step and promptly trips over a fallen board, but he catches himself, pushes more of the debris away with his cane, plants it, and tries again. He's sore all over but apparently ambulatory. "Damn cat," he mumbles at Caicos as he tap-steps gingerly past the tips of the crouched felines' noses on his way to the wine rack.

"I'll bring my cane, is all," Guy sputtered. "And, hell, maybe I don't even need the damn thing anymore," and he tossed it down with a clatter. That at least got Trick to pull his nose out of the refrigerator. He shook his head at his father and pointed at the ceiling. Okay, that'd been a bit loud, but what the hell—Guy was making a point. And he still was: he took a determined step but then winced and had to catch himself with a hand on the kitchen counter. "Shit," he wheezed.

Guy selects a bottle—a nice Graciano, Merlot and Tempranillo blend—and looks around for the wine opener. It isn't in its spot but he finally notices it on the cement at his feet. He bends over to retrieve it, stuffs it in the waistband of his sweats, and tucks the bottle under one arm. Then he tap-steps over to a stack of old ladder-back chairs, pulls one clear, and plops down on it, sending up a puff of dust. Turks comes slinking out of his hidey-hole to join him as he works the cork screw to open the bottle; an invisible Caicos sneezes.

Trick came around the center island, stooped to reclaim the cane, and handed it to his father. Guy could never help feeling a bit intimidated by his son's close proximity; except for the glasses, the young man looked every bit the Yavapai warrior, stocky and muscled, and he towered over him. But Trick's words were gentle: "I got this, Dad," he told Guy. Then he pulled out one of the bar stools. "Come on and sit down before you fall down."

But, "Damn it, Trick, I'm not an invalid," Guy said instead of obeying him.

Trick's "Yeah" was noncommittal; he was back in the pantry now, putting bags of crackers and chips into another of Mariana's canvas grocery sacks.

"You planning on being gone a month?" Guy asked, but his son just shrugged.

It has been many years since Guy's chugged wine from the bottle, but the technique comes right back to him. The light bulb has finally stopped its dizzying sway and he looks around at the clutter and destruction between swigs; man, he's made a mess of those stairs. Guy isn't at all sure how he's going to get himself out of this hole, but the cross hanging there gets him thinking about constructing a ladder of some kind. Turks is nosing around past the circle of light; Guy can hear him swatting at something—a mouse? A moth?—but Caicos remains in his spot under the metal shelving. "Damn cat," Guy says again. Maybe he could haul that shelf over under the remnants of the steps and climb?

I think Guy trusts unsupported, old, metal shelves too much, too, especially since, as soon as that first bottle's empty, he limps his way back to the wine rack to grab another.

"You don't know where to even look, Trick." Guy shuffled over to the bar stool Trick had pulled out for him and half-fell onto it. "He gave the craziest directions—do you think he was drunk?"

"Ha—stoned, more likely," Trick snorted. But then he lowered his head and added: "And scared shitless." He must have finished his gathering because he crossed his hands over his broad chest, gave a massive yawn, and leaned back against the counter. "I'll head out toward the Imperial Ranch. It's a place to start, anyway. He mentioned water—there's water there. And, I don't know—maybe he was hiding in that same cave Mariana told us about."

"I never seen no fucking cave anywhere around here," Guy stated sourly.

Trick considered that. "Well, maybe it's a mine. There's lots of old Mexican silver mines about—you're the one who told me the Total Wreck mine was how the Imperial Ranch financed *their* operation for a while. And when I tried redialing the number JC used to call us, I got an answering machine saying to leave a message—in Spanish."

By the middle of the second bottle of wine, Guy's shoulder is feeling fine, and neither his tooth nor his ankle is giving him any trouble, either. But his heart still aches. He's worried about both boys, feeling guilty about letting JC run so wild and not being the one to be out there trying to find him, and apprehensive about what Trick might encounter when—or rather, if—he does. There's only been the one call from JC; no word from Trick since he left in the middle of the night five days before. But Guy's afraid that what Trick said was true: he's just a slow-to-heal old man who's in everybody's way, and totally incapable of rescuing anyone anymore anyway.

Plus after scouting around the dusty shelves and counters, Guy has come up empty on any ladder-construction materials. He has the boards, plenty of boards, but no tools, no nails or screws or bolts. So he makes his way back to the chair and swipes the orange cat off it, sits, and drinks. After a while he gets confused about whether he's drowning his sorrows or celebrating, but since the solution's the same, he just keeps on drinking.

"Maybe I could take the truck . . . ."

"Hell no, Dad."

Had his son's voice always been such a deep rumble in his chest? But Guy didn't let that deter him: "Why not? I mean, I could just follow along, you know, like your wing man . . . ."

"No." Trick hoisted his accumulated goods and stood before his father again. "I don't think JC is standing on some road all this time with his thumb out. Besides, you can't drive, either. Not yet. It takes a good four weeks to heal a fracture, six, if you're old—like you. More if you tore the ligaments . . . ."

"I'm not even 50!" Guy sputtered.

"Yeah, like I said . . . ." Trick made for the front door and deposited his gear by the backpack, then nearly ran into his father on his way to the hall closet. "You're in the way, Dad. I need a bedroll. Is there some extra Sterno in there?"

Guy dozes for a time and when he raises his head again there's a small rectangle of grey, morning light high above the shelf Caicos is still hiding under—a window vent just above the foundation. Guy sets the nearly empty bottle down on the cement beside his chair, stands unsteadily.

Guy put a hand out to stop his son. "Don't go, kid," he told him. "I don't want you to."

Trick surprised him by pulling him into an embrace; Guy thought for a second that the squeeze was going to snap his spine, but the young man finally let go. When he did, Guy grabbed a breath and said: "I couldn't stand to lose both my sons—I just couldn't take that."

"He's not my brother."

Guy took a step back. "Uhm, I'm not sure why I said that." Guy nearly stumbled, stepping back again.

"Is he?" Trick wanted to know. "It would kind of explain things . . . . I mean, why else did they ask *you* to take care of him? And 'Sweet' Kate, right?"

Yes, Guy always thought of her—and spoke of her, apparently—as Sweet Kate. And there had been that one time, not long after he'd arrived at her ranch . . . . But, "None of your damned bidness," is what he said to his son. He said it like that —"bidness"—on purpose; his son would know that meant he was serious.

Actually, what it meant was that he was being an asshole. Okay, to be kind: It meant he wasn't ready to talk about that possibility with our son yet, which is understandable, as this was the first time the thought had ever even crossed his mind.

"Come to think of it," Trick said, his arms folded across the expanse of his chest again, "he looks a lot more like you than *I* do. Is it possible?"

"I'm . . . I'm . . . Well, I . . . ," Guy sputtered. He gave up and his son turned away. "You, ah, you got your cell phone, right?"

Trick's snort came from deep inside the closet; he was bent over, rummaging around in a box. "Of course I do."

"And the charger?"

"Yeah. There's one in the backpack," Trick assured him as he stood, a two-pack of Sterno in his hands. "But there probably won't be any reception out there, anyway, Dad."

"Ah, Jeez," Guy sighed. He rubbed at his eyes. "Well, take my coat at least—the heavy Levi jacket. It's cold . . . ." He brought his hand up to his chest to cover the burn there, then dropped it and stepped aside as Trick, his arms full, strode past him and backed out the screen door. "Be careful," Guy called after him, then under his breath: "I wish to hell I was going with you."

He'd rather be the one to suffer whatever was to be required of Trick. But Guy does *trust our son—just enough to let him go.*

Trick tilted his hat back and raised his eyes to the vast, dark sky, then held his breath so the cloud of condensation would not obscure his view of the stars; they were splashed across the blackness from horizon to horizon, and the weight of his father's concern lifted with his soul at the sight of them.

Then Amigo started his weaving again as they traveled along the side of the highway, and Trick's, "Easy, now. Back off, Amigo," was having little effect. Dice kept lifting his tail and flicking it, and Trick was afraid he might get a rope burn from the trailing rein or—worse yet—let go with a solid kick to Amigo's nose. The two horses were stable mates and companionable, so Amigo should be able to get the hang of it, but instead of keeping to one side, his head at Trick's knee, he kept dropping back, slowing Dice down, or surging forward on their off side, making Dice jump into a canter.

"That's enough, now," Trick told both horses in exasperation. Then "Everybody just settle down," he added after a long stretch of musing; this time he was including himself in the exhortation. Finally, "Half-brother, huh?" he said quietly. "Dad, you dirty dog."

CHAPTER FIFTEEN

JASMINE

I didn't mean to kill that horse, I really didn't. And maybe it wasn't totally my fault. I mean, yeah, I rode Sweet Pea hard on rough trails without letting her eat or rest; I was cruel. But the last time I saw her, she didn't seem anywhere near cashing it in. And she got me back double eventually because after a while I just could not keep my eyes open anymore, and as soon as I dozed, she backtracked. I'd startle awake—the first time just after the sun went down—and look around, trying to figure out where the hell we were, and it would always look a little too familiar.

My son, Trick, was only 10 when I died; his move to Stanford School was all part of the settlement of my affairs. Unfortunately, young Jasmine did not like the idea of a new addition to her family and appointed herself his chief tormentor right from the start. She teased him about his coal-black hair, his too-blue eyes, and seemed determined to trip him up in class, even though he was studying hard. And although Trick had been on horseback at his Uncle Henry's since he was little, she nearly succeeded in unhorsing him during their riding lessons multiple times.

I'd check the current in the river—we were following the trail that followed it—and instead of going downstream toward Phoenix we were upstream within sight of that old stand of cottonwoods again where Sweet Pea had heard Guy's voice. I'd swear at her and yank her around, but I couldn't stay awake all night. And, sure enough, morning found us still on the Rez by Trick's Uncle Henry's house, right back where we'd started again. If she'd just stopped or even slowed down to graze, it would have woken me up, but that damn mare was too smart for that. She just angled herself around without a pause and tried again and again to get back to him.

She was a regular Penelope, patiently undoing all the weaving I'd done.

But at least Jasmine paid attention to Trick; she was the only one. The other kids at the school were all older, so they ignored him. His foster father was only good for calling him into his study and giving him stern lectures; his foster mother was already vacant-eyed most of the time. This is when Trick figured out how to call his real dad, Guy, up in Winslow at Kate's buffalo ranch, and tell him he didn't want to be a foster child anymore. But for one reason and another—including his father's decision to ride his horse instead of renting a trailer— it took Guy months to get there.

So then I got mad, and when I'm mad, I'm mean. I slapped Sweet Pea with the reins, kicked her in the sides, even landed a few punches on her shoulders. But I didn't win that fight;

Sweet Pea crow-hopped twice, banged me against a low branch, and scraped me right off. Then she reared over me like she was going to tromp me good; I instinctively curled into a ball, raised a scraped-up arm in futile defense. But then she didn't hurt me, after all; she just ran off and left me there. I spent the rest of that night squished inside a hole in an old Arizona sycamore and cried until I was an empty husk. By the next day I'd had enough, but I wasn't done running away. I just had realized I needed to update my mode of transportation.

Since I'm dead, I know the whole of it. Like a hummingbird, I flit through time (I'm there when she sticks a foot out and causes Trick's stumble, leads the laughter at his sprawl, but also when the other kids have passed through the classroom door and she reaches out a hand to help him up), through space (I see her weary trek through the brush, hear the noise of the I-17 freeway overhead, feel the gravel underfoot when she finally makes the side of the on-ramp toward Phoenix and sticks her thumb out), through mind (I know her confusion when the battered sedan stops and the driver leans over to give her a good look.)

Yeah, I knew a fifteen-year-old girl in a mud-smeared T-shirt and cut-offs, with leaves and sticks in her hair, scraped and bloodied, might attract the wrong kind of ride. What I wasn't clear on—and remember, I hadn't eaten anything but dog food for two days and I was so crazy dehydrated I couldn't think straight—was if the "wrong" ride would be the cops swooping in to forcibly return me to my zoned-out mom-of-despair or this guy, giving me a real up-and-down.

Unfortunately, she gets in.

Yeah, so I thought about it. And then I got in.

A pint of Gatorade and 1 ½ hours later, I know the poor girl is squirming around in the stranger's car because she needs to pee. That she needs to pee badly. She's needed to pee since they'd hit the outskirts of Phoenix, and now they are deep in the city, with no way to just pull over, and she really has to pee. But she's too afraid to say anything, just shifts onto one hip and then the other, until after a while, she's too afraid not to tell him: "Hey, mister, I'm really sorry, but I'm gonna piss all over myself if you don't pull over, like right here, or real soon. I don't even give a shit where . . . ."

Larry's backhanded slap surprises her, squirts urine into her underwear.

I didn't even know Sweet Pea had died until Trick and some lady named Star showed up at one of the juvenile detentions centers I was being held at, quite a while after I'd run away. I'd made good on my promise not to go back to my so-called home, ever, but I hadn't gotten anywhere else, either—anywhere good, that is. But I had managed to disappear into a ward of the court, and if it hadn't had been for that asshole, Trick—with his what? Heroic sense of duty? I don't know—and the crazy research skills of Guy's new girlfriend, I would have stayed that way. Well, and my dad dying in the car accident, of course—they felt like they *had t*o tell me, for some reason. It meant Trick finally got all the money from his mom —that's how they bought the place in Sonoita. And it meant all of a sudden I had visitors one day.

Larry stands a ways off while Jasmine waters the side of the freeway just into the Gila River Indian Rez on the south side of Phoenix; they're still a good 90 miles from his dumpy rental in Tucson. He shakes, stuffs, zips and comes to tower over her, tucking a clump of stringy, yellow hair behind one ear.

"That seat wet?" he demands of her, his hands coming to his hips. When she just moves her head, no, he tsks and pulls the sucker stick from his mouth and points it at her. "If it is, girl, you'll pay."

And why the hell did I end up in custody? Just luck, maybe bad but probably good luck, as it likely saved my life, so "dumb" luck, I guess. Larry, the guy who stopped to pick me up when I was finally stumbling along the macadam of the Interstate's on-ramp only miles from the school with my thumb out, all hunched up over my aching, empty belly and literally weaving with exhaustion, was a not-so-nice and certainly not law-abiding sort. You'd *have* to be sketchy to pick up an obviously under-age, certain-sure runaway who looked like she'd just been dragged through hell on her way to some even darker place that the preachers haven't even found out about yet—which I was.

She thinks she has no choice but to tag along with him through all his petty thievery. "I have to pee," Jasmine tells him. "Really, Larry. I've had to pee since we left the god-damned park and you told me you wouldn't wait."

Larry stops messing with the padlock and turns around to snarl at her: "You always fucking have to pee."

"Yeah, well, this makes me fucking nervous, and when I get nervous . . . ."

"Shut up." Larry grabs her shirt front and yanks her forward; his straggly mustache nearly brushes her face, and she squints her eyes and pulls back. "You stay here and stand guard, you got it?"

Larry. What an asshole. Still he did me a great service—

drove me all the way to Tucson—and then gave me a livelihood, of a sort. He started me out begging from the white-collar guys downtown, then riding busses, where I stuck my hand in a lot of purses. He taught me how to pick a door knob lock with a paperclip, slip window latches with a credit card. The deal was, as long as I brought something home, he'd feed me, and if I kept out of his hair and didn't talk back, he wouldn't hit me. Well, usually.

Jasmine shifts her weight from one foot to the other, her hands stuffed in the pockets of the jeans Larry bought for her at the Goodwill store, and listens to him move stuff around inside the storage shed and swear. Pickings have been light this week, and Larry has a habit to feed. "Come on, Larry," she whispers under her breath. As soon as he finds something—tools, hopefully; they're easy to sell. Or electronics. Maybe they have some old jewelry stashed in there. Copper, any metal, really. Once he'd stolen a clothesline, complete with little wooden laundry pins, which he'd used to tie the dealer up when Larry decided to rip him off for a change. They need to get the hell out of there; she hopes he'll be happy with the haul and stop at Taco Bell to get something to eat. So she can pee.

Anyway, when I saw Trick with his hands folded in front of him on the table in the rec room they straightened up for visiting day, I was beyond pissed. Star introduced herself and then went to chat up one of the staffers and pretended not to eavesdrop on our conversation, but I knew she was listening when I told Trick I didn't give a shit about my dad dying, about my mom being even more of a basket case, and that I didn't want or need his help then and never would.

Yeah, well, I was wrong about that last part.

But Larry is taking his time, too much time, and finally

Jasmine yanks the buttons on her jeans and squats over the weeds. Of course that's when the cop-for-hire comes around the row of storage sheds and lights her up with his flashlight. The charge is only indecent exposure—it could have been worse. Larry gets caught trying to make off with a pair of binoculars slung around his neck and a squeegee stick, which—because of his priors and the underage girl in his company—lands him in Florence for a good amount of time.

I don't think Trick would have even mentioned Sweet Pea if I hadn't started in on how my serial incarcerations were all her fault, that she was a shit horse and that crap about what a great, noble beast she was was just that—a load of crap—because any good horse would have just plodded along and gone where I told her to go. It shut me up to hear she'd collapsed just a day or so after our stupid adventure, that Guy had used up whatever I had left of her trying to find—you guessed it—me.

Trying to find a worthless shit like me.

So it felt good, these many years later, to be the one to do right by Guy. I mean, Jesus, how convenient was it that good ol' Larry had turned me into a juvenile delinquent-type who knew how to shift the screen door in its frame just right and toggle it open? Then since the ranch's heavy front door was just a simple knob lock instead of a dead bolt, I pulled, jiggled, lifted and pushed just right, and it let us into the entryway.

I don't think the lackey my PO sent down with me was too happy to be the witness of Guy's rescue—I had to use my paperclip trick on the inside door because somehow Guy had gotten himself stuck in his own damn basement, if you can believe that—but I kind of thought of the whole deal as paying it backwards, you know? When we showed up at the address

Trick had given me for their place in Sonoita, and nobody answered our knock, and then we heard Guy hollering and figured out he was down there, I knew right what to do.

I busted him out.

Besides, I'd drunk about a gallon of water on the drive down there from Tucson—nerves, I guess—and I really had to pee.

CHAPTER SIXTEEN

DREAM WORLD

Mariana dreams:

The match flares, but when it's tossed, it flames out, and she hears JC say: "Damn."

She had been in the deep, restorative state of stage four sleep, practically comatose, for almost half an hour when she jerked under the covers and climbed briefly back to consciousness. She had turned onto her side and watched the match, heard the word, her eyes scanning, back and forth, beneath closed lids.

The boy jumps onto a ledge then scrambles down the slope to stand beside the overturned VW. He brushes the dirt from his hands on his jeans, and because he's panting from the exertion, the raw panic, he extinguishes the next match with his breath. "Damn," he gasps again.

Tenku Ania is a private world; only Mariana sees JC palm-smack his head, shudder in the cold, from the fear, and strike another match. This one he holds cupped until he is sure it has caught.

Unscrew the gas cap, Mariana tells him wordlessly. *Pull your gym-sweaty T-shirt out of the backpack you left in the back seat and stuff that into the fuel filler neck. You want to start the car on fire? Light that.*

But the boy has morphed into *Yebu'uku Yoeme*, the first man to hunt deer, and instead of trying to start a car on fire he is drawing water from the lagoon near his and his mother's home. He has lived alone with her his entire life, and with no other woman in their house, it is the young man's job to carry water to her every morning. But the young man doesn't mind. First of all, this is the only way of life he's known. And second, after this one, simple chore, he is free to roam into the mountains and venture among the animals there. He has great power over them, especially the deer. Although they are very dangerous, very wild, he has the ability to tame them; he has even yoked them together and driven them like a team.

Mariana is suddenly at her husband's side; he is laughing and patting their son on his back because Juanito has done something very brave, something that makes his father proud, that would make even their namesake, the great Yaqui leader, Juan Banderas, proud. Mariana isn't sure what, but she knows he was very, very . . . .

The match fizzles out. JC says, "Damn," and strikes another.

Mariana's heart races and her breathing goes fast, then slow, then fast again. She is slack-jawed, immobilized, racing toward a precipice and leaping. That's when she realizes *she* is Deer, running for her life, dodging arrows.

No, not brave. Her son has done something stupid, but her

husband is laughing and patting him on the back. Now it is *her* back her husband is patting; he holds her in his arms, and while they sway, back and forth, he pats softly and tells her: "It's okay. He lives! That's all that matters."

Yebu'uku Yoeme steps into the clearing and lowers his *olla* to the tiny, lapping waves of the lagoon. Only then does he notice the young woman on the opposite bank, her head dipped to the water, and realize she is washing her long, black hair. "Hel . . . hello, Woman," he stutters.

Mariana feels the spray on her own arm as the woman flips the wet hair from her face and says, "Hello, Man."

JC works his way through most of the box of matches: snap, sizzle, fssst. "Damn, damn, damn," he says, and Mariana hears her husband laugh and laugh; perhaps he has been drinking.

"Why are you washing your hair in my drinking water?" *Yebu'uku Yoeme* asks the strange woman.

She just shrugs and says: "I don't know."

Mariana's body is cold but her brain is on fire, and her eyeballs zip side-to-side. She hears the splash of the water as *Yebu'uku Yoeme* fills his vessel, sees the vivid yellow dance of the flame with its phosphorus-blue center, the gray wisp of smoke it trails as JC tosses it—the last match, feels the jolt as her hooves meet earth and, spraying mud, she darts and lunges and crashes through the bracken. Her husband is on her heels, his laughter maniacal; he will eat her if he catches her.

"How did you get here?" *Yebu'uku Yoeme* asks the young woman next, but her answer is the same:

"I don't know." She tilts her head and squeezes water from the length of black hair. "Don't you have a woman at home to draw your water?"

Yebu'uku Yoeme stands and shoulders the strap of his *olla*. "Only my mother, and she is old."

JC leans down and sees his book bag on the roof of the over-turned VW; inside the pack is a lighter as well as the evidence he is so desperate to destroy. Mariana watches him crouch beside the car and reach in; she is next to him as he unzips the front pouch and fingers out the lighter. He hesitates, considering, then also takes out the baggie filled with little blue pills and. stuffs it down the front of his jeans, then he tosses the pack back into the vehicle. But when he flicks the lighter, again and again, he realizes it's empty.

"Take me home to your mother," the young woman tells *Yebu'uku Yoeme*, and she also stands. "Tell her you want me to be your wife."

The woman is Deer now, and Mariana. They slog through the water after *Yebu'uku Yoeme*, following him home, but the lagoon has become a mud hole rimmed with quicksand, and it sucks their strength as they lift one leg, slog forward, lift another, and sink. Mariana tries to soar above the muck, to run, but she can only move in painfully slow motion. She looks down at her feet and wills them to go, go fast. *Hurry, they are coming after me*, she tells her slender, mud-caked legs, her dainty hooves.

His mother is sweeping when *Yebu'uku Yoeme* appears with a wife in tow; she's happy to hand over her broom to the younger woman. "*Yebu'uku Yoeme* need gather water no more," the old woman tells her. "Now all his day will be spent in the *monte*. He will hunt Deer and feed us well." Now Mariana and the girl are in their husbands' arms, their heads thrown back, their torsos arching into an ululating ecstasy again and again.

"*¡Ahi está!*"

Mariana gasps as JC looks up, then drops to his knees beside the car.

"*¡Agárralo! ¡No lo dejes ir!*"

"It doesn't matter what you've done," Mariana's husband assures JC. "You are my son, and I will always love you." But the words are coming out of Guy's mouth, shouted after the boy who is making a mad dash for it, scrambling through the dark, tripping, wrenching himself up, and throwing himself forward through the wash again. There are bigger, darker shapes moving all around him, but the boy is going to make it. He's ahead of the snarling pack at his heels; his feet slip in a patch of mud, but he's small and skinny enough to shimmy into the crack in the rocks beside an old Emory Oak, scared enough to suck his breath in and hold it, hold it, hold it, as he edges in, past the puddle of water, and in, and even farther in.

Mariana gets up from her marriage bed and pads barefoot to the bathroom, but when she reaches the toilet, she sees the bowl is filled to the brim with writhing snakes, so she slams the lid down.

She is in a private world. In *Tenku Ania* anything is possible.

And everything is forgiven.

It is just a hint of light that strikes Mariana's eyelids, but it rouses her enough to open them. She sits up, feels for her robe with one hand, her slippers with both feet, then she scuffs her way to the bathroom.

She turns on the light, something she normally would not feel the need to do, but on this early morning, for some reason, she is worried about snakes.

CHAPTER SEVENTEEN

FOURTH SUNDAY OF LENT

March 6, 2016:

The Prodigal Son

". . . The younger son collected all his belongings and set off to
a distant country where he squandered his inheritance on a life
of dissipation."
Luke 15:1-3, 11-32

"Since when do the casita guests eat dinner with us?" Trick demanded, blue eyes blazing. He totally filled the doorway into the dining room with his arms akimbo like that.

Guy stopped with the ladle hovering over Jasmine's bowl as he looked at his son. The young man's search for JC had been unproductive and arduous; Trick had returned the day after Jasmine's arrival at the ranch, after seven days of traipsing all over the countryside, sun-browned, badly scratched, and starving. He'd stayed in his room most of the past week in a kind of funk, huddled over his textbooks—at least that was what Guy assumed he was doing. He'd come out to raid the refrigerator and cupboards at odd times and was obviously avoiding contact with the entire household, but especially Guy—or so it seemed to him. This was the first meal he'd appeared at all week; maybe he didn't realize Jasmine had been at the table with them for all three squares the whole time she'd been there.

So Guy didn't answer his son. Instead, he dumped the green chili stew in the young woman's bowl and dipped the ladle into the pot to scoop out a serving for Sally, then himself, replaced the pot on the mat, pulled out his chair, shook out his napkin, and sat down. "You're going to need a bowl, son," he finally said, the spoon at his mouth. "There's plenty left."

Trick huffed, turned, and disappeared down the hallway.

"I don't think *Truco* likes you anymore," Sally mumbled with her mouth full, spurring Guy's soft, "Hey, now." The five-year-old liked to peel her tortilla into strips and chew them into gobs which she would either eat or deposit in her napkin, depending on how hungry she was. Tonight she seemed to be swallowing.

"Doesn't seem like '*Truco*' likes anyone anymore," Jasmine commented, but she kept her head down, her eyes on her bowl.

I know she doesn't blame my son, Trick—or little Sally—for their attitude; Jasmine knows she's imposing, and that it was only by making many, many bad decisions that she's managed to squander her own inheritance. She has no right to horn in on Trick and his family—and no other choice.

Guy was gradually getting used to all the tattoos and piercings on the young woman sitting across from him at the table; he'd only asked her once if the things hurt—that ring through her eyebrow, for instance, and especially the one through one side of her nose—and been shushed by Star for being impolite. He wondered about the significance of the letters on her forearm, the half shapes he could see ringing her neck, the swirls of black and red that disappeared under her sleeves, but he'd kept his questions to himself out of deference to Star, and now that she and Mariana were back up in Tucson for the weekend, he kept out of the young woman's business as an example to Sally. Guy knew *he* didn't relish inquiries into some of the messier aspects of his past, and he wanted his daughter to respect that kind of privacy.

He lifted his bowl and drained the rest of his stew. It was delicious, thick and meaty with a nice, slow, Hatch green chili burn, one of Star's specialties, and she'd made a double batch especially for him on her last night at home. She'd served it up with an admonition: "You've got to talk to your son, Guy. Something happened out there that upset him—I'm not sure what. I'm not even sure *he* knows." That despite the fact that the day before, Guy had seen Star corner the young man in the kitchen and hold him there with a hand on his arm for a lengthy discussion; Guy kept pacing past the kitchen's opening into the dining room and glancing in at the two of them. He'd stand a moment beside the big, oak table, then stomp-step back again —past the need for crutches or a cane, now, but still wearing the boot-cast. He couldn't make out their words, but they were clearly talking.

Which is more than he'd done on Saturday. So today was the day—or rather, tonight was the night—if he was going to do as Star had asked and find out what the hell was going on with his son; the women were scheduled to return first thing Monday morning.

Star had placed her hand on our son's arm and asked him to tell her what had happened out there, to start at the beginning. But in the telling of it Trick grew so frustrated that he pulled free of her grip and stormed from the kitchen, grumbling that it made no sense at all:

The night Trick had started out on his search for JC it had been cold and clear, and once the moon had fully set, he'd had the company of an amazing number of stars; he kept having to catch his hat because he was tipping his head back so far to trace the Milky Way, to guess at which of the planets were up there, guiding him. And even though he had only the sketchiest idea where he was going, he did feel like someone—or something—was right there with him and Dice and Amigo, showing them the way.

And the one was many.

There was no traffic at that hour, and they didn't have to follow the highway long before they came to the dirt road that led to the Imperial Ranch. Once Amigo finally settled into his pack horse role, Trick was able to relax a little, even doze a bit. They were traveling northeast, and within the hour the sky had lightened over the Whetstone Mountains and Trick turned in the saddle to look over his shoulder; behind them over the western horizon was the dark curve of the planet—earth's shadow, cast into space. But that was the last of the sky Trick saw for a while because, as the sun rose, a mist came up off the damp ground and swallowed them all—the rolling hillsides of thick grasses, scrub oak, rocky outcrops, and ravines—gulped them down whole; he could barely see to follow the road.

Moving through the mist, the landscape would slowly

reveal itself, and Trick watched Dice's ears, his turning head, knowing the horse was taking it all in, just as he was. The leafless trees made him think of billowing smoke as each appeared, dark grey against the white of fog. "Damn, Dice. I never seen it this thick," Trick remarked, and the horse lifted its head and stepped up smartly, making the trailing Amigo huff a little to keep up. Still the going wasn't difficult, and *This isn't so bad*, Trick told himself.

He'd whispered to Star in the kitchen, head down, that he'd decided to check in with the volunteers at the Imperial Ranch first to see if they'd seen the missing teen, then scout through the Imperial Gulch and backtrack up Cienega Creek, the nearest sources of water. If that didn't work, he'd start looking for mines or rock caves, places the kid might have found to hide. "Instead of sweating blood to get there, I was suddenly thinking it was going to be easy, after all," he'd told Star. "I was sure I'd be bringing him home with me, that it wouldn't be more than a day, two at the most."

My son did not anticipate the non-sense of time in this world..

JASMINE HAD CALLED down to Guy in the cellar: "Hey! You okay down there?" Then when Guy moved some of the boards out of the way so he could get in her line of sight she added: "Jesus fucking Christ, what the hell did you do to the stairs?"

His rescue had been quite a production which had started with Jasmine running to fetch José and his oldest son—which embarrassed Guy very much. They brought a mallet to knock down the remnant steps and a sturdy rope. The tabby had leapt from a shelf onto what was left of the steps and scrambled out as soon as Jasmine had finagled the door open, but the white cat had been hard to coax from his hiding place and Guy had to grab him, then he strapped himself to the old chair he'd been dozing on and held the cat on his lap; they'd hoisted the two of them up to the doorway and tipped them unceremoniously onto the hallway tiles.

Then they'd helped Guy to the kitchen and gotten some coffee into him, but he'd still been wobbly drunk. He thought he'd disguised that fact pretty well when they'd gone ahead and had him sign the paperwork that put Jasmine in his temporary custody, but the reasons for which and the responsibilities pertaining to such—although carefully explained to him in great detail by the nice Hispanic lady who'd driven Jasmine down from Tucson—were totally lost on him in his current state.

"EAT YOUR STEW," Guy told his daughter. "Don't just play with it." He'd finally noticed the mess she was making on the tablecloth, squishing potatoes with the back of her spoon. Sally leaned down, gave the table a good lick, and sat back up with a nose-crinkling grin on her face.

"Eating with you is like slopping hogs," Jasmine observed.

If the comment was made to correct Sally's behavior, it didn't work. She just widened the grin and went at the lumps of potatoes again with several remarkably authentic snorts and grunts, most likely picked up from visiting one of the neighboring ranch's pigsties.

"Jesus," Jasmine sighed, a disgusted look on her face. Then

she addressed Guy: "Do all of your children have this weird ability to become other animals? I know I've seen Trick do it . . . ."

For some reason, instead of Trick's incredible bird calls or Sally's monkey attributes coming to mind, Guy thought of JC at her question, and how, on the buffalo ranch in Winslow, the little boy had barked and neighed and pounced and hopped. The memory made him bring his hand up to his chest to rub the burn there, then he moved it to his bearded jaw where the dentist had extracted his molar. Somehow the ache there had become part of his anguish over the missing boy.

"Well, shit, I guess that makes me a pig, too, since I'm sitting at the trough with you all." Jasmine stood up and reached for the pot of stew. "Is it okay if I eat like one?" she asked Guy.

He held up his bowl. "Have at it, and give me some, too. Might as well finish it."

"What about *Truco*?" Sally asked. "Maybe he'll be hungry later."

"He comes down here and wants me to, I'll fry him a nice, juicy steak," Guy told her. The "talk" they were supposed to have loomed over him, as talking was *not* Guy's specialty—never had been, and almost certainly never would be. "Now finish up and get the dishcloth—you get to wipe down the table, young lady," Guy admonished her, then he huddled back over his refilled bowl.

TRICK HAD STUDIED up a bit on the surrounding ranches when his father had moved down to the Sonoita area, and he knew the Imperial Ranch Headquarters was an historic homestead surrounded by BLM holdings, the Las Cienegas National Conservation Area, and a nice swath of state lands beyond them. It had been one of the largest ranches in the country in its heyday, 100,000 acres reaching down into Mexico and covering most of southern and central Arizona, with its own silver mine, the Total Wreck, up on Imperial Mountain.

It had been whittled down to 160 acres over the years, but it was still a working cattle ranch; they ran a trademark Hereford/Brahma bull mix spread out over the historic ranch's three ranges: right now the cattle would be in the southern section he was approaching, where the Sacaton and salt grasses were still thick; come summer they'd move them to the benches along Cienega Creek; then they'd winter them in the foothills of the Imperial and Whetstone Mountains. Trick and his dad had helped the Imperial hands move the herds from one range to another a few times a year since they'd been living down there, so he was fairly familiar with the spread.

That's why he pulled Dice up so sharply that Amigo ran right into his butt. Something was wrong. Trick stretched up in the saddle, worked his cell phone out of his front jeans pocket, swiped it on, and stared at its lighted screen. No reception, of course, even though he held it over his head and turned it this way and that. The bigger problem was the clock said it was approaching 8 a.m. Trick knew they'd left his father standing on the porch of the Far View around 5 and had been traveling at a good pace, despite the fog that continued to close off the horizon and reduce the sun to a filmy disk still low in the sky; they should have encountered the cattle guard and the old pole and branded board sign that marked the ranch's boundary by now, even if the bowl of land the ranch sat in was still fogged in, the out buildings and windmill over the stock tank lost in mist.

Trick found it very strange that he could make out nothing but the hock-high grasses and the occasional oak or alligator juniper, even standing in the stirrups and removing his hat to give their surroundings a good 360. Nothing.

Actually there were many, many things within his view, but none of them had been made by men.

JASMINE SELECTED the casita at the far end of the row, closest to the old swimming pool, for her temporary residence. She only had a black duffle bag full of stuff which she insisted on carrying over there herself—not that Guy would have been of much assistance. Sally, still in her pj's, had found him stretched out on the couch and was sitting on his chest and devouring a slice of pizza she had discovered in the refrigerator; Guy kept his head turned—he was still mightily hung over and the smell of pepperoni was making him nauseous—and watched the young woman re-approaching the ranch house through the big living room window; he'd instructed her to check in with José as soon as she got settled, and apparently there hadn't been much to unpack from the duffel.

"Who is that?" Sally wanted to know. She craned her neck to see, then stepped up onto the coffee table, still holding the mostly-devoured pizza slice, to get a better look.

"Get offa there," Guy told her. He stood, which made his head throb, but still he grabbed his daughter up and limped over to open the door, then stepped out onto the porch with her in his arms. He was thinking Jasmine might actually be of some help around the place; Guy knew she'd been given the same equestrian training as Trick during her years at the school outside of Prescott, so she should know what she was doing around horses. And the young woman had assured him that being a stable hand—for him and perhaps for some of the neighboring ranches—would qualify as "engaging in gainful employment" and satisfy one of her parole requirements. She was wiping her hands on her jeans—black, like her short-cropped hair and her T-shirt—and walking back toward them from the far end of the lane; José must have sent her to the front pasture to fill the water troughs.

"She walks mean," Sally observed; she tried to hand him the gummed-up crust of the pizza she'd been gnawing on, but Guy set her down on the porch instead. He'd been thinking much the same thing; the young woman had quite a swagger to her. "I don't like her," his daughter added.

"Be nice, monkey," he told her, leaning a shoulder against the post by the steps. "She's in a tough spot." Because he'd decided to step up and help the girl. She'd rescued him from his predicament in the cellar, after all, and needed a second chance—well, more like a fifth or sixth chance—and he believed in sixth chances.

GUY HELD the bottle of Jack Daniels by its neck and used the hand that clutched a couple of juice glasses to tap on Trick's closed bedroom door. Actually it was JC's room, and it was unusual for Trick to appropriate it—he usually slept on the second twin in Sally's room—but ever since his return from his search, that's where he'd been holed up. Guy heard the desk chair scoot back and Trick's, "What da ya want, Sally?" and tapped again.

"It's your dad," he said to the thick, oak door. "Open up."

Guy waited, but when he didn't hear any more movement he tried the knob, and it turned in his hand. He couldn't help the gasp at what was spread out before him: the rug was covered in maps; he recognized his own topo map of the area he'd bought when they'd first moved down there, but others looked to be hand drawn and the rest seemed to be printed from the Internet; there were notebooks spread over these and on the desk and the bedspread; and lining the walls were sticky tabs filled with Trick's scribble and strung together by what looked to be dental floss pinned to them.

Guy walked over to the nearest wall and fingered the waxy strings to be sure; yep, floss. He set the bottle and glasses down on the dresser below the display. There was a yellow note with a big "VW" scrawled on it in the center with floss radiating out to several blue notes, one that said: "book bags"; another had the word "dent" on it; the third said "blood," Guy realized with a wince. Other notes strung together with the stuff were just questions: "How call?" and "Border Patrol = ?" and one had just the word "fog." Trick must have raided both upstairs bathrooms' medicine cabinets to get all that string. "What the hell?" Guy said, turning with his hands on his hips to confront his son.

"Why are the cops letting JC's girlfriend off the hook?" Trick asked him. He was back to wearing contacts—his eyes were a fierce blue against the deep brown of his skin—and he still wore a few of the welts and scabs on his face from his unsuccessful search. "Heather has got to know what happened —she was there."

"Well, they say she don't remember nothin'," Guy responded.

Trick crossed his arms over his chest and leaned back, making the wooden chair squeak.

"That deputy lady called," Guy told him. "Star and I both talked to her." For all the good it had done—but Guy didn't add that part out loud. He was frustrated by the marshal's lack of progress, and from the looks of the walls around them, Trick was, too.

"But why doesn't she remember? Because of the head injury?" Trick asked next. He was still seated at JC's little desk; both JC's and Trick's own laptop were opened before him. Trick had bags under his eyes and Guy thought he looked older than his 20 years; he was pretty sure the young man wasn't sleeping well. "So she gets to claim memory loss, vertigo, and just be no fucking help at all?" Trick demanded.

"Ah, yeah. She had lots of bruises, too." Guy eyed his own son's injuries, then turned back to the dresser, unscrewed the cap on the bottle, and served up two generous helpings of the whiskey. "Star and I did go over there and try to talk to her while you were—out there." Guy still didn't know why Trick had been gone so long and had returned so beat up and empty-handed, but he'd been too testy about it to ask. "Heather took one look at us and started crying—I mean, *hard* crying—and her dad told us we'd better get out. He's a surly bastard on the best of days," Guy lifted one glass and took a swig, and grimacing, swung around to hand the other to his son, "and this wasn't his best day by a long sight." Guy sighed, thinking about the sobbing girl. "Only saw her for a minute, but you could still see where she'd had stitches, like a cross carved into the middle of her forehead."

"Not the middle; toward the left." Trick pointed to the spot on his own forehead, then reached out, took the glass, and knocked the whiskey back in one huge swallow.

"Yeah, that's right," Guy said, watching his son but holding back a comment about the use of his good Jack Daniels. "The family's saying she hurt herself in a fall trying to get home after she and JC had a fight, that he stole the car and wrecked it. The old man told us he's still thinking about pressing charges."

Trick gave a sour laugh. "Yeah, right—charge a ghost." He handed Guy his empty glass and turned back to his computer. "That's not what happened, Dad."

"No, probably not." Guy studied the braid running down his son's broad back, then brought a hand up to rub the thick whiskers over his jaw as he pondered the mystery of the missing boy.

Trick lowered himself to the saddle again, the creaking leather the only sound in the isolating fog. When he finally thought to use the flashlight app on his phone to get his bearings, its beam of light showed him a white world of heavy, drifting mist in all directions. Dice pawed the ground and Trick lowered the beam to show grasses and earth underfoot. Apparently, they weren't on a road anymore—Trick twisted again in the saddle, looking around—and maybe they hadn't been for a while.

The phone's ring was loud and startled all of them, but Dice most of all. The gelding exploded straight up and landed hard on his forelegs, jarring the phone from Trick's hand; he heard it land with a soft thud in the dirt. Then it rang again, and while Trick was trying to calm Dice, Amigo decided to dance from one side to the other, sawing the rope over Dice's croup and sending first one and then the other animal spinning. There was a crack and the ringing stopped, but Trick was so focused on keeping hold of Dice's reins that when Amigo jerked back the lead rope slipped from his grip, and although he nearly unseated himself in the lunge to retrieve it, he felt it slither away. The sound of hooves receded quickly; their pack horse—and all his supplies—had disappeared.

So much for an easy rescue; the seeker had become the lost.

JASMINE MUST HAVE SEEN Guy and Sally watching her from the porch because she angled over toward them instead of heading back to the horse barn. Sally was scaling the railings and then tight-rope walking between posts, her arms out for balance, and seeming to ignore the young woman as she stalled out a few feet from the steps. Jasmine folded her arms over the black T-shirt and Guy realized he was in the same pose; he lowered his hands to his side. "I'm sorry I killed your horse, Mr. Thornton," she said. "I know I told Trick that, but I'm pretty sure I never told you, 'specially since I haven't even seen you since I was a kid."

Guy didn't say anything in response; he'd forgiven the girl, but he certainly couldn't say he hadn't minded, that it was okay. He moved farther down the porch, shadowing his daughter as she swung around another post and traveled along the railing.

"My crazy old lady told me you went out looking for me on Sweet Pea," the young woman went on. "She appreciated that; she'd tell me about it over and over on the phone once she got the dementia, like that was the last good thing that ever happened to her, the last time somebody helped her out . . . ."

Guy had learned from Star that Jasmine's mother was in an institution, but he hadn't known it was dementia that had put her there. Still he didn't feel like he had anything to say to the young woman about that, either.

Jasmine toed the dirt in front of her with one of her black biker boots and Guy looked down at his own dusty boot-cast and scuffed up slipper. "I know I've been a big disappointment to her and, well, everybody, I guess. I really don't deserve your generosity."

"Don't sweat it, kid," Guy told her, snatching up his daughter and swinging her under one arm. "Star and Mariana will be home any minute now; they'll make us a nice lunch, and we'll have us a little celebration, make you feel right at home." Sally was squirming to get free, so Guy set her feet down on the boards of the porch.

Jasmine's smile was more of a smirk, but she nodded, then rubbed her black hair into spikes with one hand and turned. "I guess I'll keep working for a while then," she said over her shoulder as she swaggered off toward the barn again.

"Why are you being so nice to her?" Sally asked, calling his attention back to her. Now *she* had her arms folded across her chest. "She doesn't belong here. You don't let *my* friends move in here."

"Your friends are welcome anytime. You know that," Guy told her. "Go on upstairs and get dressed; your momma will be here soon." But she kept the pout on her face and stood her ground. Guy was thinking about how to explain to his daughter that Jasmine had taken a wrong turn early in life, but that she'd paid her dues and was now trying to get back on track. What came out was: "She was lost, honey."

That made the little girl squirrel up her face. "Like JC?" she asked.

He shrugged and rubbed the sore spot on his jaw through the whiskers. "Yeah, like JC, I guess."

"And now she's found?" Sally persisted, her head tilted way back to look up at him. "Like JC will be, right, 'cause *Truco's* gonna find him."

"I don't know, baby," Guy responded with a sigh. He was worried about both boys; JC had been missing for almost three weeks, and there'd been no word from Trick since he'd headed out after him days ago. "I hope so."

GUY ROUSED HIMSELF, took another sip of his whiskey, and did a slow pirouette to examine the walls of JC's room again. "So you think you know what *did* happen?" he asked his son.

Trick just heaved a gargantuan sigh in response.

"Well, did you ever think of asking the resident psychic?" Guy asked. Putting two and two together and filling in the gaps —that was right up Star's alley.

Trick raised an arm in a backward arc. "She just said to do this: compile the evidence, construct the timeline, and map it out." Then he hunched lower over the desk: "Not that it's helping."

Guy peered over Trick's shoulder at the computer screen. "Well, you have some information . . . ."

"No!" Trick shouted. "The evidence is no good because I have no timeline and no map, and I have no timeline and no map because things are so fucked up over there," he raised his open hand toward the north, "until they're not." He lowered it back to the keyboard. "It's fuckin' . . . ." He shook his head so hard his heavy braid swung, then he snapped his laptop closed and turned in his chair. "I don't know what the fuck they were up to, but I sure as hell know it wasn't something good."

"Okay," Guy persisted, "maybe you think you know what *didn't* happen."

"I know JC wasn't driving—it must have been Heather who hit something—or someone. And she must not have been wearing her seatbelt because that cut . . ." Trick pointed to the spot on his forehead again. ". . . that's from the metal piece on the VW's driver's side head visor."

Guy nodded, sipped, waited. He'd been stewing over the same facts of the case for many sleepless hours, and hearing his son say it out loud only deepened the sense of desperation—of incompetence—that had already been hounding him.

"I don't know what she hit," Trick went on, "but I know the county impound lot returned the VW minus its fender."

That got Guy examining the sticky tabs covering the wall again, looking for that one word that had made him shudder. He'd emptied Sally's jean pockets and laundered the T-shirt she'd been wearing when she was climbing around the wrecked VW as soon as they'd gotten home from having his ankle booted, as if a dose of bleach was going to erase the foreboding that had descended on him at the sight of the red-brown smears on it.

He finished off his own whiskey and set both empty glasses down on the dresser again, then he took the Jack Daniels up by its neck. He was either going to pour another round or take the bottle back down to the kitchen and put it away, depending on what Trick said next.

"They kept it for further testing, didn't they?" Trick asked. "The fender. Because it had blood on it, right?"

Guy hung his head and looked at his son through the side of his eye. Then he raised the bottle and poured.

SECOND SCRUTINY

There are good reasons our son keeps the story of his misadventures in the cienega *to himself. They are the same reasons he keeps going back, trying to understand what he simply cannot:*

Now Trick had no idea where he *or* JC was, but he did know that entire ranches didn't just disappear. It was the fog, he assured himself; he just had to wait for it to lift so he could see the mountains and get re-oriented. He didn't even know if he'd go after Amigo; the horse could find his own way home once he got hungry enough.

Of course, the horse could eat grass; all my son has left of his supplies is the old canteen he'd hung from Dice's saddle horn.

The first thing the young man had needed to do was to get Dice to stop his twitching and turning; he wanted to find his phone and check its condition. Once his father's settling words had worked their magic on the gelding, Trick swung a leg over and had the mixed blessing of landing right on it, cramming it a little farther into the dirt with his boot heel. He wound Dice's reins around his wrist so he could bend over and dig out the phone's various pieces—the back had popped off the badly cracked screen and the battery had fallen out. Trick brushed the parts on his jeans and blew out the grit as best he could before reassembling it, then he shoved his glasses back on his nose, held the device close, and studied the screen. Nothing. He thought to turn it off and on again and a crazy hieroglyphic of its start-up routine showed through the cracks. All in all, it didn't look good, but Trick sighed and slipped it back into his front pocket anyway.

They heard the owl just as Trick remounted. The fog was starting to lift, but the bird's ghostly "Woo, woo, woo" still sent a chill along Trick's spine that seemed to continue right on down through Dice, who shivered and pawed the ground. There it was again—Dice turned his head to the right—"Woo, woo, woo"—and when the horse took a step toward the sound, Trick relaxed the reins and let him take the lead. The cottonwood limbs took filmy shape ahead of them as they approached; a large, hunched form was on one of them. So it was not just any old owl but a mature Great Horned Owl on its perch.

"Impressive," Trick whispered as he pulled up a respectful distance from the tree. "Can't tell if it's night or day in all this fog, can ya, buddy?" Then he imitated the bird's vocalization, waited the same amount of time it had, and repeated the sounds: "Woo, woo, woo." The bird graced them with a 180 degree turn of its head; even through the thick, white air Trick could make out its black tufted ears, wide-ringed eyes. It regarded them silently for some time, and the young man and his horse remained almost as stationary, Dice shifting his weight only once.

Be careful, my son. It isn't just Native Peoples who believe Owl is a harbinger or a messenger of Death.

GUY WAS NOT a good conversationalist in person and even more tongue-tied on the phone, but he dutifully called JC's mother, Kate, every evening as the sun set, after yet another day had gone by and the fifteen-year-old was still missing. He never called the boy's father, Richard—he didn't even have that number, hadn't even known the couple was separated—but Kate assured him that she kept JC's father informed, not that there was much "informing" to do.

Despite the depressing news he had to give her—or lack thereof—Guy actually enjoyed talking to Kate, especially since she seemed perfectly happy to do most of the conversing. And he must have felt a little guilty about their extended half-conversations because, if Star was home instead of in Tucson, he always made the call while she was busy helping Mariana in the kitchen or engaged in a yoga or healing session in her studio space. He'd take the phone and a beer out to the porch with him and watch the last light leave the roll of the land and fan a sunset over the Santa Ritas; Sally would usually join him there on the swing they'd hung from the porch rafters, lugging along the current favorite stuffed animal in her menagerie.

Once Guy had stammered out his update, Kate would sigh and sniffle softly for a few moments, then thank him—she always thanked him—and launch into her own account. A few times she'd had something about the case to tell him—both she and Richard had been interviewed by a federal officer. But the rest of Kate's stories were about lunch with her lady friends, some book she was reading, what the weather was like in Flagstaff, or a great TV show she wanted him to check out. For a woman who had suffered—and was suffering—such losses, she was pretty upbeat. Guy had been shocked by the news about Grace: Kate's daughter had been staying with one of Richard's sisters while she took a course at the university in Tucson with plans to enroll full time in the fall, but there'd been an accident—Kate couldn't talk about it except in sobs that Guy couldn't quite understand. She'd had a fall or been pushed. So Kate was all on her own now, but she stayed positive.

In fact, the whole time she was speaking Guy felt wrapped up in her familiar, homey, cultured life, in her days of meals and recitals and readings at the local bookstore; it made him miss her and the kids and the years at the buffalo ranch they'd shared. And all he had to do was utter a "huh" or a word or two: "Great," "No kidding," even a whole: "Yeah, I remember all right," from time to time.

Mostly he imagined the thick waves of Kate's hair, still a reddish brown because he hadn't witnessed the new streaks of grey, her capable hands cupping the receiver, the way she'd bite her lip—he knew she was doing that every time she'd pause to think of something else to say. She'd drag the calls out until all the light had left the sky. In the dark, that's when he'd think about that one encounter not long after he'd arrived at her family's ranch outside of Winslow. They'd both been drunk; she'd had a fight with Richard and, after he'd gone to bed mad, they'd killed off the bottle of Jack Daniels in her kitchen. Guy had risen unsteadily from the table, intending to stagger off to the old bunkhouse where he slept, but Kate had grabbed him by the shirt.

It was kind of like that again, talking on the phone with her, no real news to share, just assuring her they were all doing everything they could to find JC, and then her hanging on, not wanting to let him go (he'd laughed and tried to loosen her grip, then laughed again when he couldn't), even when Sally started pulling on his hand: "Come on, Daddy. It's supper time." Even with first Star's and then Mariana's voice (she'd said his name, again and again, softly, pleading), calling from the dining room: "Time to eat!" Even with the dinner smells wafting through the screen door (the whiskey on her breath as she pulled herself up the length of him). Even though he'd said, "Well, I should go" two or three times by then ("Kate, no. We shouldn't. Oh, sweet Kate.") But the conversation would go on. (That one time, right there in the kitchen. Only that one time.)

He wondered if Trick's guess was true. He wondered if she wondered—or knew.

* * *

TRICK CAME to sprawled on a pillow of thick grasses. He groaned his way up to a sitting position with *Where's my horse?* then *Where's my hat?* jangling through his brain; just over there, munching on salt grass, and about a foot away from his right hand, resting on its crown. But when Trick reached to grab it, he got so dizzy he groaned and lay back down.

He opened his eyes sometime later to a blurry, early morning sky; Trick felt his face and realized his glasses were also missing. "Shit," he wheezed as he sat up again; he reached over, snagged the hat, and put it on. The back of his head hurt and his left shoulder felt bruised; he rubbed it while getting to his knees and then lumbered the rest of the way up. He crouched there a while, brushing off his jeans and trying to get his head to stop spinning.

He finally straightened and took a step toward his horse. That crack underfoot—he lifted his boot and reached down— was, sure enough, his missing glasses. One hinge had snapped off the frame and one of the nose pads was bent; when he tried to straighten it, it broke off in his fingers. "Shit," Trick said again and tried them on; they tipped cockeyed with only one ear hooked, one nose pad in place, so he took them off and put them in his shirt pocket.

Dice hadn't wandered far; Trick used his dad's whistle to call him—"Wee oh wheet!"—and the horse lifted his head, long strands of grass dangling from his mouth and tangled in his bit. He seemed to think about it for a moment, but then he snorted and came up slowly. "What the hell happened?" Trick asked the horse when it nosed him in the chest, leaving a smear of green slobber on his dad's Levi jacket. "I find it hard to believe I just fell off you, mister. What'd you do, spook? Take a roll?" Dice nodded but Trick wasn't buying it; he remembered perfectly the last time he'd been bucked off a horse—old Sweet Pea had been startled by a jumpy calf squirting right under her belly. That had been a good six years ago. It had been a unique event. Trick did not think it possible for him to just fall asleep and tumble off; waking up on the ground made no sense at all.

That's all the young man had told Star in the kitchen because this, and the next several parts of his adventure, hell, the entirety of it was like some weird version of reality that could not actually have happened. But then what did?

GUY LAY IN BED, his head swirling from all the whiskey, trying not to think about Trick or JC or blood—only it wasn't working. His son's hunch about why the marshal's office had kept the fender was right, but the Deputy lady had told him they were having trouble identifying the sample because there was so little left of it; they assumed that was due to the rain that had come through the area before they'd been able to raise the vehicle from the ravine. For some reason Guy hadn't wanted to tell Trick about the matches and the lighter Sally had found. The Deputy never mentioned any efforts by the teens to destroy the evidence in or on the vehicle, but Guy was pretty sure that was what they'd been trying to do. The "why" of it all still eluded him though, that and the involvement of the Border Patrol whose agents had stopped by with their third set of questions just a few days ago.

Trick had observed this discussion from the top of the stairs, keeping just outside of both their and Star's view—but not Guy's. And that's the topic he had broached next in JC's bedroom as Guy refilled their juice glasses with Jack Daniels. "Border Patrol means Mexico," Trick said softly. "Mexico could mean a lot of different things—including drugs, or guns —but if the kids were riding around wild and hit something, it'd more likely be immigrants. Or their *Coyote*." And Guy knew Trick meant the guide who had led the people there rather than the animal.

Trick did that downing of his drink in one large swallow again, and this time Guy followed suit.

"Remember when JC called you, Dad, and I tried the redial?" Trick held out his glass again. "That answering machine message in Spanish?"

"Of course I remember," Guy assured his son, splashing more whiskey into both of their empty glasses. "Why do you think he sounded so rushed and disoriented? He knows this country—why couldn't he tell us exactly where he was? And why the hell was he whispering—I couldn't hardly hear him."

Trick muttered, "Fucking crazy out there . . . ."

Guy rubbed the spot on his jaw, gone all numb, now, from the alcohol. "Ransom?" he finally asked his son.

Trick swallowed his whiskey in a gulp. Guy, wincing, did likewise.

"I'm sorry to say this, Dad." Trick shook his head several times before continuing: "But we're not much of a target for extortion. And frankly, the kid ain't worth a shit . . . ."

That had made Guy straighten and rock back on his heels.

"Well, he isn't," Trick insisted. "'Cept maybe to you and 'Sweet Kate.'"

"But not you?' Guy fumed. "What if he *is* your half-brother?"

Trick turned back to his computer. "Like I said."

That had ended their discussion, but not Guy's drinking; he'd frowned at his son's broad shoulders, grabbed the bottle by its neck, and carted it into his bedroom with him.

Trick winced his way back into the saddle and turned the horse to look for the owl—the last thing he remembered—but he couldn't even find the big cottonwood it had been roosting on, just a copse of young juniper rising out of the thick grama grass that obscured the ground and any tracks Trick might have been able to use to retrace their steps—or determine where Amigo had gotten off to. The mountains were still whited out, but the sun was definitely burning off the remnants of fog in the foreground and lighting up the landscape in its own surreal way: every strand of grass glistened with a diamond drop of moisture at its point; every seed-tipped mesquite branch glittered and turned iridescent as they passed. The world they traveled through was all aglow, bejeweled with unworldly riches, and totally unfamiliar to him.

Finally my son sees, truly sees. But of course what lies before his eyes is strange to him—it's the world of the Surem.

CHAPTER NINETEEN

JASMINE

I had one day—*one day*—of the good life at the Far View Ranch before Trick returned from his weird adventure and started messing things up for me. He was supposed to be up in Tucson finishing his stupid degree in veterinary science while I *seemed* to fulfill my work requirement and the last months of mandatory parole with his easy-going dad as my sponsor. If Trick had been where he was supposed to be, I could have just lazed around, then fed my PO a line of bull during our every-other-week phone calls. Instead I had just one glorious day to revel in my luxurious surroundings—of course, it wouldn't have taken much to beat that crappy halfway house up in Tucson where I had been living—before Trick, not even fully recovered from his injuries and debilitation, spoke to José and told him to crack the whip.

On *me*.

But that first morning, luxuriate I did. It started off with an absolutely amazing breakfast of ham and eggs and biscuits, jellies and jams that their Yaqui housekeeper, Mariana, made. When I finally pushed back from the table I could hardly stand up I was so full, but I managed, and then sat in the swing out on the front porch petting one of the cats for a while, digesting. I finally decided to stroll down to the horse barn just as José was finishing the chores that I had been supposed to do—feeding and watering and raking and spreading clean straw around—so I just went from stall to stall and scratched horse noses. And then—why not?—I saddled up one of the mares and lit out for a good, long ride. I hadn't ever been to Sonoita, wasn't really aware of this lush, grassy part of Arizona, and I and my little pinto didn't straggle back in until hours later. But when we did, I could smell the tamales all the way down at the horse barn; that made me incredibly hungry all over again, so I rushed through my horse's rub down and literally ran back up to the house, launched myself over the porch steps, slapped through the screen door, and was first to pull out a chair at the dining room table for lunch.

Mariana's nice—she laughed at me when she set the plate down in front of me and said: "*Jovencita, no te preocupes.* There's plenty for everyone." And you know what? There really was: enchiladas and refried beans and a salad as well as the tamales I'd smelled; I kept marveling at it all as I shoveled it into my mouth.

But then my wonderful day went a little sour because Star joined me, and she wanted to talk, of course, so she asked me lots and lots of questions, not general ones like: "How are you doing?" where you could say, you know, *Fine,* and she'd shut the hell up. No. Star asked: "How often are you talking to your mom?"

Well, not often 'cause she can't even form complete sentences anymore, but I told her: "Oh, once or twice a week."

Star studied me, put her chin in her hand. "It must be hard to understand her." Then she wanted to know if I'd been able to complete my court-ordered restitution.

No. Not even close. But I answered: "Oh, yeah. That's all taken care of now."

This earned another long look and the comment: "I'll talk to Guy about giving you a better wage. That should help." I have to admit, I liked the sound of that, but it was pissing me off that she seemed to be hearing my thoughts instead of my words. Then she asked: "Are you still feeling really angry? Have you been practicing your management techniques?"

Hell no. And I'm about to rip your head off, lady. "Oh yes, every day."

"I'll help you get started again," Star assured me. Then she went there, and she—probably more than anybody—knows I don't talk about him: "How are you feeling about your dad these days?"

Fuck you, bitch. I didn't even attempt to answer that one. Luckily Guy stomped in with his daughter in his arms right about then—he was still wearing that leg cast—and after setting the kid down he went clear around the table to rub Star's shoulders before he sat beside her, then who knows what they were doing under that table, and he kept scooting his chair closer to hers—I swear to God. Even Sally got jealous after a while and left her chair to crawl up in her mom's lap to get some attention.

There's something wrong with the kid, I'm pretty sure, some "identity issues" I think one of my shrinks would call it: most of the time Sally will moo or meow or squawk rather than speak, and she always has some kind of stuffed animal in her arms—or two or three. And it took me about a micro second to understand why Guy calls her "monkey" instead of using her name most of the time: she's always scaling any cliff she can find, like bookshelves—I came in one time and found her dangling from the top shelf of one of the really tall ones beside the big fireplace—and Star told me later that she can't hide a thing from the girl, even in the highest cupboards.

It took me all of that first full day to tell Sally didn't like me, and that's okay—I don't have any fondness for kids, either. And I'd had to put a good scare into her the previous morning because I'd caught her snooping around my casita, testing the doorknob, peering in the windows. I know how to be pretty intimidating, pitching my voice low and growling, shoulders hunched, tatted, muscled arms out wide at my side—I've been lifting weights regularly since my first incarceration—a furious scowl on my face. And it worked. She ran—well, actually, she kind of hopped—all the way back to the house squealing—I'm telling ya, there's something not right, there—that I was going to "fail" her alive.

Actually, I'd told her I would "flay" her alive, but she'd gotten the point all right and has pretty much left me alone since.

That first day, Guy didn't really seem to register that I was there at the table with them until just before we were done eating lunch when he rousted himself enough to list a bunch of chores and errands he wanted me to run. But on that first day I took his instructions to be more like suggestions, and although I imagined I probably would get around to doing at least some of what he was asking of me, I certainly wasn't in any hurry. I had developed a habit of taking a nap after my mid-day meal over the past few years, for example—nothing better to pass the time of incarceration—which usually took up most of an hour, and after that I'd planned to take my bath towel and a book off one of Star's shelves and lay out by the little swimming pool they'd dug out around the back of the house and read—another practice I'd learned in captivity. Star actually encouraged this; her books were all self-help and psychobabble shit, and she thought I was "improving myself" when in reality I was having a good laugh. My shrinks had pretty much tried *all* of it on me, with no obvious effect.

So I was nodding at Guy, like *Okay, I'll get right on it*, as I rose from their table for the second time that day. And about five hours later when I smelled the casserole Mariana had pulled out of the oven, I slid back into the chair I'd appropriated as my own and started munching on the carrots and celery she had put in little dishes around the table cloth, well rested, well read, a little tanner, and ready to dive in to some great chow again. There's a small flat screen TV in my casita, and I planned to sneak a bottle of wine over there with me right after dinner. I'm not supposed to be drinking during my probation—mostly because my sentencing judge was an honest-to-God sadist—but my plan was to get roaring drunk or at least nicely tipsy while I watched any fucking thing I wanted on that little screen.

That's exactly what I was doing when Trick got back. He rode in well after midnight, but I was still awake, just finishing the bottle, when I heard horses greeting their stable mates with some really anxious-sounding whinnies, and when I pulled aside the drape to look out my window, I could see him, way out at the end of the yard, riding one horse—well, hanging on to one, all slumped over—and leading another into the horse barn. Then over the whole compound came these rooster shrieks out of Sally: *"Truco! Truco! Truco!"* She must have been leaning halfway out her upstairs bedroom window, sounding the alarm. But it was still all a big *So what?* for me at first, and I was snoozing in the chair by the time Guy rousted me with a hammering on my door. I hollered, "Go away" at him, but he just pounded some more and then shouted through my window that I was to take care of Trick's horses, that Trick was in bad shape, and the horses needed immediate attention.

So I slogged around in the dark that night. And I've been slogging every day and even some nights since, thanks to having an asshole slave driver back in the house, and Star's been making me just as crazy with all her yacking and her wacko crystals and stuff. Luckily she's got a sick dad up in Tucson, so she's not around that much.

Since that night, the end of my one good day, I have gradually gotten used to this place and my role here. I was certainly not a happy camper as I was slamming my way out of my casita that night, but then I saw Guy struggling to help Trick to the house, the bigger man's arm slung over his shoulder, and Trick's legs buckling, and I had to help; I mean, Trick is an asshole, but he's in *my* posse of assholes, and I could tell they weren't going to make it across the yard, let alone up the stairs, without assistance. So I hustled over and got Trick by his other arm, and between us, we did it, slowly, one step and a rest, then the next, across the porch, into the dark house. Then when Guy jerked his chin at the couch, I readjusted Trick's weight and kind of squat-walked with the bulk of his heavy load toward it. The landing was not graceful, but Trick's groan of relief satisfied me.

Then Guy had to go and turn on the light.

I'd been prepared for Trick to be a mess; half-carrying him, I'd gotten a clear message that he hadn't washed in days. But there was also this other, strange smell. I don't exactly know how to describe it. Some kind of herby perfume or fragrance? Maybe something Christmas-y, I don't know.

Guy pulled off Trick's muddy boots and lifted his legs up onto the couch, eliciting a gasp from his son, then gently removed his hat and adjusted the sofa cushion under his head while I just stood there gaping at the gouges and scrapes all over his face, his neck. But really it was the blood that shocked me—the amount of it, for one thing. The whole front of his Levi jacket was covered with its wine-black stain, as well as his cuffs and his hands. I looked closer—and I wish I hadn't. That was blood smeared around his mouth; he looked like a wolf that had gnawed his last meal from the bone. I couldn't help the shudder.

Guy had resorted to moaning and pacing, his hand over his mouth and beard. I reached over and pulled the blanket off the back of the couch, intending to cover Trick's shivering, but Guy froze and said "No!" He held out a hand for the blanket. "Go see to the horses," he insisted. "I'll tend to him."

Then Sally slid down the banister, shrilling the whole way: "*Truuuuuco!*" She landed in a sprawl at the foot of the stars, and wouldn't you know it, that crazy kid—hell, *one* of Guy's certifiably crazy kids—had knocked herself out cold.

CHAPTER TWENTY

FLOWER WORLD

Mariana has finished tidying the house and has gone out to work in the yard. She'd been humming snippets from hymns as she swept the painted concrete, enjoying the cool air of the spring mid-morning, and is now moving with the hose from planter to planter, the sun warm on her back as she bends to pluck a weed here, snap a dead blossom off there. The birds at the feeder and bath launch with a whirl of wings at her approach. She turns off the water, coils the hose, then moves to straighten the lawn chairs back into their cluster around the metal table at the center of the patio—Jasmine has been reading out here, and she likes to put her boots up on a facing chair. There are the hummingbird feeders to refill; that takes several trips in and out of the kitchen, as there are many. Then Mariana takes the broom with her through the house and out onto the front porch where she begins sweeping the old, worn boards. There is an after-breakfast hush over the property, and she is alone with the voice in her head, reciting her daily devotions in silent words that keep time with her swaying movements.

She prays for Trick. JC needs her attention more, she knows, but that doesn't dissuade her from focusing on Trick. An argument could be made for Star's dying father—but that could be disputed, as well. Jasmine, unfortunately, strikes Mariana as a lost cause, but she does not neglect her entirely. She doesn't believe healthy, well cared for little children like Sally need much from a loving God, and Star has told her she does not wish to be prayed for, so Mariana does not.

She lifts the mat by the front door, sweeps under it, replaces it, then moves down the steps and starts sweeping the flag-stones that line the front flower beds. It used to be Mariana prayed for Guy a lot; she's concerned that, although he's such a good man, a very kind man, he feels unworthy, unneeded—and recently—all used up. He's behaving like Wise Deer in the tale her father told her about the huge deer that was so strong and wise none of the hunters could ever find him. He would hide so well they could track him for hours, for days, and never see more of him than his over-sized hoof prints. Even when large groups of hunters went out in pursuit, he would know they were surrounding him and stay hidden.

This went on until Wise Deer grew so old he became disen-chanted with his life; he wished to lay it down. But when he presented himself to the old men who had sought him in his youth, they turned away, saying: "He is too old, his meat too stringy now—even the dogs couldn't chew it." Wise Deer followed the hunters' trails, searching for a trap in which to ensnare his vast rack of antlers, entangle one of his big hooves, but he couldn't find one. Finally, overcome with weariness, he called out in anguish to the twilight: "I have given myself up" and died. Even coyotes shunned his carcass, and it took a very long time for it to rot away.

Mariana knows it will not come to this; Guy is only in the middle of his life, not the end. But she senses his belief that he is aging out of purposefulness, when in fact, she's pretty sure this Easter—if the family survives this trial that has befallen them during the weeks of Lent—he will prove his worth and rediscover his family's need for him. And more than that—she hopes that the events about to transpire will restore his confidence in his own vigor. She does still pray for that.

Dawn's glittering dew dazzles my son; he doesn't notice Dice's head tossing and general alarm until the horse wrenches hard on the reins and Trick is nearly jostled from the saddle. Before he can correct his horse he hears it, too—a rustling through the grasses—then sees it: a zig-zagging lightning strike that erupts into the clearing in a blur of fur and tall ears. Dice, already agitated, rears with a terrified scream, and although Trick has a good wrap of the reins he's not prepared for the next explosion from the grass or for the pounce that pushes him sidewise out of the saddle, the claws digging into his shoulders, his neck, the big cat's vicious snarl. He's on the ground, the wind knocked out of him, his hands wrapped around the animal's throat, squeezing, both of them spitting and gasping, the cat—a bobcat, a small one, just a juvenile— scratching with all four legs until Trick slings it clear and hears it slap with a crunch of bone against a tree.

Mariana notices the earth around the flowers Star planted has been turned up, the blossoms trampled, and she drops to her knees and sets down the broom to resettle the petunias, gather the broken snapdragons. She speaks to the *Surem,* the guardians of *Sea Ania,* the Flower World that lies hidden below the dawn: "Keepers of all that is beautiful, all that is good in the world, send *Saila Maaso*, Little Brother Deer, with his blessings to visit us." She brushes the dirt from her hands and sits back with a sigh. She knows it is Trick who has done this destructive thing, early every morning, on his way to haunting the place that haunts him. This is why Mariana is so worried about him. She's not sure how or if he will recover from his encounter with the *Surem*, for that is what she believes happened to the young man out on the *campo*.

It's an occurrence not entirely out of Mariana's realm of experience. Her own son was taken—thank God. He had fallen under the influence of evil shortly after he'd begun his EMT training. Somehow the drugs that were meant to save other people gained a hold over him; Mariana wasn't sure how. Her son had stayed away from her during this time, become a stranger to her, and when she did chance to see him she could hardly recognize him; he was too thin, too shaky, his eyes dull. It went on for months.

My son rolls to his side, wincing—my poor son, oozing blood down his neck. A puncture wound—from the cat's claw or tooth—is too close to the carotid artery and is surging with each heartbeat. Trick clamps his hand over it, lies back down. When he turns his head he sees the jackrabbit calmly nibbling the grass only a few feet away from him, even though Dice is still pacing and bobbing his head above the both of them.

Then one day Mariana's son returned; he came walking down the dusty alley toward her husband's adobe home in Old Pascua on the outskirts of Tucson. Mariana was in the back of the lot, hanging clothes on the droopy clothesline, and watched him approach. He was still much too thin, but his steps were sure, he was smiling, his eyes had their old luster. She opened the gate for him, pulled him into an embrace, turned with him to the house and presented him to his father, standing just outside the door. The two men regarded each other wordlessly, and finally Mariana pushed past them to put some food on the table—her son looked like he hadn't eaten in weeks.

Trick finally stills his breathing enough to try to stand, manages a weaving, half-crouch, his hand still gripping his neck, stumbles once and takes a knee. But he is determined to catch Dice's reins and lunges up again, grabs them left-handed, and rests his forehead against the horse's shivering neck. That's when he hears the owl again: "Woo, woo, woo."

But it wasn't true that he hadn't eaten, Mariana's son told them later. The food of the Surem was like a manna that appeared every morning; it was his daily bread. That comforted her, but then he went on to tell them how he had been tested in the wilderness, and that he had very possibly died, not once, but several times. More than this Mariana's son would not tell them for many years, and from this Mariana understood Trick's reticence: the animal encounters, some benign, some terrifying, do not make sense outside of *Sea Ania.*

Bird noise wakes Trick and he opens his eyes to what appears to be yet another dawn. He sits and his head is clear again. When he thinks to examine his scratches they seem to have scabbed over much more quickly than he would have expected; only his neck wound is still slightly bloody to the touch. He traces the crusty lines along his collarbone, his cheeks, then turns to look for the bobcat's carcass.

In Mariana's son's case, once he'd survived his test, eaten the flesh of Deer, drank its blood, he was able to find his way home, cured of his affliction. But she remembers that he was disturbed for many months afterwards and only gradually came to terms with what had befallen him. She believes it was the *Chapeyka* dance that finally wove his schizophrenic experiences together in his mind and heart.

Somehow Trick's not surprised when he sees the deer, instead. It's a magnificent eight-point buck, with flowers draped through the candelabra of its antlers. It steps into the clearing, now dotted with the yellow bloom of wild roses, its nose working, and dips its head at Trick. He hears the drumming of its heart; the metered tapping of its breath is the exhale of a thousand blossoms. He smells something herby, spicy, other-worldly—a sacred incense.

In the dance Mariana's son is at once God and human; he is Devil and human, as well.

In the dance her son is evil, and yet the God of all-good loves him dearly.

How was Trick to understand these things?

So kneeling there beside the broken flowers Mariana prays:

Sea Ania, *world of the good and beautiful, place where all things merge and find their balance, help him to forget, or if that is not possible, to reconcile his inner churning.* Saila Maaso, *you lay down your life to feed the Yaqui people; your sacrificial blood springs into flowers as it touches the earth.*

If all else fails, teach him how to survive the knowing.

CHAPTER TWENTY-ONE

FIFTH SUNDAY OF LENT

March 13, 2016:
Christ's Forgiveness

"Let the one among you who is without sin
be the first to throw a stone . . . ."
John 8:1-11

Guy was at his perch on the couch, the casted leg propped up on the coffee table, staring out the big front windows absently, as was his custom these days—well, on weekends when Star and Mariana were gone. If they were around, he'd be chopping wood for the casita's fireplaces—although they still didn't have any guests booked—repairing leaky faucets, cleaning the fountain, feeding the stupid Koi—although there was also a turtle in the pond, and he liked feeding shrimp to the turtle—and keeping the pool clean—for Jasmine, he guessed, because she was the only one using it. In short, he was a house servant and a handy man since he still couldn't drive, let alone ride a horse. And he'd just about had enough of it.

But Sally was happy when he was hanging out with her. He had carried her down the stairs that morning on his shoulders, and she'd leaned over to giggle in his ear: "I'm riding a mountain!" Then she'd brought him some books and they'd sat on the couch together and read for a good half hour before he made them breakfast. Now she was on the floor at his feet, managing her own zoo-farm hybrid, moving giraffes into the lions' cages and running cows and sheep all over the old Navajo rug. "The lions are going to eat those guys," Guy warned her, but Sally didn't even look up. So much for his opinion.

Trick had pretty much done the same thing to him earlier that morning. Guy had had an inspiration—he was sure he'd figured out the mystery of the missing boy. Well, maybe he should give some credit to the show he'd been watching on their bedroom TV the night before. It was a crime drama that Star liked—one of the few complicated enough that she usually couldn't figure out the perp before the show's characters did. Guy mostly dozed through the episode, only to be roused by Star's "whoop" of accomplishment when she *did* get it right. But Star had been up in Tucson making the hospice arrangements for her father, and Guy, who'd been unusually antsy all that day, had still been awake for a change, at least enough to follow the plot.

In this installment, the Mexican drug lords were looking for ways to fill in the cuts that increased border surveillance had taken out of their income stream, and they'd landed on a new drug: the synthetic opioid, fentanyl. It was cheap, easily sourced from China, and 50 times more powerful than heroin. And of course, that was the problem for the TV cops—people dying right and left.

Guy had sat up in bed, then stretched across it to the end table on Star's side where she kept the pen and little notebook for logging her dreams, and scribbled the word: "fentanyl" so he'd remember to tell Trick in the morning. But when he'd tapped on his son's door in the early light, it had swung open, revealing Trick's own ever-expanding sleuthing in the form of sticky tabs and notebooks strewn everywhere, but although the bed looked to have been slept in, there was no sign of Trick, and when Guy brought his daughter downstairs on his shoulders he'd seen the young man's hat was missing from the coat rack near the door.

My son has taken to leaving the house before dawn; he doesn't wash or eat for fear it will wake the others, he just rolls out of bed, pulls on yesterday's clothes, and, boots in hand, creeps down the dark stairs, through the shadows of the living room, grabs his hat, and slips out the door, closing it soundlessly behind him.

Guy had made coffee and burned some toast for himself and Sally and even cleaned up the kitchen by the time Trick had reappeared. Guy'd caught him halfway up the stairs, headed back to his room, he surmised. Trick hadn't wanted to hear about fentanyl, and following him up the stairs, explaining, hadn't seemed to change that.

"Maybe that's what was in the backpacks," Guy said as Trick resolutely shut the bathroom door. "It's worth a lot of money. He could be running from a cartel of some kind."

"Even JC's not that crazy," came muffled through the thick

wood. "And the marshal's report doesn't say anything about fentanyl or any other kind of drug."

"What about Heather's asshole dad?" Guy asked him. "And the chief marshal did say there was stuff about the case he wouldn't tell me."

"He wouldn't tell you your own son was suspected of running drugs?" And then Guy heard the noise of a flushing toilet.

So that's what his son thought about Guy's "drug lord" inspirations.

As Trick heads out the stars are salt scattered over black velvet; he stops at the bottom step to examine them. There is the Milky Way, right where it's supposed to be. He skirts the house, trampling the petunias and snapdragons Star has planted so as not to trip the motion-sensitive yard light. He ducks and crosses the driveway, hustles along the pole fence of the corral, and steps into the entryway of the horse barn. There he turns, hands stuffed in the pockets of his father's bloodied Levi jacket, and searches for the Big Dipper, then uses it to pinpoint the North Star; it, too, is in the right position, not dancing and weaving, spinning out of control.

So Guy decided to stop pestering the young man and ride the couch the rest of the day. He'd tried to raid the refrigerator but had come away with just a relish tray of olives, and since Sally liked them, too—if he dressed each of her fingers with one—those were soon gone. After watching Sally play for a while, he'd picked up a copy of *Farm and Ranch* magazine from the end table, but it was resting open on his chest while he kept his eyes on the view out in the yard.

He sat up when he saw Jasmine leading Pedro around on a cool-down walk; apparently Trick had taken one of the horses somewhere again this morning. The girl had started to seem like she was taking a genuine interest in her work lately, and Guy wasn't unhappy he'd agreed to her sponsorship—unlike Trick, who was very vocal in his doubts about her. But taking her in had been Trick's idea in the first place, Guy kept reminding him, and Trick was the one who'd decided to keep hanging around the ranch instead of heading back up to the university where Star says he was supposed to be doing research for one of his animal science professors. The young man had been so moody, a real sourpuss, ever since . . . .

In the deeper dark of the stable Trick is greeted by the horses with huffs and stamping; they are expecting to be fed, but only the mount Trick chooses for his use will be. He passes Dice's stall and the horse whirls away from him; Amigo warns him off with a throaty growl. He has ridden neither horse since . . . . He is fairly certain he will never ride either horse again. Trick stops and pets Armonía's nose, the mare he rode out on the day before; she shivers and lifts her head away from him. The only horse he has not selected for this purpose is an old Pinto gelding they called Pedro. Trick sighs and turns to collect the horse's tack.

Jasmine had turned Pedro out in the corral and was making her way back up toward the house, smacking the dust from her gloves on her black jeans. Most of her uniform was the same— black everything—except for the battered, dingy white Stetson. That was a new edition, courtesy of Guy's closet. He had counted the rings and things in her ears at the dinner table, the piercings dotting her face, and come up with about 14; the tattoo swirls on one arm had finally revealed the shape of a dragon; on the other arm were numbers that Star had told him represented a certain date. She was a moving canvas most of the time, but for some reason this morning the young woman had just stopped in the middle of the yard. She stuffed the gloves into her back pockets and then stood there, waiting. Guy lowered his booted leg from the coffee table and stood to look.

"Woof," Sally said. Then she made a very authentic growling sound; Guy realized she was standing now, too, sharing his view out the window.

"I can't figure out what she's doing out there," Guy confided to his daughter.

Sally tilted her head way back to look up at him. "*Truco says I'm to throw stones at her if she stops working.*"

"What?" Guy said, frowning down at her. "Don't you dare do that."

Sally just shrugged, her eyes on the young woman, still as a statue, head down as if examining the ground before her biker boots.

Trick leads Pedro through the double doors at the rear of the horse barn, along the back pasture fence, and only mounts the horse once they are on the lane leading to the highway. He removes his hat, checks the stars again; they remain as before. He taps the hat back on, pulls the coat tight, and urges the old gelding into a fast walk. They will be retracing Trick's path to the Imperial Ranch—again. They will be looking for an owl perched on a cottonwood tree—again. And most of the way there and all the way back, his horse, no matter which horse, will turn its head from side to side, its ears constantly swiveling, start and stare, wrench to a stop and suddenly jump into a trot. And although, try as he might, Trick can't see anything unusual going on, his mount will grow increasingly agitated and distressed until it froths and shakes beneath him.

Guy sighed and made his way to the door with Sally at his

heels. The view didn't change from the porch; Jasmine stood with her head down, and Guy knew something was going to be required of him, something he was most likely ill-prepared to respond to, but he continued down the porch steps anyway, crossed the yard, and stood before the young woman with his hands on his hips. He looked over at Sally, doing her "Minnie me" impression of him, but she also wore a scowl on her face. Guy rubbed his whiskered jaw and made a fierce attempt at a smile. "What's goin' on," he drawled at the young woman.

They never make it. Each attempt thwarts Trick with a different challenge: the mist fails to appear and the stars stay right where they're supposed to; the limbs of the cottonwood are empty; there are no diamonds littering the grass; there is no exploding rabbit or crazed beast lunging into an attack. There certainly is no majestic deer stepping into the clearing, and they easily find the branded board sign of the ranch. The sun will rise and the mountains will stand tall in their proper places. Trick will turn his traumatized horse back towards home, vastly disappointed and incredibly relieved.

"There's somethin' you oughta know," Jasmine said quietly, still speaking to the ground.

"What did she say?" Sally demanded. When Guy shushed her she insisted, "Well, I can't hear her if she's going to whisper."

"Why don't you bark off?" Jasmine snarled at that, and Guy raised his hands between the two of them in a settling gesture.

But that just incited Sally: "You can't yell at me. You're bad. You killed Daddy's horse. You . . . ." But she didn't get to finish because Guy scooped her up and took her jaw in one hand and stopped her words.

"That's enough out of you," Guy warned her.

But Sally wrestled her face free. "*Truco* says she does 'adult' stuff—bad stuff."

"And you don't ever do nothing bad, huh?" Guy asked her. "How about me? You think I got this broken ankle by doin' right?"

"Sometimes you can do the right thing and still get hurt," Sally objected.

"I'm not out here to fucking talk about me or you two assholes," Jasmine fumed. She wrenched her hat off and held it at her hip, squinting up at him. "Sorry," she spat out, paused, and then she said it again, softer: "Sorry." Her spiky black hair stuck out all over the place but Guy was careful not to smile. Instead he did his best to shush Sally and waited.

Finally she came out with it: "It's Trick. I'm not sure what he's doing to the horses, but I'm sick of trying to get the spook out of 'em when he brings them home. Maybe you could talk to him about it—where's he takin' 'em off to or, I don't know. Tell him to stop."

It wasn't news to Guy, so he didn't pretend it was; José had been very worried about Dice and Amigo, and he'd let Guy know that hadn't been the end of it. But what to do? What to say?

"He's searching for that JC kid, right?" Jasmine went on. "Over on the Imperial Ranch somewhere?"

Guy bent down to set Sally on the ground and took a knee. For some reason he started writing in the gravely dirt. "I'm not sure it's even about JC anymore," he told them. "Star can't get much out of Trick, just a few words."

"Owl," Sally read over his shoulder. "Why'd you write that?"

Guy raised his eyes to Jasmine's instead of answering his daughter. "Weird shit happened. Something about a deer, too. He told her he kept waking up dead, over and over."

That sent Sally in a run for the house, squawking: "*Truco? Trucu? Truco?*"

Guy stood, wiping his hand on his jeans.

Jasmine sighed out a long, "Okay," and they stood in silence for a time.

"Well I'm not going off on an owl hunt," Jasmine said finally. "And Trick's not dead, but who knows if JC is." That made Guy wince, but she went on: "My thinking is we go back to where you found the wrecked car and see if we can find some sign of him there. Star thinks there might be something there too . . . ."

"*We?*" Guy quizzed her.

"I'll need you to show me where it was." She settled her hat back on her head.

It was Guy's turn to sigh. "The marshal's people have been all over that place . . . ."

"Fuck, Guy—neither that asshole marshal nor those Border Patrol idiots have accomplished shit," Jasmine scoffed. "And it's pretty clear that your beloved son Trick is not cuttin' it, either. So if you want, I will help you try to find the kid."

Guy looked down at his dusty boot cast; the Velcro straps were dangling and frayed, the bottom scuffed slick. The thing was on its last legs, anyway. "Well, you're right about that," he said slowly, scratching at his beard again. "They think he just ran away." He remembered Jasmine's mother's words, essentially the same, that had sent him out on the search for her: "They think she's a statistic!"

"I know I'm not the most trustworthy character to go out on a hunt with," Jasmine added.

"No one's said you've been anything but trustworthy, so far . . . ," he assured her. But there was still a lot of hesitation in Guy's mind. He was pretty sure Star wouldn't approve—he wasn't supposed to put any weight on the unsupported ankle unless the x-ray next week indicated it was completely healed, and Guy doubted the boot cast would fit through the stirrup.

Jasmine saw him looking down at it and offered: "I bet I can rig a sling from your saddle horn for that leg; you'll just have to hang on tight with the rest of ya. And if we head out soon, we'll be back before you have any explaining to do to the ladies."

At her words Guy lifted his head. "I guess so," he said, coming to a decision; he'd been cooped up long enough. "I'll tell Trick to watch Sally—and to lay off the horses."

"Okay. I'll get Dice and Amigo saddled up." She turned toward the stable but then stopped and swung back around. "Guy, you probably already know—the kid's right. I've done some really shitty things."

Guy straightened, regarding her. "Well, hell, who hasn't?" He felt the familiar burn in his chest and, rubbing it, added: "Just don't do it anymore, I guess."

CHAPTER TWENTY-TWO

SALLY

THIRD SCRUTINY

Wake up, Son.

Trick opened his eyes and found himself flat on his back in the thick grass. The world was a blur—his glasses had broken, he remembered; he patted his front shirt pocket and was reassured to feel them under the fabric. Then he rolled to his knees, woozy as he'd been each time before. There was his hat, upturned on its crown, there was his horse with the long grasses dangling from its moving mouth. He whistled—again—and the horse hesitated—again. "Damn it, Dice, don't give me any shit—I'm warning you," Trick snarled at him this time; he was in no mood for this déjà vu crap.

If only it was *déjà vu, my son. Instead you are outside of time, beyond space, past mind.*

. . .

"WHAT THE HELL is the problem now?" Jasmine asked Guy irritably. He'd gotten the sling she'd rigged for his boot-cast tangled up in the stirrup again and had stopped—again. This was the third time, so he wasn't surprised by her impatience. Unfortunately, he couldn't quite get the hang of riding this way; either he was slipping off one side of the saddle or the other, or he was snarled up in something. "I wasn't planning on an overnight, here," she complained to the rolling grassland surrounding them.

The other problem was getting Dice to go; normally he was a very well-mannered animal, but Guy hadn't been on him for a while, and he wasn't behaving like the horse Guy remembered. He obviously didn't like the sling from his saddle horn and was swinging his head around to eyeball it, he kept surging ahead and then pulling back because he didn't like Amigo taking the lead, and he didn't seem to have any inclination to go where Jasmine was leading them—back to the site of the overturned car. Guy wasn't too happy about their destination, either, but he could see why Jasmine would want to start back at the beginning. Too bad the horses didn't; both had started out jumpy as hell. Amigo had settled down some when they'd turned for the highway instead of toward the Imperial Ranch, but not Dice. Guy was definitely getting the feeling that the horse was trying to tell him that this was a very bad idea.

But he was out and about in beautiful country, the spring sun was warm but not too warm, and there was a nice breeze. If only they were going on that picnic Trick had wanted those many weeks before; if only they weren't hunting the boy who had become a ghost, instead.

THE HORSE CAME FORWARD as Trick slowly gained his feet again, smeared the Levi jacket green again as Trick took his reins. "We are going home," he told the horse. Strangely, he wasn't hungry or thirsty, but he sure as hell was sore, dirty, scratched and punctured. And worse than that, he was confused; he needed to get back to the familiar, then maybe he could try to find JC another time. Trick grunted with the effort of tightening the cinch and gingerly mounted the turning horse.

"Steady," Trick angrily corrected Dice and backed him out of his nervous circles. "What is it?" he asked him, "What's bothering you?" and just then he saw the dismembered rabbit, a mess of fur, bone and shredded flesh, and smelled the blood— but it was on *him*, on the hand that came up to cover his nose, on his whiskered cheeks. He normally only had to shave about once a week, so the stubble in itself was odd.

Wake up, Son. You must wake up and rid yourself of the stench of death.

JASMINE'S MOUNT obviously wasn't happy about their outing, either; Guy saw him balking and turning in circles as he caught up with them. The string of obscenities she unleashed on the horse was impressive, even to Guy, and he was glad he'd insisted Sally remain at home with Trick, even if neither of *them* had been happy about the arrangement; they'd stood side by side on the porch and watched him limp to the horse barn with the old, black backpack slung from one shoulder, both of them with their arms crossed over their chests, scowling and pouting up a storm. But Guy had been resolute: "You've done your best to find him, son. Time to let Jasmine and me give it a go."

"What the hell is wrong with you?" Jasmine was demanding of her horse as Guy urged Dice past them.

"It's not far now," Guy said over his shoulder. "I can hear the highway."

———

TRICK LOOKED up when he heard it: "Woo, woo, woo." But instead of an owl he saw the blur of movement again and ducked instinctively, then slowly lowered his arm and raised his head when nothing broke from the thick grass, nothing pounced. Dice was moving in circles again, huffing and jerking at the bit; it gave Trick hope that the stars weren't really spinning above them, clumping together and then spiraling off to the horizons. But they kept at it when he stilled his panting horse and took his hat off to stare up at them; it made him dizzy.

A muffled ringing started in, adding to Trick's confusion. He searched the clearing in a panic until he finally realized it was his phone, stuffed in his front jeans pocket. He stood in the stirrups, worked it free of the denim, and squinted at the cracked screen but couldn't make out the number, or swipe it to answer. He finally remembered his glasses and fumbled them onto his face, but they didn't do much good—the screen was a spider web. Trick punched his finger at it again and again.

Oh, my son, wake up! You have to wake up now!

———

BY THE TIME Jasmine and Amigo joined them, Guy had been sitting on Dice at the edge of the ravine for several minutes. He tilted his hat back and turned in the saddle to regard them: "You didn't hurt him, I hope."

"Damn horse," Jasmine grumbled. "I tell ya, you've got a stable full of these rabbits, now, thanks to your wonderful son."

Guy was thinking it wasn't his son's fault that something seemed to be spooking the horses out here, but he just turned back around. "You can see where they winched the VW up; it was right down there."

Jasmine dismounted and came closer to peer over the edge of the ravine. She lifted her hat, rifled a hand through her hair, and gave a low whistle. She looked at him over her shoulder and asked: "You jumped that?" Guy shrugged and she barked out a laugh. "All right, old man." She replaced the hat and backed Amigo up.

"Now what?" Guy asked her.

"Well, I'm not crazy," she said as she remounted. "So me and Amigo are taking the long way around. You boys are welcome to come along, although you don't have to, now that I know where to start."

Go back and sit on the couch? Not likely, Guy thought as he turned Dice, cued him, then slapped him with the reins, then gave him a good jab in the ribs with his heels to get him going again.

TRICK WOKE on his back again, swearing this time. It was hard to even drag himself onto an elbow, but eventually he managed to sit up and spit out a wad of what looked to be half-chewed, uncooked flesh. He touched his stubbled face, felt the crust of dried blood around his mouth, then sputtered and moaned his way to his feet again and called Dice over.

He could barely stand, so he had no idea how he was going to get on the horse, but finally he led Dice over to a bent sapling and was able to leverage himself into the saddle. But then he just swayed there, without the strength to cue the horse with his legs or snap the reins, or utter more than a feeble, "Haa." And then Dice started dancing in circles again. And then the stars joined in, twirling, faster and faster.

You must *wake up, Trick. You must.*

"ARE you sure this is the same ravine?" Jasmine demanded.

It was just a wash at this point, and honestly, it was hard to tell, but Guy nodded and said, "Yep."

Jasmine was leading Amigo—having given up on managing his spins and half-bucks—and was struggling almost as much just to keep his reins in her hand with all his wide-eyed head-jerking. Dice was shivering under Guy, but as long as he kept his comforting whisper going—more tone than words—the horse would walk forward in this crazy, high-stepping, nervous gate. "I'm beyond spooked, too," she continued, looking around the boulder-strewn wash. "What do they know that we don't?"

Guy couldn't answer that, so he didn't.

IT WAS VERY dark this time when Trick opened his eyes. He was lying on his back, and he tilted his aching head from side to side and squinted until he found the half-moon in a gap among the moving branches of the trees; it was no longer full as he remembered it being when he'd set out. His ribs hurt when he inhaled deeply of the strong, almost medicine-like incense that filled the clearing, and he felt the deer's presence but he could not see it. He was startled when, out of the blackness, a whirling sound grew closer and a hummingbird came so close he could feel the fan of its wings. It was strange enough to see the little bird after dark, stranger still for it to come so close. Trick raised a sore arm, then he fingered his broken glasses out of his pocket and put them on in defense. He waved the little bird away, worked his way up, and managed, eventually, to climb on Dice.

Then he heard the owl: "Woo, woo, woo."

Trick, wake up. Your father is going to need your help.

"OKAY, THIS IS RIGHT," Jasmine said. "I can see the highway. Let's leave these poor excuses for horses here and go the rest of the way on foot." When Guy reined up beside her, she looked up at him and amended what she'd said: "Well, right, so *I'll* go ahead and check things out and come back and let you know what I find." She led Amigo over to a mesquite and wrapped his reins around one of its flimsy branches.

"To hell with that," Guy responded. He was about to dismount but then hesitated, turned in the saddle, and unstrapped the old, black backpack he'd tied to the cantle. "Here," he said, gesturing Jasmine over. "There's some water in here."

"Ugh," she said as she accepted it. "Apparently that's not all. We're not staying a week, Guy."

Guy didn't say it, just thought it, with the missing JC and the recovering Trick in mind: *You never know.*

THIS TIME TRICK turned away from the owl; he closed his eyes, not wishing to see it, and instead of letting Dice move toward the big cottonwood it perched on, he backed Dice out of the clearing in the direction he was pretty sure they'd come. He made a conscious effort to undo each action he could remember: He did not pull his cell phone from his pocket and try to use it to illuminate the ground around them; he did not imitate the owl's call; and he kept his head down and flattened himself against Dice's neck as much as he could at the rustling of the grasses. "We're going home," he insisted in a hoarse whisper. Then he cleared his throat, spat the bloody mess from his mouth, and raised his voice: "We are going home!"

He did work the phone from his pocket when it rang, though, out of habit. But the ringing stopped when Trick held the device to his ear. "Hello?" he said in the profound silence. "Hello?" Dice took a step forward. "No!" Trick insisted, jerking back on the reins. "My father needs me to come home." Then Dice lifted his muzzle and let out a nicker just as Amigo, muddy and droopy-headed but still loaded with all Trick's supplies, stepped into the opposite side of the clearing.

JASMINE DROPPED the pack at her feet and held out a hand. "Need some help there?" she asked Guy. He waved her away; he wasn't a god-damned invalid. But then just as he was getting his right leg clear of the saddle, Dice stepped sideways and Guy's boot-cast got tangled up in the sling again. There was a moment when he thought he'd regained his balance, but his "Steady" to caution the horse ended with a "shit!" as he swayed sidewise. He made a grab for the saddle horn, missed, and fell backwards, landing in the dirt with a loud "Ouff," his booted foot still caught in the stirrup. Dice skittered and dragged Guy after him, despite his, "Whoa. Dice! Whoa!" and Jasmine's, "Holy shit! Asshole horse!"

The commotion got Amigo yanking backwards, and Jasmine turned to secure him instead of leaning down to help Guy, but the horse's rein slipped free of the branch before she could get to him and the big Saddlebred reared with squeal, whirled, and dashed back down the wash the way they'd come; Dice—despite Guy's "Whoa, now. Whoa!"—bolted after him, with Guy in tow. He could hardly hear Jasmine's fading, "Guy! Guy! Aw, fuck!" over his own: "Whoa. Ow. Ow! Dice! Whoa! Shit!" as he was dragged over the rugged ground.

CHAPTER TWENTY-THREE

JASMINE

I took off after them at a run. Well, I guess I did hesitate a second while I looked down at the backpack Guy had handed me and wondered if I was supposed to take it with me, but one heft of a strap and I knew it would slow me down too much. *Then* I was off, dodging boulders, spraying sand. I tripped and landed in a sprawl right next to Guy's hat, grabbed that up, and scrambled back to my feet. Guy's "ow's" and "whoa's" had stopped by then, so I figured he was either out of earshot, knocked unconscious, or disentangled from the horse, and thank God it was the last one—I skidded around a bend in the wash and there he was, sitting up, covered in dirt and holding his head in his hands.

I staggered over to him, panting, and tried to hand him his hat, but now I could see the blood—lots of it; it was matting the hair on the back of his head, his face on one side was scraped raw, and there was a rent in his shirt at the shoulder where the fabric was turning red. He finally looked up and took the hat, but instead of putting it on he just held it in his lap. And what do you think he asked me? Yep: "Where's the backpack?"

"Are you all right?" I asked him instead of answering, watching him brush some of the dust and gravel off the side of his face.

He turned with a wince and looked over his shoulder.

"They're long gone, Guy," I assured him. "I guess we're on foot." And then we both looked down at his now-entirely-brown-with-dirt boot-cast. "You got your cell phone on ya?" I asked him after considering a bit.

He patted a pocket, then sighed and went back to holding his head. "No reception out here anyway." I knew his head hurt bad by the careful way his put his hat back on. "Let's find the backpack." Then he rolled to his knees like he was going to try to stand up.

"Maybe you'll let me help you this time," I offered, and I held out a hand.

I'm pretty strong, but hauling Guy up was not easy—he's tall, and he's put on some weight these past years. Then he started off, but he kept swaying and stumbling, so I grabbed his arm and slung it over my shoulder. It wasn't long before I felt the sticky-wet of his blood on my arm, so I stopped him and lifted his shirt to see if there was a way I could staunch the bleeding from the wound on his back. I thought a second, then took my hat off and drew my T-shirt over my head. "What?" I said at his shocked expression. I mean, I wear a bra, especially to ride, so it wasn't like I was flashing my boobs at him or anything.

"I just—I never saw the whole, ah, lizard-thing before."

"Jesus, Guy," I scolded him. "It's a damn dragon. Now turn back around."

I've seen injuries and shit before, but I really wasn't prepared for the amount of damage that being dragged had been done to Guy's shoulder. There was a flap of flesh hanging lose over a long, gaping slice that was still surging blood, so I balled up my shirt and tried to brush off the wound, but that made Guy give a low growl and pull away from me. I pressed the fabric over the gash, then pulled his right hand across his body and put it over the wad. "Can you hold that on there?" I asked him.

"Backpack," was all he said. Now there was blood seeping onto the band of his hat from his head wound.

It was slow going back to where I'd left the backpack with him leaning so heavily on me, and frankly, I thought the whole exercise a waste of time until I parked Guy in a tiny bit of shade on the side of the wash and brought it over to him. I could see why he'd wanted the water—we both gulped down a bottle each—and then he rinsed off the side of his face where he'd gotten the road rash and poured some on the deeper slice that ran down his back. But then he kept pulling other stuff out of the backpack, and I remembered its "magic" reputation. In fact, I had been in possession of this very pack—or some earlier version of it—as a teenage runaway on Guy's horse. Unfortunately, I'd lost it before I'd even opened it.

So now was really my first chance, and I grabbed it out of his hands. He told me there was a tarp at the bottom; so I dragged that out and spread it on the ground, then helped him scoot over so he was sitting on it. Then I took over the job of dumping the rest of the supplies out beside him and kind of sorting through it all. He pointed at the pack of wet wipes and took off his hat.

"Can you get some of the blood off?" he asked me, then he picked up a small pill bottle, bounced several into his hand, and knocked them back with another slug of water; some kind of pain reliever, I imagined.

So I set to work. I found a pair of tweezers and some reading glasses in a little case—they must have been Star's; I've never seen Guy wear glasses—and was able to pick out most of the cactus spines and little rocks lodged in the side of his face. He had a big old knot on his head, and it was really too tender for me to do much but get the worst of the dirt off with the wipes and pat it gently with some of the iodine. The Swiss Army knife had a good blade and even a little pair of scissors, which I used to mangle Guy's shirt into a bunch of strips. Then I wrapped Guy's forehead, and sitting back to examine my work, I thought he looked like he was wearing a weird, bloodied cotton crown. He pointed out the duct tape, which I used to secure the bandage. When he gestured at the little sewing kit, I thought he wanted me to fix all the ripping I'd done to his shirt, but he just barely moved his head, no, and scooted around so his back was toward me.

"I think it's still bleeding—I'm getting woozy," he told me.

Well, he was right about the bleeding; he'd been holding my t-shirt against the wound, and it was soaked. But I didn't get the point of the needle and thread until he made a stitching motion with one hand. "You've got to be kidding me," I told him. He just dropped his head, so I threaded the needle, which always takes me a while but took even longer this time because I was shaking so bad, then I leaned closer. When he said: "Wait" I couldn't have been more relieved. But he lifted his hand like he wanted something and said: "Whiskey." I looked through the pile and found the pint bottle of Jack Daniels. He just chuckled when I asked him if he wanted me to sterilize the needle, and then he sipped and did some heavy breathing while I worked at reattaching the flap of skin.

This whole experience haunts me: His skin was slippery with blood, as well as all the sweat—and frankly, tears—that I was dropping onto his back, and my fingers cramped up. I hated the stick part when I poked the needle through, but I hated the feeling of the thread traveling through his flesh as I pulled it taut more. He just kept breathing, slow and steady, but when I was about halfway done I had to lurch to my feet, walk a few feet away, and hurl all that water I'd drunk onto the sand. But I came back, wiped my mouth with the back of my hand, and finished the job; I have never been happier to tie a knot. "Okay, that's the best I can do," I said, and Guy tilted his head back to finish the bottle and then turned around on the tarp to face me; his cheeks were wet above the beard, and I realized he'd been crying, too.

"I'm so sorry, Guy," came out of me then, and that was a big deal for me—I *never* say I'm sorry for shit because I don't know how that helps; you still did the bad whatever you're sorry for. But it was finally dawning on me that this was all *my* doing—I'd been the one to propose this disaster of an outing; I'd rigged the sling for his boot-cast that, for all I knew, would still be the thing that killed him; I'd turned to the horse instead of the person lying on the ground. So I cried, I cried a lot, and Guy just sort of looked at me.

After a while he said: "Stop blaming yourself, girl." His laugh was just a whisper. "And if you did do anything wrong, I forgive you." He paused and touched his bandaged head, then straightened and did the craziest thing: He coughed onto his fingers, motioned me forward, and rubbed the little bit of moisture onto the center of my sternum. I kind of expected to be grossed out, but a weird warmth immediately emanated from the spot and I sat back with a "Shit, man—what'd you do?"

Then I realized that Guy was starting to slump and his skin tone had turned a little grey. I leaned over and got him sitting upright again, but then he was shivering, despite the late afternoon sun that had invaded our tiny spot of shade. "Are you cold?" I asked him after I'd used one of the tissues—there were, like, five packs of those—to wipe my nose, and yeah, my chest. He just hugged himself and shook, so I hurried to finish wrapping and duct- taping his shoulder and dug the red, long sleeve shirt from the bottom of the pack and helped him get into it.

"M-m-maybe some food," he said in a shaky voice. "Then you better get going."

"Ah, food—okay," I said, "Sure. But I'm not going anywhere."

I handed him a packet of peanuts, and took it back when he couldn't open it, then jostled them handful by handful into his palm. I joined him in finishing off the crackers; he was shaking too hard to get the protein bar to his mouth, so I hand-fed him that. "Hey, look," I said, "There's a box of wine in here. What do you know? I never seen a little box like that."

"Hand it over," he said, slurring a little. "Then you get going."

"I don't think drinking all this alcohol is what you're supposed to be doing right now," I chided him, but I opened it and handed it to him, anyway. "And I'm not leaving you alone, Guy."

"You can climb . . . ." He stopped, leaned back against the shelf of rock behind him, and hugged the emptied backpack to his chest. ". . . climb out at the highway bridge," he said."Get help." He took a swig of the wine then closed his eyes. "Take the flashlight." And I realized he was right—the sun was getting close to the horizon, and if I really did hike out, it would be past dark before I'd make it back to him again.

"Guy, I can't just leave you," I protested.

All of a sudden there was a whirl of wings and then a little hummingbird flew right at my face. "Jesus!" I said, ducking and raising an arm as it came back on another strafing run. "What the fuck!" I jumped to my feet and took my hat off to wave it away. When I looked over at Guy, he just shrugged, then winced from the pain of the motion.

"Daddy!" came from down the wash next. Then "Daddy!" again in her little girl shriek that I normally found so annoying but this time sent a thrill through me.

Guy groaned, and when I looked over I could see he was trying to stand, but he only made it to one knee before collapsing onto his side. "What . . . ," he wheezed out, "What are you . . . ."

Then I could see them, and I cupped my hands around my mouth to yell: "What the hell are you doing out here all by yourself?" Sally was the last person I would expect to see riding in here on a horse. "It's Sally on Pedro," I told Guy over my shoulder. "And would you believe it—she's got Dice by the reins." Suddenly our situation didn't seem so desperate, in fact, maybe not desperate, at all.

"Daddy! Daddy! Daddy!" Sally squawked again and again as she trotted up, bouncing like a toy on Pedro's bare back, heels flying. She gave the horse an earnest "whoa," dropped to the ground before he'd come to a stop, and started for Guy, but I grabbed her.

"Hey! Whoa, yourself, kid. When Dice ran off he dragged your dad; he's hurt."

Sally shot an angry look at the horse over her shoulder, then glanced at me. "Where's your clothes?" she asked me before turning back to her father. "Daddy?" she mewed. "Mommy called again. She said I was to tell you not to come out here, that something bad was going to happen. She said to tell you not to go." She clasped her hands under her chin and chirped again: "Daddy?" but Guy didn't respond.

"Go ahead. Just be gentle," I told her. "I've got to get these horses tied up."

I led Pedro and Dice a way off where they wouldn't stomp all over Guy, and while I was securing the reins—careful to select a bigger branch, tie bigger knots—I heard a *tchee tchee tchee tchee tchee*. There was the hummingbird coming around a bend in the wash—and what do ya know? Behind the stupid bird was good ol' Amigo. He whinnied to his buddy, Pedro, and when the old Pinto answered, Amigo came trotting up, so I tied him off, too.

My heart burned. It was a strange, totally foreign feeling, like joy, in the midst of all this chaos. I rubbed the spot, muttering, "Okay, I got this, I got this," as I walked back over to them, even though I still had no idea what to do. Sally was curled up against Guy's chest on the tarp; she'd pulled one of his arms over her and was humming some little kid song and fiddling with his pony tail.

The situation certainly didn't look desperate, more like an after-picnic nap.

But then I got closer.

III. RESURRECTION

There will be a great light after what seems like days of darkness. You will open your eyes, shake your head to clear it of all the dreams, and see a beam shining through the cracks and down the chimney of rocks; it will take your breath away. The illumination will turn the damp cave of your terror into a cathedral.

You will scoot, shimmy, slide your way toward the light, irresistibly drawn to it. You will still your breathing, suddenly so loud in your own ears, and listen for your enemies' voices but there will only be light emanating from the outside, only light and a strange, spicy smell like incense.

Is this, too, a dream, you will wonder. The darkness has been a tormenting series of visions: Heather's bloodied lip, her father's drunken demands, headlights headed straight toward you. Then the blood on the dead man's jeans, on your hands from rolling him over, dripping into Heather's eye. Lighting match after match after match. And then running, running, waking with your legs still twitching.

But then you'll look down at the baggie at your feet and know it wasn't a dream.

It was a nightmare.

You will step over the baggie and use your knife to pry loose the boulders you've stacked over the cave's opening. You will squeeze through the narrow gap in the rocks and emerge into the clearing, squinting and blinking, sun-blinded.

Spanish words will assault you, then the knife will be knocked loose, your wrist wrenched behind you, and you will be taken, your hands bound behind your back. After a sack that smells of oats is thrown over your head, you will be led, stumbling, over rocky, uneven terrain. You will fall, be yanked up by the arm, and fall again and again. Finally you will be shoved onto a wooden bench in a shed of some sort that smells of horse and be given water, a warm tortilla.

And sometime later, back in blackness, you will be handed a phone. You will pull the handset under your hood, punch the buttons, and give Heather their message: bring back the money and the drugs, or you will be killed. *Tell her I will slit your throat*, the man will demand you add in heavily accented English, *with your own knife*.

You will know what her father will do when he hears this.

So before they can grab the phone away, you will make the second call, the call you hope will save you.

CHAPTER TWENTY-FOUR

PALM SUNDAY

"*Gracias, Señora.*"

"*De nada.* Napkins and forks are right over there."

A roar goes up from the crowd, and when Mariana raises her head she sees people moving toward the plaza, shaking their fists. After a morning and noon of anticipation, the *Pharisios*, the enemies of Jesus, have arrived. They are dressed all in black and black scarves cover their faces; they hold sticks like swords. These are Yaqui men the Madonna has saved, and they are sworn to her, so they participate in the dances as Her son's accusers, necessary actors in the redemption of all mankind.

The drum beats twice and Mariana watches them line up at the center of the square; when the flute starts up they begin to file in. She is at the far side where she's been helping a friend serve home-made red and green chili burros from the tiny booth the two women constructed that morning out of two-byfours and a plastic tarp. Mariana motions to her friend, then removes her apron and hangs it from a splintered board.

The *fiesta* did not end until very late the night before, and Mariana and many of the others who stayed to see Deer Dancer and the *Pahkolam* emerge have had little sleep, but the lethargy of the morning has been erased, now, with the arrival of the *Pharisios*, Pontious Pilate's soldiers. Soon the *Chapeyka*, devils and wicked creatures, will join them in the square, but the people will dispatch the evil ones. Then there will be the procession with blessed palm leaves. The Deer will dance, and they will carry the Christ statue across the plaza and into the Jerusalem of His church.

Mariana is tall, but so are many of the others in the crowd, so she presses through the gathering, past the rows of grannies in their folding chairs, holding umbrellas. She wants to be close enough to see her son's ferocious mask, hear his snarls and rattles.

The musicians launch into a metered number and Mariana claps along with the others. Finally she spots him; even under a tusked boar's head, he is certainly her son. She is proud of his high steps, his frightening lunges that make the children squeal and scatter. They have been waiting all morning for this, holding the *cascarones*—eggs filled with confetti—and paper flowers they will use to defeat the evil *Pharisos* and their terrifying *Chapeykas*, who are spreading out around the plaza and taunting the crowd, seeming only part human in their varied costumes; she is grateful the elders are there to wave palm fronds and deter them from causing harm.

Mariana isn't expecting Star, so her appearance startles her: her halo of curls is so white in the noon sun as to seem nearly transparent, her flowing blouse makes her seem to float through the crowd. "Star!" she calls with a smile and a wave. But it's Trick, like a mountain towering behind Star, who sees her. He nudges Star's shoulder and points with his chin.

"This is wonderful," Star says over the music as she hugs Mariana.

Has she always glowed like this, Mariana wonders as she steps back from the embrace; even in the throes of grief, she seems luminous. Perhaps it is just the darkness hovering around Trick that makes her seem so bright. He has a scowl on his face, big hands hanging at his sides. His eyes are shaded by the low brim of his hat, but Mariana knows they are focused on the distance, as if he is searching for something he left out there in the *campo*.

A cheer comes up from the crowd and Mariana leans close to Star to be heard. "How are you holding up?" she asks her.

Star responds with a tight smile and a shake of her curls. "Where's your son?" she asks.

Mariana points him out, and the two women stand side by side as the dancers move past them, shimmying, jingling bells and clackers. The dust rises around them on the notes of harp and violin, flute and drum, and the emotions that have swirled inside Mariana over the past week lift with it. She turns around, hoping to see Trick's gaze returned to them, his heart stilled, too, but he is looking over the tops of everyone's heads at Mount Lemon looming at the eastern horizon.

Mariana sighs, leans down, and calls to a child standing nearby. She speaks into his ear, tilts her head to indicate Trick, then when the boy scoots off she turns to Star: "Are you staying here in Tucson tonight?"

Star nods. "I have to meet with the lawyer tomorrow." She is smiling at the antics of one of the *Chapeykas* who has stopped a short distance away; he has taken a cigarette out of the hands of one of the men and is pantomiming his smoking. Now he's stomping and jiggling, making the insects in his waist and ankle rattles sing and dance.

"Have you started back at the university, Trick?" Mariana asks over her shoulder.

"I smell fry bread," Trick rumbles behind them in response. "Do either of you want anything?"

Star shakes her head, no, and lifts her hand to her throat; Mariana also declines then watches the young man stick his thumbs through his belt loops and slowly make his way through the throngs to the food stands that line the perimeter of the plaza.

"I don't know if he *is* going back," Star says to Mariana in a low voice. "All this . . . ." She shakes her head and sighs. ". . . has got him worrying about his grandfather up on the Yavapai Rez. He says he wants to go take care of him, like I took care of *my* dad." Star looks down at her sandaled feet. "How can I argue with that?"

Shouts ring out, reclaiming their attention: some of the children have grown brave enough to chase the *Chapeykas*, their arms raised, ready to launch their confetti-filled eggs. When Mariana looks down to remark on this to Star, she sees the tears in her eyes and says instead: "Where are you holding the services? Do you want me to ask the priest here if he . . . ."

But she stalls out at Star's frown. "He wasn't Catholic," she says curtly. After a pause she adds: "We're just going to do a cremation, no real service. I need to . . . ." Her voice is so soft that Mariana can't hear the rest.

The drummers increase their tempo; more children are racing around the square. Soon there is an eruption of color and noise and *Jesucristo's* adversaries are chased with the holy palms from the plaza.

"What's taking Trick so long?" Star asks, looking around. Then she puts a hand on Mariana's arm. "Guess who's taking care of Sally?" She gives Mariana that sad smile again. "I told Jasmine I'd pay her to babysit—and she said 'yes.' Can you believe it?"

Mariana laughs. "Well there's one good thing that's come of all this. I admit I didn't have much hope for her, but she's really changed."

"It's like she and Trick have traded personalities," Star concurs. "He's still so obsessed with what happened. I told him I don't think we're ever going to really understand it all . . . ."

"Some things are understood only through faith," Mariana observes.

There is a pause in the music. When the drum starts in again the crowd quiets, knowing the procession is about to begin. Once again there is a commotion at the opposite side of the plaza, and at the dreamy swirl of the flute, Deer Dancer appears, eliciting a collective gasp from the People that rises with the music into the air. He wears clanking hooves at his waist; jingling cocoons wrap his ankles. He is skirted, bare-chested, and carries a gourd rattle in each hand. His white head wrappings nearly cover his own eyes, and his height is exaggerated by the young buck's severed head perched atop his own. Deer vaults into the center of the plaza, graceful and proud. He leaps and twirls, then dips his head to graze, every movement choreographing the movements of an antlered, regal wild creature in his prime. He raises his head when he senses the hunter's approach.

Star leans close to Mariana and asks again: "Where has Trick gotten off to?"

Mariana smiles and points with her chin. The child she'd spoken to earlier is at the edge of the plaza; he has taken Trick's hand, just as she had instructed him, and is moving him toward a group of three other men, selected for their height and strength, who will carry the Christ statue seated on his throne. It is a great honor to be asked to bear that burden. Many of the Yaquis will weep at the sight of Him, knowing the torment their Savior was to endure during the coming week, beginning with the *Tenebrae*, the whipping, on Holy Wednesday. Mariana bends down to Star and says, "There he is."

"Oh, my God," she breathes. "Is that Trick? What's going on?" She brings her hand up to shade her eyes then lowers it to rest protectively over her belly.

Mariana has already guessed it, but at that reflexive gesture, she knows. She puts her arm around Star's shoulder, and together they watch the men mill around the wooden platform they will raise to their shoulders. Trick is shaking his head, no, with his hands up, but he's smiling—an uncharacteristic look for him, lately—and eventually he removes his hat and hands it to the boy beside him. Then he looks at Star and Mariana standing across the plaza, and when Mariana waves, the boy takes off running toward them. She finds a candy in her pocket and hands it to him when he comes panting up, then she plants Trick's hat on Star's bare head. The drumming rises to a crescendo, and she turns just in time to see the Deer Dancer lay down his life to feed the People. At that moment, Trick and the three other men bend and hoist a pole to their shoulder and enter the plaza at a stately walk.

The music swells again and the crowd roars its approval.

The four men are very tall, and the platform seems to float above them all. They parade to one end of the square, turn, and then proceed up the center toward the church. Bringing up the end of the procession is the priest and a group of the faithful holding baskets of blessed palm leaves.

"This is such a great privilege," Mariana tells Star. "A Yaqui father would be so proud." When Star looks up at her, Mariana sees the tears again, but this time she believes them to be tears of joy.

As the bearers approach, Mariana watches Trick turn and bend his head and search the crowd for them. When their eyes lock she feels a jolt of wonder. He isn't smiling anymore, but he does not scowl. He looks bewildered, focused, definitely out of his element but also, somehow, at home.

Star must see it, too. "What a week we've had," she says.

"Yes," Mariana responds. Then looking around at the somber Yaquis, heads bowed, filing behind the priest into the church for mass: "And what a week there is to come."

CHAPTER TWENTY-FIVE

HOLY THURSDAY

Guy is a little kid again, sitting in a church pew. He knows he's very young but not *how* young, and he knows it isn't his uncle beside him—the man who raised him, if you could call it that—because that son-of-a-bitch had never been in a church in his life and bragged of the fact fairly often.

Guy hasn't been to church more than a handful of times himself, for a wedding or a funeral. And when he was *this* young, it was a very long way down a series of very rough ranch roads to get to *any* church, so this must be a special occasion, Christmas, maybe, when their Mexican cook—who actually *did* raise him—would take off to attend mass. Or maybe it was Easter.

And suddenly Guy knows it *is* Easter—that's why he's smelling incense, frankincense and myrrh, the burial aromatics.)

. . .

JASMINE HADN'T LIKED what she'd seen under that mesquite at a distance, and when she came up, she reached around Sally and put her fingertips to the artery in Guy's neck. She felt nothing, and she hadn't expected to; he had turned the grey color of death and his mouth had gone slack. "Move," she told Sally, then when the little girl just scowled up at her, Jasmine pulled her from Guy's weighted embrace, put a hand on his chest, and leaned down to put her ear by his mouth.

"What are you doing?" Sally asked. "Leave him alone. He's sleeping." Then when Jasmine sat back, she tilted her head and asked: "Are you crying?"

Jasmine rubbed her face, surprised at her display of emotion. "No. I'm fine," she sniffed.

Oh God, oh God, oh God. Oh no. Shit. Oh my God. What the hell should I do? What the hell am I going to do? She was surprised when a voice in her head answered—it was Guy's:

(Get help—what else? And for Christ's sake, get Sally out of here.)

Jasmine swallowed the wail that threatened to rise, not from her lungs, but from a deep place in her belly, but she didn't want to freak the little girl out. So she took a breath, another, composing herself, and when she finally said, "Let's let him sleep, then. Come on," her voice sounded almost normal.

I've got to get help. I've got to get Sally out of here.

"No," Sally objected.

Jasmine reached out a hand to the girl. "Come on," she repeated.

Sally screwed up her face into a scowl and said: "You can't make me."

"The hell I can't," Jasmine retorted, but there was no heat

in it; somehow she couldn't seem to muster the anger that had habitually taken over at moments like this. Instead she looked at the little girl and felt a profound sympathy for her; Sally was much younger than Jasmine had been when she'd lost her dad. She changed tactics: "Come on. Let's get you home. We'll let your daddy sleep for a while." Jasmine's brain wouldn't stop —*This is crazy. This is horrible. This can't be happening*—and she felt sick, but she swallowed hard, stood up, and held out a hand again, and this time Sally took it.

"I don't like horses," she told Jasmine in a whisper. "Don't tell Daddy, though. He likes them."

"Well, you rode out here on one and dragged two others along with you." Jasmine couldn't believe she was having an almost normal conversation with the kid; her brain was whirling, her stomach churning. She pulled the girl up, then leaned down again to grab the two sets of hobbles from the pile of stuff they'd emptied from the backpack; there was a ragged T-shirt in the pile which she pulled on over her head. Then she glanced at Sally, took a breath, and leaned over the body to pick up Guy's hat. "How'd you even do that?" she asked the girl as she returned to deposit the hat on her head.

"Hey," Sally giggled. She tilted it off her eyes and looked up at Jasmine. "Mommy said to tell him something, so I had to come find him."

"Yeah, but *how*?"

(NOW GUY IS BACK at the bedside of the old O'odham woman in her stifling *ki*, watching the flies enter and leave her gaping mouth. He doesn't want to be there, but she did something to him; she hocked up some kind of egg into the palm of her hand

and then rubbed it onto the hairs of his chest. The searing heat of it had made him sit back with a gasp. Now he can't leave her, as he had been planning to do. He has to sit there, slaughtering flies, and wait to do what she's asked of him. He smells sage, and something else—maybe cedar.)

DICE TURNED and huffed and shook his head at Jasmine and Sally as they came up, and the little girl shied away, hiding behind Jasmine's legs. "You like Pedro better?" she asked, and when Sally nodded, Jasmine dropped the hobbles and set about unsaddling Dice so she could put his tack on the other horse. "Who put Pedro's bridle on?" she asked the girl to distract her and to still the *What the hell do I do? What the hell do I do?* that wouldn't seem to stop rattling through her own head.

"Me." Sally followed her over to the old Pinto. "I can reach the bridles, if I move the bench over, and I can reach Pedro's head, if I climb his stall door. I let him chew a carrot, then put the stuff on him."

"Stuff," Jasmine repeated. She worked as quickly as she could; her breath was coming in pants, for some reason, and her hand shook as she tightened the cinch.

"Then I slid along on the rail between the stalls, and I kind of balanced on it." Sally held both arms out to her sides to demonstrate. "Then I hopped on and grabbed his mane."

Jasmine patted Pedro's side, then despite a nearly overwhelming sense of urgency she paused to listen to Guy's voice in her head and realized she needed to remove Amigo's saddle, too. "Shit," she sighed under her breath. Then louder: "How'd you get the stall door open?"

"No, I did that *before. Before* I jumped," Sally insisted.

"Okay, kid. Okay." Jasmine carried Amigo's saddle and blanket over to the base of the tree and set it leather-side down. "Bring me one of those hobbles." She bent down and tried to grab Dice's hock, but he must have sensed her near panic; he kept stepping away, stamping and nodding. "Stop it!" she yelled, and the horse stilled. "So how did you know where to look for us?" Jasmine asked the girl as she worked.

Sally had moved a way off—to avoid the horse, Jasmine presumed. "The little bird." Jasmine looked over her shoulder at that. Sally was making a fluttering motion with her hands, eerily similar to a hummingbird's wing movements. "She knew."

"Right," Jasmine said as she moved over to Amigo. "Whatever you say, kid." Once she had hobbled both horses and removed their reins, she reached a hand out to the girl again. "Okay. Finally ready. Let's go."

But Sally looked dubious. "So they can walk around now—by themselves?" she asked.

"Yeah, Sally. So they can eat while we're gone. Now, come on!" Sally still hesitated so Jasmine added: "Don't worry, kid, they can't go far. They'll still be here when I get back."

"Do horses ever eat people?" Sally asked next.

"No," Jasmine scoffed. "Shit, kid—have you ever seen a horse eat meat?" But the voice in her head reminded her: (Coyotes do), and she realized what she had to do next.

(GUY PULLS Sweet Pea up and dismounts carefully; he is just outside the Stanton School horse barn and still woozy from bad water and almost a week of hard travel across the Mogollon Plateau to get there. Sweet Pea has missed him during his recuperation, and as he tries to pass her she pushes her muzzle into his chest and insists he pet her, which he does willingly—she has carried him through canyons and forests and piñon-dotted rock, and he will not slight her—but when he looks up he sees movement at the far end of the barn. Silhouetted against the sun-filled doorway is 'Lizbeth—the young woman whose family has nursed him back to health—and a stocky, shaggy-headed, eleven-year-old boy.

His son.

Guy smells the fresh hay, the manure, and his heart burns.)

JASMINE EXPECTED rigor mortis to be setting in, but when she lifted Guy's arm and placed it over his chest it still felt pliable. For some reason that made her feel guiltier about rolling him up in the tarp and weighting the edges with boulders, but better this small desecration than the larger one of letting him get chewed on by some wild creature. Jasmine knew she had to get Sally home, she had to get help; let Trick take over from this voice in her head and decide what had to be done. There were still several small bottles of water, but she only took one. She was pretty sure even old Pedro could make it back to the Far View Ranch in a reasonable amount of time.

Jasmine had a terrible sense of foreboding as she jogged the short distance back to the horses which she tried to reason away: the worst possible thing had already happened, so what else could go wrong? Really—why even hurry? Amigo and Dice had wandered only a few yards in their search for forage, and Pedro was still securely attached to the juniper branch. Jasmine jerked to a stop: there was Amigo, Dice, and Pedro—but no little girl. "Shit," she breathed. "No, no, no—not this."

She dropped the water bottle and turned in circles. "Sally?" she called. *Shit, shit, shit.* She cupped her hands around her mouth: "Sally! Come on! Let's go!" For a moment she was sure she was going to burst into tears.

(GUY NEARLY MOWS down an elderly couple exiting through the Yavapai Regional Hospital's main entrance, but he doesn't stop to apologize. The damn cell phone Star made him buy has finally proved its usefulness but in a terrible way: her voice was panicked, the message urgent. It was early, too early. It wasn't happening like it was supposed to. Star had prepared for a mid-wife assisted home birth, not an emergency C-section in a hospital.

It was the last day of April, and Guy was over on one of the more remote sections of the Half-Circle N Bar checking the fence line before they started moving cattle into the area, so he was well out of range. The phone tickled his thigh with its buzzer only once he got close to the ranch, but it was such a pain to wiggle the device out of his front pocket while he was in the saddle that he waited until he dismounted. He sprinted for his truck as soon as the message started, abandoning his mount with a shout at Paul—who was nowhere to be seen—to tell him that he had to go; it was an emergency.

He raced to the hospital and now barrels across the lobby, demands Star's whereabouts, punches elevator buttons repeatedly, and runs down the hallway, but at the door to the delivery room he stops cold. He sucks in a shivering breath. He's afraid of losing Star. He's afraid of losing the baby; they know it's going to be a girl, and Star wants to name her "Sally," after

Trick's mom. He's more afraid than he's ever been in his entire life; he's nauseous and shaking with fear.

Then he hears her: a bleating that rises in volume into a full-throated cry. When he steps through the doorway he can see her being held aloft by a nurse, red-faced and squalling, smeared with white, flattened, dark swirls of hair on her head. There is a crowd of people dressed in scrubs around Star in the bed, and Guy is stabbed with fear again, but when the nurse notices him, she gives him a big smile and presents him with his daughter.

Guy cradles her against his chest and inhales the powdery smell of freshly-birthed baby and the metallic tang of blood.)

"SALLY! GOD-DAMN IT, SALLY. SALLY!"

Now what do I do? Now what do I do? Then Guy's voice was in Jasmine's head again:

(When I get like this, Star says one word to me: "Breathe.")

Jasmine abruptly stopped her twirling, closed her eyes, and filled her lungs. When she opened them she noticed something moving, and when she leaned a few inches to the right, she saw a tiny hand emerging from the rock. That sent the air sighing out of her in relief. But she squinted and approached cautiously: Sally's hand was all she could see, and it seemed to be jutting right out of the rock.

But as she got closer, Jasmine saw Sally's brown curls, so she was not *in* a cliff face but behind a boulder wedged against it or inside a seam in the rock. And there was Guy's hat on the ground. Jasmine bent to pick it up and saw a blue pill on the dirt beside it. She picked it up, and knew enough to recognize it: some kind of opioid, maybe fentanyl; she almost popped it in her mouth but stopped herself at the voice in her head.

(What the hell are you doing? You have to go get help. You have to get Sally home.)

Jasmine tucked the pill in her front pocket and called out again: "Sally, get out of there. You scared me to death."

The little girl's whole head popped out. "I found a cave," she said excitedly. "Look."

"Sally," Jasmine protested. "Come out of there."

"It's pretty dark." Sally's voice seemed to reverberate through the rock. "Better get me a flashlight."

"Aw jeez, Sally," Jasmine sighed. "No more messing around. I have to get you home, kid. Please—let's just go!"

"Look!" Sally demanded, squeezing through a crevasse Jasmine, standing right in front of it, could only now see. Sally held up a plastic baggie full of more of the pills.

"Shit," Jasmine sighed. She took off her hat and ran a hand through her short, black hair. It was dawning on her that the search she'd been considering so disastrous had also been somewhat successful, thanks to a curious little kid: this must be JC's stash—or maybe his abductors'—and it certainly raised the stakes in the game. If it *was* fentanyl, the bag Sally was handing her was worth hundreds, maybe thousands of dollars. "But this doesn't change anything," she said, mostly to herself. And despite Guy's voice in her head (Don't you even think about it. Don't you dare.), Jasmine was sorely tempted to take advantage of this new development.

Because she knew she wasn't just holding a small fortune in her hand, and it was a lot more than pain relief, too; she was holding euphoria, and Jasmine knew as well as anybody how valuable that feeling was. She had the connections, back in Tucson, at least, to change her life, to be wild and free again.

Or the opposite of free: addicted, caught and locked up again. Maybe even dead of an OD.

(No. No. You have to get Sally home.)

She took Sally's hand. "I have to get you home," Jasmine told her. "I have to get help."

"Help?" Sally asked, pulling back.

"No, I mean, I . . . ." Jasmine stuttered. "Home. Let's get you home. Come on."

"Are we going to wake Daddy then?"

"He needs to sleep more, honey." Jasmine pulled hard and Sally stumbled behind her back to where Pedro stood, swishing away flies. "You will stay right here, do you understand me?" Jasmine told her, pointing a finger in Sally's face. She'd decided to leave the drugs by the body; on her person, the temptation was just too great.

Jasmine squared her shoulders and started back toward the rolled-up tarp. She'd only taken a few steps when she heard Sally complaining about being hot and whirled around. "Go sit under the tree on the saddle then," she shouted at her. "Jeez," she muttered under her breath.

Jasmine moved one of the boulders and stuffed the baggie of drugs under the tarp by Guy's head. She straightened, paused, and then swiped off her hat. There was a flame in her heart as she looked down at him, and it occurred to her that maybe she should say a few words. "You were a good man, Guy." Her voice came out in a whisper and she cleared her throat. "You did right by me, took me in when no one else would. I just want to . . . want to thank you." She took a deep breath. "You don't . . . I mean, didn't talk much, but you sure did show by example the right thing to do. I'm glad I got to share a last meal with you."

Jasmine realized she was crying again. She replanted her hat and wiped her cheeks on the walk back to Sally. The voice in her head was repeating: *Find Trick. Find Trick. Find Trick.* But first she had to get Sally home.

CHAPTER TWENTY-SIX

GOOD FRIDAY

Unfortunately I had to get a little rough with the kid to get her to stay in the saddle; Sally really didn't want to leave Guy, and frankly, neither did I. It didn't seem right, but it *was* right—I knew it with a certainty that was totally new to me. So I wrangled her up there and kept a tight hand on her so she wouldn't squirm off the other side. Pedro kept turning his head to get a look at all the commotion going on on his back, Sally squirming and hollering about how she'd changed her mind; she didn't want to go anywhere; she wanted to stay with her dad. It made me burn inside. I wasn't used to that feeling and found it really weird.

I'd forgotten the water bottle somewhere, so when Sally stopped whimpering over being forced to leave Guy and started whining about being thirsty, I just gave Pedro a good nudge in the ribs and he picked up his plodding pace a bit. The sun was going down and Sally—who half an hour ago had been complaining about being hot—now started in about being *so* cold. Oh, my God, what a drama queen. But I didn't get mad; I kept waiting for the fury to rise in me, for the ugly words to come out of my mouth and the reflexive violence that had gotten me into so much trouble over my lifetime to seize my body and do its devilish will. But it didn't happen. I actually tried to soothe the little girl. I told her we'd be back to the ranch soon, that maybe her momma would be there, even though she wasn't due back until the following morning, because I had a hunch that the phone call Sally had intercepted had been intended for Guy and something was wrong on Star's end—maybe her old man had finally kicked.

Then the closer to home we got, the more I worried about the possibility that Star *would* be there—was I really going to be the one to tell her? I mean, the woman's a nosey bitch, but I like her, and she's been nothing but kind to me—well, in a pushy sort of way.

So I wasn't happy to see her standing on the porch as we rode up, silhouetted by the lights pouring out of the living room windows into the near-dark yard; the blond curls made a halo around her head. It wasn't just my own voice saying, *Me? Really?* inside my head:

(Don't you fucking dare, kid—don't you say nothing to Star.)

I was right back to feeling like puking again. And now I had some kind of heartburn on top of that.

Sally was leaning half out of the saddle by the time Star got down the porch steps, and Guy's hat fell off her head, crown first, onto the yard as I was handing her over, but she didn't rat me out for the rough treatment, just monkey-clung to her mom. And from the look on Star's face, I wondered if I was going to have to tell her anything—I mean, she *is* a psychic and all. Her eyes were all puffy and red; she'd obviously been crying. But maybe she'd just been worried about where her daughter had gotten off to because the first thing she said was: "Oh my God, child—I got home and you weren't here, and Trick didn't know." Then Star was sobbing, Sally's head cradled against her neck. "We were so worried about you."

I think Sally gave her a "Sorry, Mommy," but I really wasn't listening as my brain was whirling. After a moment Star reached out a hand and placed it on my leg.

"Trick's out searching for you guys," she said softly. I turned to look at the horse barn, and she added: "No. In the truck. I guess Guy told him he wasn't to take the horses out there anymore."

"He's gone back to the Imperial Ranch?" I had a hard time understanding why Trick was so fascinated with that place.

"Yeah," she sighed. "I guess he didn't find you then." Star looked past me down the lane. "So where's Guy?"

I froze; I couldn't even open my mouth, let alone say words.

"Daddy's coming," Sally lifted her head to tell Star. "He was sleeping." She held her mom's cheeks between her hands like she does when she wants her complete attention. "I'm hungry."

Star escaped the grip, then brushed her lips against Sally's hair, saying something, while I sat up there on Pedro, feeling the blush climb over my face. The way my chest burned, I started thinking I was having a heart attack. Then Star was talking to me again: "Come inside and get something to eat. I've got to feed this kid and get her to bed. Then we'll talk." She set Sally down with some sort of instructions, and the girl hopped up the porch steps.

Well, that sent a chill through me. "I . . . I can't," I told her. Part of me wanted to jump down and throw myself into her arms and sob out the whole sad story, but Guy's voice sure didn't want me to. "I . . . I'll be back," I mumbled, and I turned Pedro toward the horse barn with *Find Trick. Find Trick. Find Trick* rattling around in my head. "I've just got to get a new mount."

"What is it, Jasmine?" Star said to my back. "I know you're not telling me something." Then she called after me: "What does Sally mean: 'Guy's sleeping'? I had a really bad feeling this afternoon. That's why I called. That's, well, at least *part* of why I'm down here."

I "whoa-ed" Pedro, sighed, yanked off my hat, and turned around in the saddle to face her. But for the third time, I just couldn't tell her the horrible news; I got so pasty-dry my tongue stuck to the roof of my mouth. I swallowed hard and worked to sound normal: "You're right—I better go back and check on him," I told her. Cough. Swallow. "And I'll try and find Trick. Could you bag up a couple of sandwiches for me?" Cough. Choke. "And some water? I'll just get a fresh horse, and then I'm outa here."

"Wait, Jasmine!" Star shouted. "Is this something we should call the marshal about?"

Amazingly, I hadn't even considered that. I did then. But Guy's voice dismissed the idea.

(That marshal is an arrogant buffoon.)

"Guy doesn't like him," Star said, moving toward me with her arms clasped, hugging herself now that her daughter was no longer in her embrace. "But if there's something he should know—or something he could help us with . . . ."

I really didn't like law enforcement much, either—probably

for the same reasons Guy didn't. But I knew Star was right, and I should have let her call the marshal—*and* the Border Patrol.

"Is that what's going on?" she wanted to know. "Is Guy up to something? He's trying to find JC, isn't he?"

"No, Star—I don't know what you're imagining, but no. We don't have to call anybody." Suddenly I had *too* much saliva in my mouth, and I leaned over and spit, wiped my chin. Shit, I really needed to talk to Trick. Let *him* tell Star. And I'd much rather it be him explaining to the cops why he was in possession of a possible Schedule II narcotic than *me*, a theft and drug parolee; that would definitely screw me up. Plus I still really wanted to find JC—that kid was more lost than even I'd ever been.

By now Star was just a few feet away, and I had a feeling she might take the reins and try to send me into the house whether I liked it or not, so I pressed Pedro forward.

"Jasmine!" she called after us. "Guy—sometimes, when he gets upset . . . ."

"I know," I told her over my shoulder. "I should tell him to 'breathe.'"

So I didn't follow Star's advice; I didn't even wait for the sandwiches. I wish I had. Not only did it make for a howling-empty stomach that night, if I hadn't gone back out there, if I had waited and talked to the marshal, then I wouldn't have to live with the impossible events that followed, stuff science and logic just can't explain.

But they happened. They happened to me.

To us.

CHAPTER TWENTY-SEVEN

HOLY SATURDAY

The "La Gloria" ceremony starts at noon and does not end but evolves into an all-night vigil. Mariana is fasting and, exhausted by the long day, she often experiences vivid, waking dreams in the last hours of Holy Saturday; this year is no exception. She sits with her back against the whitewashed wall of the chapel, her rosary moving through her fingers, eyes unfocused, watching the visions and meditating on *Jesucristo's* Passion and Death, his Descent into Hell. She is not alone, but she might as well be.

I HAD a hard time picking a horse to get the hell out of there on, and I had to go fast or I was going run back to the house and tell Star about Guy, even though his voice in my head was clearly telling me not to. A big part of the problem with selecting a mount is that I knew Trick had subjected all or almost all of them to his 3 a.m. jaunts out to the Imperial Ranch and had brought them home totally freaked out. I'd seen what Dice and Amigo acted like out there, and how happy Pedro had been to turn back for home. And even though I'd found a heavy jacket and a pretty good flashlight amongst the tack, I didn't want to chance a skittish horse on a night ride. So it was a quandary.

But I had to go, I had to hurry, I had to find Trick and take him to his dad.

God, and we had to bring those two horses back.

Then there was that fortune in drugs we had to surrender to the authorities.

Probably.

I decided on the mule because Trick was too big and heavy for him, so I could be sure he'd never been out there. I was no lightweight myself, but Samson could handle me just fine. I'd taken him out before, just for fun, and he had some personality; I like that in an animal. I was a jittery mess, literally shaking in my boots, really ragging on myself about all that had happened, and I needed the company of something like a quirky mule.

And maybe, I thought, *I should go ahead and take that pill.*
But I didn't.

The moon was a little more than half-full as we set out, but the sky was clear and the stars were popping out, adding their white sparkle to the glow over the gravel roads and grass. Sam seemed excited by the novelty of a night-time outing and started out smartly, but I soon learned that my underparts could not handle that smacking gait and slowed him down to a spritely walk. He kept turning his head from left to right, really scoping things out.

Mules come in various sizes, and Samson was about average, I guess. He had the height and body size of his dam—a horse—and the big-eared, boxy head and dainty hooves of his donkey sire. Guy told me Sam had been one of the animals on the Far View when they'd bought the place, and nobody knew exactly how old he was. I asked the vet, and he said Sam was at least 25, but that mules live longer than horses, so he probably had quite a few good years left in him.

Of course, that was before I took him to the Imperial Ranch with me. I knew people's hair stood on end when they were really scared, but I'd never known an animal could have that reaction too.

MARIANA'S VISIONS as she dozes against the whitewashed wall of the church are of her Savior. In an ordered sequence she sees Him questioned, scourged, presented to the crowd in a purple robe and a crown of thorns. When she hears what the people shout, tears come to her eyes and she reaches for the handkerchief she keeps tucked into the waistband of her skirt. Mariana cringes at the images of crucifixion, but she does not turn away: she sees her Savior stripped, thrust to the ground on a back raw from scourging; positioned, arms outstretched, on the gibbet. She hears the noisy assault of a sign being hammered over His head into the wood, then the more horrific one of nails tapped into and through flesh to the board.

She feels the dragging downward pull and agony of being jostled as He's hoisted up.

She listens as He speaks to those gathered below.

She knows His thirst.

SAMSON DIDN'T SEEM to need me to show him the way with the flashlight, so I shut it off to save the battery. He was pretty steady on the short length of Highway 83 we had to travel, despite some traffic, and never stumbled once on the rough edge of the asphalt. We made the turnoff to Imperial Ranch and kept going at a good pace down the road to the ranch.

I was hungry. I was heart-sunk sad. I was as tired as I've ever been in my life, so maybe I was dozing a bit in the saddle. When some bird broke from the cover on the side of the road and swooped over my head, Samson stopped short and I nearly fell over the top of him, but I regained my seat. "Sam, buddy—you gotta stop that," I told him, and it was the sound of my own voice, like an echo, that made me look around, and that weird shit I'd overheard Trick talk about to Star seemed like maybe it was happening because there was the fog he'd described, obscuring the landscape all around us, and that incense was in the air; it was the same smell that had been on Trick that first night when I'd helped him to the couch.

I turned on the flashlight to try to see where we were, but that only made things worse: swirls of what I hoped was moisture rose from the ground all around us. When Sam shook and stomped, I heard the splash of wet earth.

I dropped down to investigate. I pulled my phone out, swiped on the camera and flash, and started taking a video, but I could see only the white swirls of vapor on the screen. Until I turned, and there was a silly old mule, giving me a big, toothy smile as if he knew I was holding a camera.

"Samson, you are a ham," I told him, and he nodded, right on cue.

MARIANA HAS WATCHED Death approach before. For her husband, wasted by disease, it was relatively quick; a day of torpor that did not let go. But Mariana's sister had been younger, stronger, and had fought the family members away as they'd tried to soothe her as if *they* were the ones stealing her life from her. She'd struggled to stand, to walk, to run away from the organs failing inside of her. There'd been three days of thrashing; there had to be at least two caregivers, one on each side, to help her to her feet, steady her wavering steps, and steer her back into bed again.

Jesucristo is even younger than Mariana's sister. He is healthy when He dies, in his prime, like Deer. He is not a middle-aged man with diabetes or a woman afflicted with cancer—*He* is *our* victim.

Used by our Father to feed us.

To save us.

So His death is not only slow; it is deliberate. His body is pulled down by gravity, distending His arms and His chest, His lungs. The men on either side of Him suffer, as well; to breathe while hanging requires a nearly impossible lifting of the entire torso.

Slowly, so slowly, in excruciating pain, from exhaustion, then asphyxiation: "It is finished."

I LED Samson around a while and soon figured out why the ground was so wet and what probably accounted for the fog: we had wandered off the ranch road toward Cienega Creek.

There were marshy patches all around us, and when I splashed into the central stream, Sam put his head down and took a long drink. I thought about it, then put my phone in my back pocket, dropped to my belly on the bank upstream of him, and joined him in slurping; I hadn't waited for Star to pack me any water bottles, either.

When I thought about her, I got really sad and sat back to wipe at my face and my eyes again. But I knew sitting on my butt feeling bad wasn't going to find Trick, so as soon as Samson had had his fill, I remounted and we set out again in the direction I hoped was back toward the Imperial Ranch. But we hadn't gone ten feet through that fog before the next weird thing happened: first there was that strong, herby smell again, then there was a thunderous boom and a wind rushed out at us through the grasses and the trees along the creek, but when I looked up, the sky was still full of stars; there were no clouds overhead. Then the ground started shaking, and Samson danced all around, totally freaked—as was I. Between the dancing and the wind and the tilting my head skyward, my hat fell off, and when I told Sam to "whoa" he did his best, but he was still rocking and rolling when I got off to grab my hat. I had just smacked it back on when the creatures started popping out of the whiteness at us: rabbits, a raccoon, a whole pack of javelina, several squirrels, a fox, a stream of little mice, a couple of skunks, and other beasts that passed us so fast they were just blurs.

When I finally remembered to fumble my phone out to record this madness it was over. I turned to Sam and his ears were sticking straight up from his head and his eyes looked like they might pop right out. His lip was pulled back in a funny way, and I guessed that was what incredulity looked like on a mule; I felt the same way.

Had I taken that pill after all? I dug a finger around in my front pocket—no, there it was.

Part of me was all for giving up and getting the hell out of that crazy place—a *large* part. But the other part was completely unfazed. That's the part of me that jumps into swimming holes from cliffs without scouting out the depth, the part that pushes other people from those cliffs when they linger and fret too long and piss me off. The part of me that runs from the cops like you can ever really get away. *That* part of me was: *Hell no. That didn't just happen*—even though it most certainly *had.* That part was climbing back on Samson and telling him: "They can't scare us off with this crazy shit, Sam. We have to find Trick."

Samson's response was big head-shake that certainly meant, "No." But that hair-rising thing when his coat stood up all over like an electrical charge was running right through him—through him and into *me*—that didn't happen until later.

MARIANA BREATHES DEEPLY and opens her eyes to the flickering dance of the many candles, the drifting swirls of two old world incenses mixing in a holy cloud. She stretches and rubs her neck, sore from letting her head droop. One of the sisters is chanting yet another decade of the rosary; two others are lighting fresh candles at opposite ends of the chapel. Mariana's neighbor is snoring softly, grandchildren pillowed on her lap. There was no mass today, and the altar before her is bare stone: there are no linens, no chalice or paten; they've placed their candles on the sanctuary floor.

Mariana nods off again, dreaming she is naked, also, in this altar's presence, her faith lying similarly exposed. It is impossible for her not to feel the lance pierce her side, to spill out her own blood and water. It is her body lowered from the cross, carried, bound with cloth and spice; her head is wrapped last and darkness descends. She hears the scrape of stone on stone and then nothing. The Lord's tomb closes in around her, and she can't see, and she can't hear, and she can't breathe.

MULES CAN BE STUBBORN, and Samson did his best to turn us toward home, but Guy had taught me a few tricks by then, and the gentle persistence and sweet-talking eventually worked. The fog seemed to be lifting, but we still hadn't found the ranch road when I saw something coming right at us, bounding erratically over the rough terrain:

One white light.

I didn't have to rein Samson up; he practically skidded to a stop when he saw it. This time I stood in the stirrups to wiggle my phone out of my pocket right away; I had this hunch that technology could make all the weird shit just go away. But that didn't seem to be happening this time: the light tipped skyward into the white air, dipped and illuminated the grasslands and brush, then shot upward again, and it kept coming, pretty fast.

Then we heard it—Samson pointed his long ears forward but took two steps back before I told him, "Steady" and made him hold still. It was a guttural roar but choppy, and then I knew: an engine, but not just any old engine. It was the engine in Guy's beater of a truck with its busted headlight and perpetual pinging, ticking and rattling headed toward us.

We had found Trick, or more accurately, he was about to find us; I just hoped he wouldn't accidentally run us down. But Samson hadn't figured that out yet; this is when all the hairs on the shaggy beast stood on end with fright.

I leaned close to one of his sticking-straight-up-out-of-his-head-ears and told him, "Sam, Sam—just *breathe*!"

THE LAST HOURS of Holy Saturday are always the worst: Mariana's eyes are too heavy and just won't stay open; her whole body aches from sitting, cross-legged, on the floor for so long; and in her visions she has descended into Hell with her Savior.

Strange beasts emerge from the blackness; they lunge and retreat, snarling, teeth-bared like rabid dogs but of ghastly decaying, half-human shapes. Mariana can't help it—she turns away. They are the sinners wasting away in Purgatory, those *Jesucristo* has come to save. Among them are those to whom God is unknown, but also those who know and despise, those who have betrayed Him, ridiculed Him, disparaged Him, even those who have tortured and slayed Him. But His Father has charged *Jesucristo* to love all of them, so He does. Despite their actions, despite their ugliness, He loves them all.

When Mariana forces herself to look again, this time through His eyes, she sees they are not monsters but people, just like her, worthy of her love, as well. It is this love—His love magnified in so many breasts—that opens the gates of Heaven.

From somewhere nearby a rooster crows and Mariana opens her eyes. Several members of the congregation exchange knowing looks in the flickering candlelight, but there are still many hours yet before dawn. Her fingers find their places on the beads of her rosary and she begins reciting her prayers again. She first holds Star's father, who has recently passed, in her mind. Then Mariana thinks about Guy. She tells him wordlessly, insistently, to *breathe*.

CHAPTER TWENTY-EIGHT

EASTER

Guy heard the word Star would say to him when she grew exasperated at his fuming over some trivial matter. Usually he'd look at her with a scowl and just stifle the rant, but this time he actually tried to obey her command to breathe. Unfortunately, there was a weight on his chest. He tried again, and a searing pain shot from his ribs to his left shoulder and made his inhale a shuddering gasp.

So breathing was not much fun, but he kept doing it anyway.

A while later Guy woke to the sound of a baby's wail. It was Sally; he was sure of it. But when he tried to roll out of bed and respond to it, he found he couldn't move. Maybe his eyes were open, maybe they weren't—it was pitch black, so he couldn't tell; he was enshrouded in something, his arms pinned at his sides.

He heard voices then, fairly close:

"No, you go—I wanna stay with Daddy."

"Sally, I'm not messing with you. Come here."

"No. I don't like horses. I'm gonna stay."

Guy tried again to move, to call out, but he couldn't. It was dark and stuffy and close; he smelled alcohol. Maybe he shouldn't have drunk all that whiskey—oh, yeah, and that box of wine—because he most certainly was drunk. He hoped he wasn't going to be sick because he couldn't even turn his head, let alone roll onto a side.

"Breathe" was just about all he could do.

When he woke again it was quiet except for the muffled sound of crickets. His entire back was on fire but it was the pain in his ribs and shoulder that made it so hard to take anything but the shallowest of breaths. At least the blackness surrounding him wasn't twirling in circles anymore, and he found he could move his right arm a bit and his head, although it hurt like hell when he did so. He tried to call Jasmine and a croak, barely audible to his own ears, came out. He attempted to swallow—no, too dry—cleared his throat, and tried again: "Hey," was pretty feeble, "Hey, Jaz?" a little better, and "Sally!" came out rather loud in the confines of his cocoon. Why the hell was he wrapped up like this?

Regardless, Guy was thirsty—and had to pee badly—so he focused on getting out of what seemed to be the tarp; apparently someone—he paused to think: Well, Jasmine. Who else? —for some reason had decided to roll him up like a cigarette.

But then he wiggled his head higher, sweating with effort and pain from rubbing his raw back against the canvas, and hit something hard with an "Ow!"; it was a rock. He wasn't able to get up on his shoulder to push it out of his way, so Guy took a painful gulp of air and twisted onto his belly. He had to rest a moment from the effort, but then he managed to move the boulder aside. Once he got the top flap open, he could sit up—with a yelp—grit his teeth, and yank the fabric from under the other rocks and branches Jasmine had tamped it down with. Was she hiding him from someone?

It was night but the moon was up, so there was still enough light to see the backpack and its contents strewn around him. He reached for one of the water bottles and drank it down. He frowned when he noticed the dusty boot cast strapped firmly around his ankle; he couldn't remember why he was wearing it, so he wrestled it off and tossed it aside. Then he took a deep breath and groaned his way to his feet. He managed only a few unsteady steps before struggling with the buttons on his jeans—his shoulder hurt so badly he could hardly move the entire arm, down to the fingers—but he managed. Then while he was relieving himself he noticed the horses—both Dice and Amigo were hobbled not far off.

If it weren't for all his injuries, all the pain of them, the sight of his animals would have caused Guy to celebrate a good turn in his luck. But walking three feet and standing up for two minutes had just about worn him out, so he satisfied himself with getting back to the rumpled tarp and sitting with his back resting gingerly against the little oak, and gave up the notion of horse riding for the time being.

That's where Jasmine was off to, he decided. He remembered hearing her and Sally—although how Sally could possibly have been there was a total mystery to him. But that's the only thing that made sense: Jasmine had taken Sally home and gone for help.

Guy found a breakfast bar, and even though he was more nauseous than hungry, he made himself eat it, then he slowly started gathering the other items jumbled around him and putting them back into the pack. It made him gasp to reach for the baggie, then he was surprised to see it contained a large quantity of small blue pills. "Holy shit," Guy wheezed. He dropped the bag and wiped his hands first on his dirt-smeared jeans then, for good measure, on his tattered shirt. The cop show he'd watched the night before—they'd shown what fentanyl looked like. It came in different forms, but these distinctive blue tablets was one of them, made down in Mexico to look like other types of prescription opioids.

His first thought was that Jasmine was using again; there had been several entries in her parole file about drugs. But then he remembered his original supposition: maybe these pills were at the root of JC's disappearance. Guy knew they were worth a lot of money, and this kind of dangerous drug would explain the marshal's continued interest in the boy and the involvement of the Border Patrol. JC could have passed right by here as he left the overturned VW. But what was the baggie doing buried with him under the tarp?

His third thought was much more personal—these were pain pills, so what would happen if he took one? Maybe he could ride. Before Guy could give it much more thought, he was unzipping the bag and picking one of the tablets out. He almost popped it into his mouth but then hesitated; the problem with counterfeit pills, he understood, was their unknown potency. If the fentanyl was pure, a couple of grams could kill him.

Guy squinted at the little tablet, gave it a lick, then waited a few breaths before trying to lift his arm again. A howl of pain escaped him. So he swallowed the pill, using the next-to-last water bottle to wash it down.

If anyone had asked Guy if he had led a happy life up until

then, he would have said, yes. He didn't much like the aches and limitations that came along with getting older; in fact, he'd been feeling pretty used up and useless lately. But he loved the Sonoita area, having his family around him, spending time with Star. After another few minutes, however, Guy would have told you he'd never truly been happy in his life. Only now was his heart this joyous, this blissful—the closest he'd ever come before to this kind of happiness was in those few minutes of extreme drunkenness before he puked his guts out. But he wasn't nauseous anymore, and maybe he was still a little stiff, but he was not in any great pain, even when he stood and did all the motions it took to shake out and fold the tarp. Then he grabbed the re-filled backpack, looked about one last time—nope, no hat, for some reason—and started for the horses. He was thinking a moonlight ride sounded like a great idea right about then.

As Guy hefted the one remaining saddle onto Dice, secured it, and tied the backpack behind its cantle, he wondered if he shouldn't keep looking for JC instead of heading back to the Far View. That bag of pills was the first possible sign of the boy he'd come across, and if he followed the wash, maybe tonight was the night he'd find him.

Hell, Guy was feeling so good as he launched himself into the saddle, he'd even put it way beyond "maybe" and all the way up to "probably." By the time he got Dice started out, with Amigo trailing nicely behind—*Huh*, Guy mused, *I wonder when he learned to do that*—he knew it was a certainty that he'd find JC. No doubt about it. He just had to ignore the wet feeling of blood dripping down his back and get it done.

TRICK INSISTED on holding the flashlight while he walked, which was stupid because I was ahead of him on Samson—he'd been too afraid the mule would overrun him to lead Sam by the reins—and it was *my* flashlight. Well, the flashlight *I* had brought along. The one Trick had taken from the glove compartment of the truck—which would not open unless you pounded it with the side of your fist just right—had worked for about 10 seconds before blacking out. It was a dud—just like everything else in and around and associated with that truck.

I hadn't wanted to ride in it, and Samson balked at being tied to the rear bumper, so we left it on the side of the ranch road and made our way back to Guy through the wash, Samson and I showing what I hoped to be the way at a slow walk. Sam was still nervous and skittish, and I let his bad behavior be the excuse for focusing my attention on him instead of telling Trick the rest of the story about his dad. All I'd been able to get out—I had that dry mouth attack again—was that I had to take Trick to him, that there'd been an accident. I could only imagine what he was thinking as that grim look overtook his face—at least, I think it was a grim look; we were still in the cab of the truck and the dome light didn't work, either.

Trick had some water with him that he shared with me, so I wasn't suffering from thirst on the way back to Guy's body, just weighed down with guilt and a terrible foreboding—what would Trick do when he saw his dad? What would *we* do once we got there? I'm really good at getting myself into fixes and really terrible at getting myself out of them, so I was hoping Trick would manage things from here on out.

I was pretty sure we were getting close, so I stopped Samson and turned in the saddle to address Trick: "Bring the light up here and shine it around over by those trees." I thought

I would hear the horses greeting Sam as we came up, but all I heard was crickets, and when Trick came up and blasted the trees with light, I could see they weren't there. "But they were hobbled," I said. "Dice and Amigo both. And Amigo's saddle was under that tree."

I dismounted but kept a good hold of Samson's reins—obviously, weird shit happened to animals out here—and together, Trick and I scoured the area. We saw their tracks, lots of tracks, but no Dice or Amigo. After a while Trick went one way down the wash, and Sam and I went the other, calling their names. Walking back toward Trick's voice I felt the dread of what was going to happen next magnifying. Not only had I been unable to save Guy, I was also a double-stupid asshole who had lost two of the Far View's best horses.

Did I not put the hobbles on right?

I tied Samson carefully—I wasn't going to lose two horses *and* a mule. Trick was standing near the oak tree where I had left Guy's body when I rejoined him. "Don't worry about it," he told me. "They'll find their way home. So where's my dad?"

I took my hat off and held it before me in both hands. "Behind you," I said in a whisper.

Trick swung around with the flashlight, and I couldn't help it: I closed my eyes. "What do you mean?" he said. "Where?"

I opened my eyes.

No tarp.

"Give me the damn flashlight," I hollered at Trick as I put my hat back on.

"Jasmine," Trick said, "What's going on?"

No backpack. No clutter of supplies.

"Damn it," I reached over, wrenched the light out of his hands, and swung it over the ground. "This was the spot," I insisted and pointed with the light at the little patch of grass under the oak that had been flattened by the tarp. The only other evidence of Guy having been there—but a telling one—was the boot-cast, tossed to one side.

But shit, no baggie of pills.

And definitely no Guy.

Breathe, I told myself. *Just breathe.*

CHAPTER TWENTY-NINE

ASCENSION

I turned to look at Trick and accidentally blinded him with the flashlight, making him squint and hold up a hand in defense. "Jesus, Jasmine."

"Sorry. Sorry," I told him, but I didn't move the light, just stared at him, my breath coming in pants like I'd been running. "He's not dead!" came out of me in one of those breaths.

"Jasmine, God, here—give me that," and Trick grabbed the flashlight back. "Of course he's not dead—you never said he was dead." There was a panicked note in Trick's voice, but I was just bonkers with joy; there was a spot between my breasts that burned so hot it brought tears to my eyes, and I just couldn't help it, I launched myself at Trick and caught him up in a huge hug, and then I was crying hard.

Trick stumbled backwards, totally caught off guard, but when he heard my sobs he didn't push me away; he held me. And after a moment he started in on those calming phrases we'd both learned from his father: "It's okay. Hey, now, don't worry. It's okay. You'll be all right. I got you."

After a while he moved me back by the shoulders and looked at me intently. "What happened?" he asked me.

So I told him the whole story, right from when Guy and I had left the ranch. Instead of dry mouth I suddenly had a case of run-at-the-mouth, and I didn't pause for him to comment or ask any questions. I told him about the horses being so skittish and Guy getting dragged and hurt, then how Sally had found us somehow with the now lost horses, and on top of that, how she'd been messing around and found a baggie of some kind of drug, maybe fentanyl. That kind of surprised me; I hadn't been sure whether I'd share that information with Trick or not. I went right on about how I'd heard Guy's voice in my head telling me to get Sally home safe, which I had, but then how I couldn't tell Star and decided to come looking for Trick instead. I even told him about getting kind of lost around Cienega Creek and the booming and earth shaking and the animals shooting past Samson and me.

That's when he stopped me: "Wait—what? You saw that?"

"Um, yeah. What the fuck is it with the animals around this place?" I asked him. "I bet Mariana knows what's going on here—have you heard her talk about those little, like, invisible people that do shit to help you when you're lost?"

"No," Trick laughed. "No, I've just been thinking I'd gone bat-shit crazy for weeks." And he pulled me in for another hug.

I'm not into guys, but I have to admit that it felt good, in a family kind of way—which was also totally alien to me. Trick's as big as a bear, with a wide chest, broad shoulders, arms like blocks, so I was comfortably swaddled, and I probably let him hold me longer than was necessary, then stepped back, feeling embarrassed. We toed our boots in the dirt for a moment, then I asked him: "So what do we do now?"

Trick had his hands on his hips. "You said he was hurt pretty bad."

"Yeah," I assured him. "Real bad. He banged his head, tore his shoulder open. I mean, I stitched him up, but he'd lost so much blood."

Trick took his hat off and chewed at his lip. "Could somebody have found him?"

I told Trick about the burrito I'd made of his father then. "It was getting dark when we left," I explained. "I didn't want anything disturbing the . . . him. I don't see how anyone could have just stumbled across him."

Trick sighed and rubbed at his jaw, and he reminded me of Guy right then, always messing with that beard of his. "So Dad and you came out here looking for JC, right?" When he looked up I nodded. "Well, he's getting kind of stubborn in his old age. There's a chance he limped home and is enjoying a nice Cabernet with Star right now, but I'd bet money he's back on the hunt. He doesn't believe JC has just run off—he thinks he's in trouble. And those pills make me think so, too."

"Yeah. So what do we do now?" I repeated.

"Well," Trick resettled his hat. "We keep hunting, too, I guess."

Mariana prays: *Huya Ania, Wilderness World, open.*

AFTER A WHILE GUY started regretting he'd taken that pain pill; he was woozy and had to keep grabbing the saddle horn because his legs didn't seem able to grip right, and Dice probably wasn't skipping from side to side, but it felt like it.

That made the decision at the divide in the wash all the more difficult: if Guy kept the horses moving to the northeast, they'd find the Imperial Ranch Road and head into the conservation area and the wilderness beyond; if he turned them south, they'd be on the trail home.

To Star. He knew she was there; he felt her.

But it was Kate's image that came to mind unbidden. She'd entrusted her wayward son to him, and Guy had lost him all over again. She'd had no one else to turn to and still didn't; it was all on him.

Guy had a fight on his hands convincing Dice and Amigo that he was making the right decision. Both horses snorted and yanked back on the reins; first one then the other would try to turn around. Guy was hanging on the best he could and kept repeating his calming phrases in a slur to little effect, so he ended up using the bit and his heels more than he liked. This made for a rough ride through the wash and even more jerking and jostling to remind him of his injuries, but eventually they climbed to the road and headed up toward the ranch and the mountains behind.

There was a partial moon, a few clouds, and many, many stars. Hatless for a change, Guy took advantage of glancing up whenever his argument with the horses let up for a time. The sight of the Milky Way always made that spot in his chest burn, but tonight it was extra hot. Maybe it was the fentanyl—it was probably the fentanyl—but Guy felt strangely strong and capable; he was certain he could accomplish this mission.

He would save JC.

The sticky wetness running from his shoulder to the waist-band of his jeans should have informed Guy otherwise, but he was too busy rising to his own expectations and disregarded it.

"If you're going to hold the flashlight, you have to walk in front of us," I told Trick. I'd tried using the light on my cell phone, but Samson's head jerking—ears-up, turning right to left—made the shadows of the oaks and manzanita bob and bounce and irritated him even more, so I shut it off and just tried to concentrate on soothing Sam and following Trick. But then Trick stopped and leaned over. He put his fingers to the ground and then brought them to his nose, tasted them.

"Blood," was all he said.

Shit.

Trick started off again, and I watched his flashlight pick out one dark spot on the sand, then travel over the rocks and brush; a few yards farther along, he'd find another. At least we knew Guy's direction for sure, but the last thing I wanted to be following was his blood trail. I kept listening, but that voice in my head had shut off, so I tried using my own telepathy and asked him: "Why the hell are you doing this? Why didn't you just stay put?" No response, of course, and, anyway, I knew the answer:

He wanted to save JC, and despite the cost to himself, he had to try. That was just who Guy was.

So the situation was grim, and it got grimmer: Trick stopped again, turned and retraced his steps toward us. Samson backed up like he was thinking he would finally get his way and we'd start for home, but after Trick played the flashlight over the ground for a while, he pointed it up the north bank of the wash, and I could see their tracks; Guy definitely had both horses with him, and they'd torn up the earth pretty good climbing up the side.

"He's badly injured, bleeding, riding one horse and leading another—up an incline like this," Trick lamented. He lowered the light and was looking pretty dejected, his big shoulders slumped, as Sam and I came even with him.

I followed his eyes up the cut in the bank. "They're going toward the Imperial Ranch, aren't they?" I asked him, but he just sighed, dropped his head, and started trudging up the side of the wash. I waited until he'd topped the crest, then started trying to get Samson to charge up after him.

Let's just say that took a while.

———

MARIANA PRAYS: *Yo Ania, Enchanted World, unveil.*

———

GUY ABANDONED the road at some point and drove the horses higher, into the humps and ravines leading to the boulder-strewn crest of the Imperial Mountain just west of the Imperial Ranch itself. It was rough country, and he had to work even harder to manage Dice. The gelding was still surging then balking, high-stepping then dragging his feet and trying to turn. Thankfully, Amigo had given up and was generally following with his head down, but he had to lift it to avoid collision with Dice's haunch each time the other horse stalled out. Guy had never seen Dice behave this badly, and he understood why Jasmine had wanted Trick to stop taking the horses out here. In the dark, on rugged ground like this, he needed a steady mount, and Dice was acting like anything but.

And the terrain was only going to get worse.

Guy was heading up to the Imperial Ranch's abandoned silver mine tucked into a hollow under the ridgeline of the mountain. He'd never been there before, but he knew it had a couple of old, falling down mining shacks clustered around a rocky ledge with a rough road that dropped steeply in the direction of the ranch. *Why* he was urging the horses up there through the brush and boulders was another thing entirely. There wasn't any voice in his head and no little bird this time, but there was certainly an outside influence driving him up, up and over. And he let it. He didn't feel like he had a choice.

By this time the euphoria from the fentanyl had worn off and all the horse wrangling had started his head and shoulder throbbing again, so the next time Dice slowed to a stop, Guy twisted in the saddle with a gasp—damn, his ribs hurt, too—to open the backpack. He ignored the snap of one of his stitches popping, grabbed the nearly empty water bottle, and fingered another of the pills out of the baggie. It sure looked innocent enough, no bigger than an aspirin, but Guy hesitated. He told himself it wasn't very high-grade fentanyl; they had to dilute the stuff to make any money from it. Besides, he wasn't dead yet. Still he bit the little blue pill roughly in half and washed it down with a gulp of water; the other half he stuffed in the tiny pocket he'd never understood the use for in his jeans. Both horses were tired and snorting, and he briefly considered leaving them and going ahead on foot. But the hazy outline of a plan was forming in his decidedly muddled brain, and he needed horses for that.

He let them rest for a few minutes and concentrated on his own breathing—it seemed more difficult than usual—and fought against an urgent need to sleep. Then when the spike of dopamine hit, Guy drew in as big of a breath as he could, then spoke more than shouted a "Yee haw!" while he spurred an unwilling Dice up the next grade.

<hr>

BY THE TIME Samson and I were up the slope of the wash, Trick was nowhere to be seen. I had a moment of panic—*Jeez, don't leave me alone out here in crazy world!* Then I heard a very distant shout, and when I looked up, there was Trick's flashlight bobbing along the side of the mountain. Samson let out his mule-y squealing wheezes, and I was pretty sure I knew what he was saying: *Aw, hell no!* I felt exactly the same way, but I gave Sam a good kick in the ribs and we started after him.

I was exhausted, and I knew Guy must be in so much worse shape than I was; I just couldn't grasp how he could keep going across this kind of rough country and now up a friggin' mountain. When we'd started out that morning, he had seemed noncommittal about our search, like he'd almost given up and didn't really expect to find anything around the site of the wrecked VW; now he was breaking trail up a pretty darn steep hillside like a man on a mission. I hoped he knew what he was doing at such great risk to himself and the two horses—as well as to Trick and Sam and me—because I had a hunch Guy had discovered that baggie of hillbilly heroin pills I'd left beside him, and he might have mistaken them for something else and taken one—or more.

Samson had been doing pretty good making his way in the half-light of the moon until he decided to take a leap over a patch of boulders rather than go around them. He nearly unseated me at the lurch and then succeeded upon the jar of his landing; I ended up on my butt. "God damn it, Sam!" I yelled at him with the little wind that hadn't been knocked out of me. At least he had the decency to stand there and look at me all innocent-like instead of running off while I moaned on the ground. I rolled to my knees, grabbed a few breaths, then got my feet under me and stood up, wincing and sore, and brushed off my ass. "Do that again and you're dog food," I reprimanded him. "Do you understand me?"

Samson backed up on my limping approach, then planted his front feet and lifted his old, boxy head toward the sky with another round of incredibly loud hee-haws that seemed to go on and on. Then he stopped and nodded at me very emphatically.

"We can't quit," I told him. "Not until Guy does. We both owe him."

MARIANA PRAYS: *Tuka Ania, Night World, descend.*

GUY HEARD voices in the distance ahead. He pulled Dice up so abruptly that Amigo actually did run into his haunch this time.

It was Spanish, spoken too fast and too far off for Guy to understand, but definitely men's voices—several men's voices. Several men's loud, angry voices.

Guy realized it would be smart to have a much clearer plan before he charged out of the dark and into their company; too bad he hadn't thought of a very good one. When he swung a leg over the saddle, Guy felt another stitch tear loose, and he noticed his tattered sleeve was dark with blood, the saddle smeared with it. It still didn't concern him for some reason, but when he tried to lead the horses over to a manzanita that was clinging to the hillside, he found it very difficult to walk, and that did worry him; he was weaving and stumbling and so dizzy he had to stop and take a knee. Dice nudged him in the shoulder, and when Guy told him, "Stop now. That's enough," the whispered words came out in an incomprehensible slur.

Okay, horses were definitely a part of the plan—since he couldn't walk—and no speaking; anyone who heard him would think him drunk.

Guy slung an arm over Dice's neck and let the horse steady his stuttering steps to the bush and fumbled his reins around a branch; Amigo he left loose for the moment. Guy wasn't planning on—wasn't *able* to—go far on foot. He thought for a second—which proved difficult, as well—then unzipped a side pouch of the backpack, found the binoculars, and slung the strap around his neck. He took in as deep a breath as he could, patted Dice's side, and pushed off, then when he stumbled onto his knees, he stayed like that and crawled, stopping to rest every few yards with his head hanging over the swaying binoc-

ulars, wheezing cool night air in and out—something was definitely wrong with his breathing.

He wanted nothing more than to pillow his addled and
aching head on his arm and curl into a ball in the dirt, but he
never stopped for long and eventually made his way to a clump
of boulders overlooking what appeared to be a camp of some
sort—there was a small fire in the center of the clearing, rocks
and tree stumps gathered around it—and a cluster of about a
dozen men milling just outside the circle of light. Guy braced
his forearms and raised the binoculars to his eyes; they were all
young men, most wearing cowboy hats, several with baseball
caps, and one wearing a sombrero. Behind them buildings
came into focus: the tumbled-down shacks of the old silver
mine.

Guy was able to make some sense of the scene now: two
groups faced each other; the Spanish words were threats.

"*¡No te me acerques!*"

"*¡Te dispararé también, hijo de la chingada!*"

"No!" rang out in English, and the sombrero was swiped
off what he realized was JC's head. "I'll find the pills. I swear.
I'll find them—I will." His voice was shrill and high—scared.

"The pills," Guy assumed, were the ones in the baggie in
his backpack.

JC's outburst started the groups mumbling, then arguing,
then they were back to shouting again:

"*Eres un imbécile, si crees en eso.*"

"*Qué demonios sabes, pinche pendejo.*"

JC's hair had grown during the weeks of his absence, he
seemed to have stretched out, and he was even skinnier than
he'd been, scarecrow skinny. Looking down at JC as he moved
closer to the fire, Guy finally saw it with a certainty: this was

his son. He may have had Kate's eyes but he had his hair color and bearing; Guy's high school friends had thought it amusing to call him "long john" or "toothpick"—either label would suit the fifteen-year-old just as well. And this situation the boy had gotten himself into was reminiscent of Guy's childhood as well.

Guy brought one hand up to the burn in his chest as he heard a cowboy-hatted man shout: *"Solo dispara al bastardo y acaba con esto"* and another chimed in: *"Ya, chíngatelo y acaba con esto de una buena vez."*

Guy's Spanish was rusty, but the menace in the voices left little doubt as to the men's meaning.

"No!" JC wailed. "Give me my knife. Give me my knife and I'll fight you all!" His boast was undermined by the high timbre and shaking of his voice, and some of the men laughed.

Then as a group they turned and looked up at the ridge. As Guy ducked behind the rocks, he heard it, too: not far off, a mule, braying.

***

TRICK WAS WAITING for us where the slope steepened, the flashlight pointed at his boots. "Do you smell that?" he hissed at me as we came up. I sniffed, shrugged. "Did you hear voices?" he asked me next. I heard Samson swishing his tail, I heard crickets, I heard a breeze rattling bushes; I shrugged again. "No, I mean as you were coming up?" Trick whispered, "Before that ass made all the noise?"

Sam shook his head, flopping his big ears all around. "Samson is a mule, not a donkey," I snapped.

"Yeah." Trick turned around to face where he must have

heard the noises coming from, careful to keep the flashlight aimed at the ground. "Well I think they heard your mule sounding off—things got really quiet after that."

"Who is *they*?" I asked him. "Any more sign of Guy?" By which I meant blood, of course—it was too rocky for tracks to be left behind here—so I was hoping he'd say "no" or shake his head, but he didn't; he nodded and said, "Yeah."

"And he's still going up?"

"I think so," Trick said to the ground. "There's a ridge up there and a mine below—I think."

"A mine? Like a real mine?" I pressed him.

He looked up at that. "Yeah, a real mine—what the fuck other kinds of mines are there?"

"Trick, we heard a big boom, the ground shook, the animals scattered." I used my pissed off voice, too. "Could those people you heard have been messing with the mine earlier, like using dynamite or something?"

"What the fuck difference does that make?" he fumed; he was yelling in a whisper.

"Because otherwise it's Mariana's little people scaring horses and causing all the other trouble out here." God—he was so dense.

Trick mumbled an "Oh jeez" and turned his wall of a back to me. Then we just stood there, scanning the hillside ahead in the hazy light of the half-moon. When Samson stamped and shook, Trick looked over his shoulder at us. "Maybe you and the noisy *mule* should stay here—I'll go on ahead and check things out."

"Like hell," I told him. God, I was so tired, I couldn't even give the words their usual heat. I sighed. "Let's just keep going. Come on, we gotta help him."

"What if he found JC?" Trick's hoarse whispering was really starting to bother me.

"Well, that would be great, right?" I answered him in a normal voice, and when he gestured at me to be quiet, I added volume, instead: "What's the matter with you, T? What are you so scared of?"

I thought he was just being a chicken shit.

I bumped Trick aside and pressed Samson up that hillside ahead of him, so I got to be the first to discover he was damn right to be afraid.

M ARIANA PRAYS: *Tenku Ania*, Dream World, awaken.

W HEN G UY VENTURED another look at the clearing, he saw that the sound of the mule had scattered most of the men. But JC still stood in the circle of firelight, holding the sombrero before him and scanning the ridgeline Guy was on. Guy lowered the binoculars and managed to stand. He raised his hand, waved.

The boy looked up, then stepped back, out of the ring of light, just as Guy tottered and fell.

He had to save his boy.

His son.

Guy crawled. The rocky ground had bloodied his hands and torn his jeans at the knees by the time he rested this time: he had to hurry; he needed to take advantage of the distraction; he had to act fast. The problem was he wasn't going anywhere quickly, and once Amigo had wandered over to him, Guy realized he hadn't even been traveling in the right direction. When the horse stepped close enough, Guy latched onto his foreleg, then got a handful of mane and leveraged himself upright. The manzanita Dice was tied to was several yards back the other way, so Guy threw an arm over Amigo's withers and had the horse walk him slowly back there.

The binoculars went back into the pack; the whistle and all the flashlights—there were several, one larger one and two LED pen lights—came out. He wrenched the tarp from the bottom of the pack, methodically unfolded it, then arranged it over his shoulders and secured it with some duct tape. He stuck the whistle in his mouth and jammed the flashlights between his fingers. It was now or never with "the plan," shitty as it was.

He managed to untie Dice but then found he couldn't get back in the saddle; the gelding's back seemed impossibly high, and the stars that showed through the patchy clouds above it were twirling and dancing maniacally. Guy took the saddle horn in his hand, determined to get his foot in the stirrup, to swing his other leg over the cantle, to settle against the leather, a series of movements he'd made thousands of times. But he couldn't leave the ground.

"Shit," he wheezed.

Breathe, Star's voice in his head said.

He made one more embarrassingly wimpy attempt to launch himself onto the horse, then sighed and lowered his head.

There was no other alternative.

If he wanted on that saddle, he was going to have to risk taking the rest of the pill and waiting for the jolt of euphoria to hit.

SAMSON and I had just about made it to the ridgeline when something erupted from the ground ahead of us and flew right over it. It swooped down and away from us, something huge, with many legs, eight at least. It was twice as tall as a man and much longer, and as it moved down the slope its broad wings unfurled with the flapping sound of canvas and it emitted a shrill bird of prey's screech—like a whistle—almost deafening at first but Doppler-ing lower as the monster moved down the steep hillside, with strange lights strafing the sky all around it. It was surreal, part large animal, part bird, part alien space ship. I saw sparks of metal striking rock and heard the noisy scatter and clank of that, and the sound of horses not just whinnying but screaming in fear. When Sam raised his head and joined in, it was pure chaos.

Even Trick was shouting something: "Dad! Wait!"

I personally did not scream or call out in any way; I was very proud of myself for that. But I did drop to the ground and cower there, my hands over my ears. When I finally got the courage to straighten up for a look, the apparition was at the bottom of the slope and screeching, strobing, and flapping into a clearing around a small fire. The huge mass became a circle below us, and now I could discern two horses, not one enormous beast, and one was being ridden by a hatless rider, caped like some superhero. I squinted. Yep, Trick was right.

Guy on Dice trailing Amigo.

"What the hell is going on?" Trick wheezed as he came up beside me.

Shouts in Spanish rang out. For a moment my heart leapt as a boy or small man wearing a sombrero jumped onto Amigo's bare back and the two horses with their riders oriented, gathered, and charged off. But there was a gunshot—I ducked again instinctively—and another shout, and the second rider—the one on Amigo—turned his horse and raised his hands. Guy must have realized he was no longer following because he reined Dice to a stop.

Then Trick and I watched as Guy dropped shoulder-first from the saddle to the ground next to his horse's dancing hooves.

I was back on Samson before I could think about whether he could manage the leap or not and the next moment we were taking it, following the rough scar of overturned rocks and bent mesquite Guy and the two horses had created. Sam lost his footing and slid; his grunts and wheezes were panicked and so loud I couldn't make out what Trick was hollering after us, and I was too busy trying to stay in the saddle to listen anyway. We were maybe halfway down when I heard another gunshot and more yelling ahead, and Samson tried to rear but fell back and kept sliding and shrieking, then somehow he planted his front hooves and braked to a sudden stop and sent me flying over the top of his head.

So for the second time that night, for a lifetime record, I was dumped in the dirt, and I was still sprawled there when Trick came stumbling up, whispering: "Jaz, you okay? You all right?"

I didn't know the answer to that, either. He was getting darn good at asking me questions I couldn't respond to. I let him prop me up on my butt, and I put my hat back on when he handed it to me. When I could breathe again I told him, "I'm fine," even though I wasn't, just to stop all his hissing: "Are you okay? Jaz? Jaz? Are you okay?"

Then he shifted to: "Are you fucking crazy?"

"Where's that damn mule?" I asked him.

"Shit." Trick whirled around and moved closer to the mining camp in a crouch. He swiped his hat off, kneeled down, and motioned for me to join him.

That wasn't easy; I was going to be bruises layered over bruises for a couple of weeks.

"Get down," Trick whispered. "Take your hat off—we're close."

I could remove my hat just fine, but when I squatted down, I found I was too sore to move like that, so I dropped to my knees and crawled the rest of the way to him.

"Oh, God," I sighed because there was Samson, several yards away and limping toward the firelight. I was hoping he wasn't hurt too badly, but also worried that he was just fine and about to let everyone in the camp know we were out here and then take off for home. He stopped when he heard something— probably the nickering of his stable mates—but I couldn't see the horses or Guy from this vantage point, and Sam soon continued on, head bobbing, past the fire and out of the circle of light. "What's he doing?" I muttered at Trick. "What the hell are we looking at?"

"It's the mine I told you about." Trick spoke close to my ear. "There's not supposed to be people here—something's going on, something bad."

A second after those words were out of his mouth we were ducking again as a mechanical whirling came up from behind us and zoomed overhead. It was another spaceship, I was sure, until Trick asked: "What's a drone doing up here?" We both looked up as approaching headlights cut across the opposing hillside. The light bounced over the tumbling-down buildings at the back of the clearing, and next I heard the big engines on the heavy duty trucks the Border Patrol uses. "Maybe not bad —maybe something good is happening," I said to Trick, and I stood up to see better, despite his, "Get down! Jaz! Get down— they'll spot you."

Yeah, he was right, but I ignored him. I should have stayed hunkered down next to him, watched to make sure it really was the Border Patrol and that they found and assisted Guy, then crept away into the dark. If I'd done that I would have been able to go back to the ranch and sleep what was left of the night away in my own bed.

But somehow, in all the excitement, and because of my newfound need to be so damn helpful and all, I momentarily forgot I was a recent parolee with multiple priors, including a drug conviction.

But mostly what I forgot was that I still had that stupid, fucking pill in my front pocket.

Just my luck.

<hr>

MARIANA PRAYS: *Sea Ania, Flower World, unfold.*

<hr>

GUY FELT HIMSELF RISING. He was flat on his back, but he was being lifted up somehow, off the dirt, over the brush at the edge of camp, past the low branches of the old oaks.

He forced himself to take a gulp of air and found himself resting on the earth again with his son leaning over him—JC— his son, saying, "Breathe, Guy. Come on, just breathe, man.

You can do it. Just pull it in, okay? Just breathe—breathe. You got me, dude? Breathe. Keep on now. Don't you stop. You breathe, you keep breathing."

The damn kid wouldn't let up, and so Guy obeyed him.

He squinted against a blinding light in his eyes and another voice said, "Pinpoint pupils," then after a moment, "Bradycardia. You on anything, mister? Did you take any drugs?"

Guy almost said, "No," reflexively, but then remembered. "Pills," he breathed. "Blue. Backpack." There was an increasing amount of commotion all around him, lots of voices, Spanish and English now: "Found the bait in his backpack," "Hey, watch them!" "*Esta fue una jodida trampa,*" "What's this kid doing here?" But no matter how hard he tried, Guy couldn't open his eyes.

"Get me Narcan, now!" the nearest voice shouted, then more quietly: "This your dad?"

"No, my mom's . . . ." JC tried to respond, but Guy spoke over him: "Yes. My son."

Something was inserted in Guy's nose. "Take some deep breaths now," a man's voice said, and Guy did his best. Breathing secmed the only thing he *was* capable of at the moment.

"Wait, they're not his," JC insisted. "The drugs are mine. He just found them. It's not his fault. It's *my* fault. Really—don't arrest him."

"Somebody get this kid out of here." There was more motion around him as JC's voice receded, still protesting, and then Guy found himself jostled at the shoulders and legs and then rising off the ground again.

"You're lucky we're here, mister. Really, really lucky," the voice said. Then he leaned in even closer and whispered: "And guess what: the bait's not the good stuff. You've got a chance. Just hang in there."

CHAPTER THIRTY

PENTECOST

Mariana sets the plastic medical device down on the coffee table beside Guy and says one word: "Breathe." When he raises his head from the pillows and frowns at her she straightens to her full height and folds her arms across her chest. "Sit up," she insists. Then she repeats: "Breathe."

Guy drops his head and rubs the stubble on his chin; he's recently started shaving again, per Star's request, but he was too lazy this morning and his skin itches. He sighs, then elbows himself up with a groan. This makes the tabby cat rise and stretch, and Guy brushes him off his belly with a "Go. Get." He reaches for the spirometer—he's supposed to use it multiple times a day to measure his breathing and strengthen his damaged lung—but that's not good enough for Mariana.

"You have to sit all the way up, Guy," she reminds him. "Sit tall."

Mariana had been walking home from mass, head down under her *rebozo*, smiling in reflection: it was the last Sunday of Lent, and a foreboding mixed with an intense excitement had permeated their small village church; even the hands of the Priest as he'd held the Eucharist high had trembled. Of course, he was also getting old and feeble, with the acolyte assisting at his elbow for every step up to or down from the altar.

Her thoughts suddenly turned to Guy, then Jasmine—which surprised her—and she stopped in the middle of the dusty lane that led to her home in Old Pascua on the outskirts of Tucson. She seldom carried the cell phone her son had bought her, but today on impulse she had taken it from the dresser drawer where she kept it, charged it, and tucked it into one of the pockets in her voluminous skirt before she left for the short walk to church. She found it now and checked its screen: Star had called.

To retrieve the message required her to bend low over the phone to shade it and punch in what she felt was a ridiculously long series of numbers. Several people from church passed her with greetings, and Mariana, of course, looked up and smiled and nodded at each one of them. But finally she'd navigated her way to Star's hysterical message, and it was not about Guy *or* Jasmine. It was about Sally. Sally had gone missing.

Mariana had to find some shade. Leaning against her neighbor's fence, her fingers shaking, she punched more numbers. Star did not answer, so she left a message: "I am coming. Sally is fine. It's not Sally, and it's probably not Jasmine. Star, I'm so sorry—I think it's Guy."

"SIT UP, SIT DOWN," Guy mutters, struggling to pull the blanket out from under his butt, to push himself up on the cushions, "Do this. Do that." When he's finally upright he inhales until it hurts and then gulps a little more air in and expels it into the spirometer in a rush that is intended to impress his tormentor but only moves the meter on the device half-way above its resting point—still quite a way from the gauge that marks the goal she's set. "Did you move that thing again?" he asks her. Then he coughs and says, "Ow," before he lowers himself onto the pillows.

"Hmmm," Mariana responds as she retrieves the device.

"Hmmm," Guy repeats to her retreating back.

It has been almost two months since what Guy called "his adventure on the mountain" and Star referred to as his miraculous escape from death. In her version, *she'd* engineered his rescue with a panicked phone call to the marshal's office. When Star had first arrived at the ranch, Trick was in manic search mode for Sally; that's when she'd called Mariana back in Tucson. Then José told them three horses were missing, too, and Trick took off in the truck. When Star remembered to look at her phone and saw Mariana's cryptic message, her concern shifted to Guy. And as soon as he came to on a hospital bed in Tucson, Star was explaining how moments after Jasmine had dropped Sally into her arms and left again, she'd started teasing the story about what had happened to him from her daughter's sleepy head.

"WE'LL EAT IN A SECOND, sweetie. Here—let's wash your hands." Star hefted her daughter up to the sink and turned on the kitchen faucet. "Where did you leave Daddy again? Okay, but why did you leave him? Here, more soap. Get under your nails. Why was he sleeping? Did you try to wake him? They were in a wash? I don't care about a little bird, honey, just tell me where the wash was. Here—dry off." Then as Star set her on the floor: "Now, listen, missy, you are never—do you hear me? *Never*—to leave the yard again without telling us. I don't care why. No. You had us *so* worried. Okay, I've got to make a call. Get up here—here's some milk. I'll get you a sandwich in just a minute."

STAR APPEARS in the doorway to the kitchen, almost as if Guy has conjured her with his daydreaming. He can smell what's in her hands: a steaming bowl of green chili stew. She's been gratifyingly attentive ever since his adventure / brush with death. By all rights, Guy feels *he* should be the one doting on her, still wrestling with the loss of her father and beleaguered by the details of settling his estate, and four months pregnant. They are hoping for a boy this time. He watches Star slowly approach, balancing the too-full bowl, with the white cat, Caicos, trailing her and meowing loudly. Then she sets the dish on the coffee table before Guy like an offering. As she steps back she smiles and pushes a blonde curl behind her ear. "Eat," she says with a dip of her head.

Star does not have to prompt him to sit up as Mariana did. When she leans close to pull the couch pillows up, Guy lifts his face for a kiss then laughs a few moments later when she draws back, rubbing her cheek. "If you're going to shave, you have to keep doing it," she complains.

"Well, maybe you'll decide you like me better with a beard." He doesn't let go of her but places his ear against the new mound of her belly. "How you doing, buddy?" he asks, but he only gets a stomach gurgle in response before Star gently pushes him away.

"Eat," she repeats.

Breathe and eat—that was about all he was able to do in the hospital. Star spent most of every day there with him, adjusting his pillows, smoothing his hair, chanting and arranging her crystals on the thin sheet that covered him. Guy's blood pressure spiked from the second dose of Narcan, administered en route to the hospital, and they kept him for three days so they could get that stabilized. He was miserable the whole time from the headaches and joint pain the anti-overdose drug caused. But he'd been lucky: the doctor told them if those little blue pills had been pure fentanyl, he'd be dead.

As it was, Guy's prognosis was good. He'd only been slightly concussed, and of all his other injuries, the two broken ribs and punctured lung were the worst. Although he was still having trouble with his breathing, the ribs only hurt now when he stood up or lay down, and it wasn't the gasp-out-loud pain anymore. The doctors were impressed with the field dressing Jasmine had done on his shoulder; they told Star the young woman had probably saved his life by staunching the bleeding. He was actually kind of proud of the lightning-strike scar jagging redly from his shoulder to the middle of his back, which he could only see if Star held the mirror for him just right.

"You look like some bad-ass," Jasmine had told him after watching him and Star perform this maneuver the second day he was home. She was standing in the hallway outside their bedroom with Sally on her hip. The young woman had endured her own three days in hell and had beat him home by only hours, arriving in the same parole officer's car that had brought her there in the first place; it was still there when Star had driven Guy into the yard in the new truck. The nice Hispanic lady had wanted him to sign Jasmine's paperwork all over again, but at least the original sentencing judge had considered the mitigating circumstances and decided that her possession of one opioid pill was a technical violation, not a crime, and didn't require him to send Jaz back to Florence.

Guy was very glad of that. He thought the change in the young woman quite remarkable; how she'd lug Sally around now was an example of that. Even Jasmine's tone was new: "You could be a biker dude," was delivered from the hallway in an amused growl. "Alls you need is a few more spikes and tats," was added with a genuine laugh.

Star sits beside Guy on the couch as he eats with first Caicos and then Turks crowding her lap. When he's emptied the bowl, she has to shed cats to rise with it in her hands. She's been telling him about all the bookings they have for the casitas and wondering if they should move Jasmine into JC's empty room for the high season, but before she turns for the kitchen she smiles again and says: "Mariana says she'll make my dress for the wedding—it's going to be beautiful! But you're not allowed to see it, of course."

"Yeah?" Guy queries as he rearranges the pillows.

"Yeah," Star assures him with a nod as she carries away the bowl.

The late morning quiet of the house has settled back around Guy for only a few moments before Jasmine walks into the living room with the gait belt slung over one shoulder; the cats—who'd reclaimed their spots on the couch—scatter at her clomping approach. "Walkies!" she announces. Guy groans and squints his eyes shut, but he knows that won't deter her. Some malevolent streak left in the young woman has made her the perfect administrator of this particular doctor-ordered torture. "Time to walk," she says, then she repeats until he rolls to a sitting position: "Walk, walk, walk."

"You know I don't need this anymore, right?"

"Yeah, you keep saying that." Jasmine slaps the belt on her thigh. "Now let's get going."

Guy sighs and stands. "And I don't need that," he tells her.

Jasmine leans in and straps the gait belt around his midsection, yanks it tight.

Since he refused to use a walker, the gait belt and Jasmine's steadying presence were the original stipulations attached to Guy's daily exercise. But now he can move easily over the carpet, walking at a good pace around the couch, down the hallway tiles, back and around the dining room table, three loops, while Jasmine tells him what she and José have done that morning, what they plan to do that afternoon. He passes Caicos' nose poking out from under one of the big bookshelves, Turks watching from the stairs.

Breathe, eat, and walk—that's how Guy has spent most of the past five weeks of his recovery.

Guy moves toward the front door with Jasmine following closely, out the screen, but carefully—there's the threshold to negotiate, and the tabby decides to scoot between his legs and down the steps. Guy picks up steam again as he crosses the rough boards of the porch. He resists the urge to put a hand on the railing and pulls his shoulders back to walk erect, but he is breathing heavily now. He does one circuit, two, and aims for the porch swing.

"Naw," Jasmine says. "Down the stairs. We're going to visit the horses."

"The horses," he repeats.

"Yep," Jasmine says behind him.

THE NIGHT of the near death / adventure it was Trick who reclaimed Dice, Amigo and Samson and brought them home to the ranch; both JC and Jasmine were read their rights and left sitting in side-by-side Border Patrol trucks with their hands zip-tied. But Trick hadn't followed Jasmine; he'd kept under cover behind a bush and watched her walk right into the light show of the newly arriving marshal's personnel, their Lightbars flashing, as they joined the arcs and swirls of the Border Patrols' headlights and searchlights. She approached the officers surrounding Guy with her hands up, shouting: "I'm just here to help. I have no weapons. That's my—that's my friend." She'd lowered one hand to point at Guy's limp form as they moved the stretcher into an ambulance.

And nothing happened.

Jasmine explained to Trick later that with all the commands in Spanish flying around, men being herded together, searched, and apprehended, no one could really hear her. She realized the medics caring for Guy were too busy to bother with her, so she fingered the pill out of her pocket and approached a different clump of uniformed men. "Here. I think he took some of these." She turned to point a finger at Guy again. "We found a whole baggie . . . ." That got the officers' attention.

Trick had used that distraction to launch for the horses; both Dice and Amigo were so stumble-tired that they didn't spook at his big shadow lunging for their dangling reins at the edge of the clearing. In fact, Amigo came up and rested his head on Trick's shoulder in a kind of horsey hug and Dice nickered at him so softly Trick could hardly hear it over all the noise of the engines and voices surrounding them. With the horses in hand, Trick turned to look for the mule.

"Come on, Samson," Trick breathed, "Come on."

There—on the other side of the smoldering camp fire. He saw the ears move, the gleam of eyes.

"Samson!" Trick risked the call, crouched, then rose again to peer across the clearing.

Tall ears twisting, the mule stepped into the circle of light. Then at another of Dice's low whinnies Samson started moving in their direction. He had to skirt around a patrol car, then he trotted toward them, head bobbing. Trick grabbed his muzzle as he came up, fearful he was catching his breath for a series of big hee-haws.

"Shush now," Trick whispered to the animals. "Let's go."

JASMINE SHADOWS GUY across the dusty yard and into the cool shade of the horse barn. He's breathing in gasps by the time he gets there and has to rest a hand on the nearest stall door and bend down, drawing in air, before he can raise his head and square his shoulders again. First one and then another horse had nickered a greeting as they came in, the loudest from Dice, and as Guy looks up he sees the spotted Morgan standing in the middle of the aisle, saddled and bridled.

"Notice anything?" Jasmine asks from behind him.

Guy nods. The saddle has been modified. There's a back brace extending a few inches upward from the cantle, and as Guy moves forward through the sawdust, he sees the stirrups have been replaced with a padded fender and adjustable straps.

"You made this?" Guy marvels.

Jasmine's voice shows her pleasure: "Yes. Yes, I did. Now we can offer handicapped-assisted rides. I mean, José helped me—a lot—but it was my idea. Well, I kinda stole it from *Game of Thrones . . . .*"

Guy has no idea what she's talking about, so he doesn't pursue that and reaches for the saddle horn. But he can barely raise his foot to the stirrup; no way can he hoist himself up there. "Shit," he wheezes as he drops down.

"Wait a sec. I, well, I mean *you* bought these stairs, too, so we can host more kids and disabled guests, you know? It was Star's idea."

"Oh, Star's idea," he repeats. But he waits while she gets the steps and sets them down before him. Once he's climbed them he has no problem slinging his leg over the high cantle. Dice snorts and stamps as Guy settles in the saddle. He speaks to the gelding softly and pats his neck so the horse will stop bobbing his head. Then he fiddles with the gate belt, pulls it off, and tosses it to Jasmine. "Hand me the reins," he tells her.

"Um," she says, looking at the belt in her hands, then at the rubber-bottomed slippers he's wearing, then at his head, minus his hat. But "Okay," she finally says and hands them up. The horse is eager to be off, pushing a shoulder against her. This is the first time Guy has ridden in all these weeks. "Don't you want me to strap you in?"

Guy lets his "Yee-haw" and heels to the horse's ribs be his answer.

Jasmine scoots out of their way. "Jeez," she mutters to their dust. Then she adds with a loud laugh: "Yee-haw, biker-cowboy!"

The house phone is ringing when Guy dismounts onto the steps of the porch, but he doesn't let it hurry him as he ties Dice off on a railing. He works his cell phone out of his pocket, notes the two missed calls from Trick, then leans close to the screen, squinting, and thumbs a text message to Jasmine, thanking her for the ride and asking her to come get Dice for him. Only then does he make his way toward the screen door. The ringing stops, then starts up again.

Guy is pretty sure he'll be saddle-sore in the morning, but other than that, the ride has done him nothing but good. They didn't go far, just checked out the property. It was a daily ritual in the past; Mariana would hold the screen door open for him upon his return, watching him slap the dust off his hat and praising him for "riding the boundaries," but Guy didn't think she meant fence lines. It was more like heart lines; she knew he traveled the land as a way of treasuring it.

And he'd really missed that.

Guy realized on his ride that he'd find nothing more satisfying than this: the early summer sun on his shoulders and the cooling wind lifting his hair; the grass high and the grounds of the ranch well-watered; a blue forever-sky overhead. He and Dice had passed their small herd of Herefords moving along the hillside pasture, scared up a few rabbits in the wash, and upon their return the newly whitewashed row of casitas circling the ranch house had practically glowed. Guy was filled with the sense that he was right where he wanted to be, right where his family needed him to be. And maybe as he approaches 50 he's getting a little old and creaky, but at least he's a creaky, old man about to have a new baby. Ha! The thought makes him smile.

The phone rings, stops before the answering machine picks up, then starts ringing again. This is the hardest part of Guy's day: he can breathe, eat, and walk just fine, but talk has never come easy for him. Guy knows it's Trick on the other end of the line even before he picks up the phone; besides the missed cell phone calls, Guy knows no one else would call the house phone, leave a message—Guy can see the light blinking on the answering machine—then call back again, probably several times. So he says, "Hello, son," when he lifts the receiver then experiences a moment of doubt during the silence that follows.

"Yeah, which son though?" he finally hears Trick ask. There's a weight and resonance in the young man's voice, just like in his presence. The sound of it brings a burn of pride to Guy's chest, but Trick's next words snuff it right out: "We need to talk."

"Talk," Guy repeats. "Okay. Well, seems like we've been doing a lot of that lately."

The sigh Trick lets out next doesn't help, or the added: "It's about your other son."

"You mean JC," Guy states. A*gain*, he adds silently.

Trick—who's demonstrated nothing but disdain for JC over the previous three years—has become obsessed with the teen, and Guy can understand why: it fell on Trick to deal with the boy's situation while Guy was in the hospital with Star at his side. Trick told him, hat in hand beside the hospital bed, that he'd expected JC to be charged with something—maybe not possession, since Guy had the baggie—but as an accessory, or for tampering with evidence at the very least. But after just one night at a juvenile detention center in Tucson he had been released into the custody of his parents.

So when Trick sighs again and asks—again: "Did you find out why the agent said those pills were 'bait'?" Guy doesn't heave out his own sigh but answers him patiently: "Nope."

"Dad," Trick complains. "You said you'd ask them."

"I wasn't sure, Trick—I mean, ask *who*?"

"The Border Patrol. I think you were right about the fentanyl. Maybe it was a set up to catch those drug guys." Guy knows his son can't hear him nodding but he does anyway. "And I'm sure that JC's screwball girlfriend and her white trash father were really the ones responsible."

"Responsible?" Guy repeats, even though he's heard his son just fine.

"Yeah, responsible," Trick says. "We've talked about all this. *She* was at the wheel of the VW; *she's* the one who hit someone—maybe a drug dealer. A kid at JC's school told me Heather's dad was selling opioids—from his Mexican contacts. Just like you thought."

"You're hanging around JC's old school now?" Guy asks.

"I have a cell phone, Dad."

"Huh. Yeah, but you know, Trick, what some school kid says isn't proof . . . ."

"I met Heather's dad that one time you made me go pick JC up from their place—he had gang tats all over him!"

Guy responds with just two words this time: "Not proof." Then he lets the silence on the other end of the line go on a while before mumbling, "I don't know, T." He rubs at his whiskers. "I hate to think JC was involved in any of that."

"No, Dad—JC's just a pot head. Heather got him in the middle of all this; he was probably trying to protect her." Trick's still adamant, but he's calming down. "Trying to destroy the evidence in her car, hiding the pills—all that was probably to try to save her and her dad's skin." Guy hears water running in a sink, then Trick says solemnly: "JC's loyal like that, you know—he's a messed-up kid, but he's a lot more like you than people give him credit for."

It's intended as a complement, Guy knows, if an undeserved one. "I don't know, Trick," Guy says again. "Heather's whole family packed up and left, anyway, trailer and all. Why are you still getting so worked up over this—you should just focus on your studies."

"I can't stop thinking, Dad. It bothers me—I want to *know*. And that's only going to happen if you talk to him." Trick has saved this request for last once again.

And once again Guy tells him: "No. The kid's been through enough."

"Then ask Sweet Kate about it; ask her to get the story out of him." The broken parts in Trick seem to have largely healed;

he came back on a recent Sunday visit acting much more at peace. But there are certainly things the young man experienced that he's still unable to explain. That's why Star thinks he remains so focused on the particulars of JC's case—that, at least, *should* be clear enough. But it isn't.

Guy sits down on the couch and switches the receiver to his other hand; he's been gripping it too hard, and his wrist aches. "Trick," Guy sighs. He scratches the stubble on his cheeks and watches the white cat lumber over and sit at his feet; he wants to be picked up. "I'm sorry, son, but that's just not going to happen."

Because he *has* spoken with Kate—and Richard; he just hasn't told Trick. Now that Kate and Richard have reconciled, their conversations are infrequent and held over the speaker on her phone. And the couple is unified in their opposition to Guy talking with JC; Richard even told him Kate's decision to place JC with Guy had been horribly misguided. He seems to think it was Guy's inadequate supervision that was to blame for all of JC's troubles, which really hurt. But not as much as Kate's quiet acquiescence as he spoke.

"Maybe someday, but not now, son," Guy tells Trick. "For now you're just going to have to let it ride." Guy switches phone hands again. "So how is school going?" He can hear Trick moving around, grumbling something. "Just let it go. Okay, Trick?"

"Shit, I guess I gotta get going," Trick says at last. "I've got an appointment with my professor so we can figure out how I'm going to make up all those hours I missed."

"Okay?" Guy asks him again.

"Yeah, okay. Okay. Love ya, Dad."

Guy drops the phone and picks up the cat once the line goes dead.

A few minutes later Mariana comes in from the back patio, goes in and out of the kitchen, then sets the spirometer and a sandwich on the table before Guy, wordlessly this time. He's blown into the damned device and eaten his lunch and is just about to settle back into a nice nap when he hears Star's BMW coming down the drive; she must have been off picking Sally up from kindergarten because the little girl soon comes pounding across the porch. She flings the door wide and charges, head down, toward him, arms open, shouting, "Hug! Hug!"

Guy barely has time to rise and protect his groin with a half turn before she's smashing against his hip and throwing her arms around his waist. "Okay, okay, kiddo. Hug."

Out of all the rest—breathe, eat, walk, and talk—hug is definitely the most enjoyable action required of him.

Star comes in and drops her purse and keys on the entryway table, stands tip-toe to give Guy a kiss on the cheek, then moves to one side, watching, because a Sally hug is not some passive embrace. Guy has to stand with his legs braced wide apart while his daughter chatters about her day at school and makes a jungle gym out of his arms and shoulders; he considers the activity—which goes on for several minutes—another form of exercise and laughs at her upside-down dangles and swings. About half-way in he starts breathing hard, then when he's had more than enough he lobs her at the couch, sending the white cat flying over its back. He goes hands to knees, panting.

(Sally had been inconsolable during Guy's stay in the hospital and had snuck into his room at every opportunity once he was home. She'd "Daddy? Daddy? Daddy?" at him until he woke up, then clamber up onto the mattress, jostling his sore ribs. If he kept his eyes closed, feigning sleep, she'd stand inches from his face until he couldn't take it anymore, and he'd open them to her unblinking stare. "Are you okay, Daddy?" she'd ask him, again and again. Star finally had to start locking the door, and when she did that the 5-year-old would sit in the hallway, and whine: "Daddy? Daddy? Daddy?" Then when Sally figured out she could avoid the door by climbing up onto the porch railings, scaling the lattice to the roof, and slithering through their opened bedroom window, Star said she'd had enough; Sally started kindergarten at the Montessori school in nearby Patagonia the next week.)

Sally is jumping on the couch, arms out. "Again! Again!" she's demanding. "More! More!"

But Guy says, "Not again, baby. No more."

Mariana comes out of the kitchen at all the commotion. "That's enough now," she tells the kangaroo on the couch. When Sally keeps bouncing she claps her hands and says, "*Eso es suficiente. Parar ahora.*"

Then Jasmine opens the door. The tabby cat slices through her footsteps as they cross the room to greet Star. The two women converse for a moment, and then Jasmine lets out her loud laugh and Star joins in with her wide-mouthed ha-ha-ha.

The phone is ringing, but Guy is busy trying to catch Sally on the next jump, so Trick's voice is added over the answering machine: "Hey, Dad, I got to thinking. Maybe the two of us should head up there to Flag; I'd like to meet Sweet Kate. We could go to Winslow, too; I've never seen that old buffalo ranch you worked on up there. I should have my hours made up by late June. There won't be a baby yet—maybe the two of us can sneak in a little vacation . . . ."

It's pandemonium. But as Guy listens it resolves into the individual timbres and resonances of the people he loves most in the world. He drops with his daughter in his arms onto the couch and stretches out his slippered feet, his heart thrumming in accord.

EPILOGUE

THE YOEMEM

I n the long ago, the *Yoemem* flourish in their homeland, the place they call *Hiakim*, along the banks of the *Yo Vatwe*, the Enchanted River, the northernmost river of life. They live in *hukim,* small houses made of sticks and mud, and inhabit not just one world but the many separate but overlapping realms and dimensions of *aniam.* Before the Talking Tree, before *Yomumuli* interprets its message to the people, this is where all *Yoemem* reside, fishing, hunting, farming. But *Yomumuli's* warning that the conquistadors would come divides them: before the *Konkista* some of the People become the *Surem* and vanish into their caves and under the waves, leaving the rest, who now call themselves the Yaqui, wandering the *Hiakim* and waiting for the rest of *Yomumuli's* prophecy to come true.

This is when *Saila Maso,* Little Brother deer, comes to them. Through him they can still communicate with their brothers, the *Surem.* He travels with them, and they go with a purpose: to know their lands and to be possessed by them.

They sing as they walk the boundaries. They sing to claim with their feet their forever home.

The knowledge *Yomumuli* bestowed on them was not welcome, but it prepares them for the Spaniards. The Yaqui see dust in the distance, then the pin-prick shine of the tips of lances, then the glare of sun on helmeted heads trailing one another through the washes and along the river bank like a multi-headed centipede. The Yaqui have never seen the strange weapons these conquistadors carry, the strange animals they are carried upon, but since *Yomumuli* had warned them there is no surprise in the Yaquis' minds, only determination; there is no awe in their hearts, only courage. They do not hesitate or imagine them Gods as many others will—they attack.

Three times the Spanish soldiers come to their lands in this way. Three times they are repulsed.

When the Jesuit brothers arrive carrying a healer called *Jesucristo* like bread in their hands, the Yaqui are prepared for this, too. Just as *Yomumuli* predicted, these newcomers insist the Yaqui adhere to their many rules and customs. But instead of being changed by the new stories, the Yaqui adapt them to their own purpose; the dying-rising god becomes their beloved Little Brother deer, *Saila Maso*. The Yaqui form eight sacred pueblos and continue to travel their lands, conversing, connecting, an evolving People of the Word. Now both *Saila Maso* and *Jesucristo* are with them and in them.

When the Mexicans come, coveting the water that feeds the lush acreage along the *Rio Yaqui*, the Jesuits intervene. They tell the Mexican soldiers: "These People have walked with angels the whole length and breadth of this land. It was given to them by our Divine Father in Heaven."

For a time they are spared, but the Mexicans keep coming.

Many of the Yaqui are ripped from their families, from *Hiakim*. Many of these Yaqui die.

But others tuck their bundles under their arms and move north, bringing *Hiakim* with them into what will become Arizona.And the Yaqui are here now, their communities rooted in ceremony, anchored by their church, and informed by the many worlds of *aniam*. *Saila Maso* still dances, not only for the Yaqui but for all humankind.

And the Yaqui still walk the land; they sing the boundaries.

– THE END –

ABOUT THE AUTHOR

Jan Kelly is a native Arizonan with an MFA in Creative Writing from Arizona State University where she taught for 30 years. She has one daughter and lives with her husband in Scottsdale, Arizona.

ACKNOWLEDGMENTS

Brazil, Mary Ann. "Yaqui Easter."
Brink Creative Digital 3 Apr. 2015.
http://www.brink.com/thoughts/yaqui-easter/
Evers, Larry and Felipe S. Molina. *Yaqui Deer Songs, Maso Bwikam: A Native American Poetry*. Tuscon: Sun Tracks and the U of Arizona P, 1987: 62-64.
Giddings, Ruth Warner. *Yaqui Myths and Legends*. Tucson: U of Arizona Press, 1959.
Shorter, David. "Yoeme (Yaqui) Ritual." *Encyclopedia of Religion and Nature*. Ed. Bron Taylor. NY: Continuum, 2005: 1780-82. http://www.davidshorter.com/up-loads/1/0/9/3/10932014/shorter--ernyoemeritual.pdf
St. Clair, Jane. "The Five Enchanted Worlds of the Yaqui People." *Jane St. Clair* 7 Feb. 2014.
http://janestclair.net/enchanted-yaqui-worlds/